The SECRETS WE KEEP

CASSANDRA DIVIAK

Book Cover by Melody Jeffries Design (Whim and Joy)

Editing by Cassidy Hudspeth and Sophie Fitzpatrick

First edition 2025

Contents

To all the people who think they are "too much" or "too broken"
to find love. You are **not** unlovable.

Content Warnings

Dearest readers,

Welcome back to the A Love at Royal Ridge series for Book 3! Please enjoy your stay in the California sunshine with a side of romance. *The Secrets We Keep* is under the contemporary romance / romantic comedy umbrella; the book's overtones are meant to be more humorous and sexy. However, the following subjects in the narrative may trigger some readers.

- on-page PTSD representation; PTSD-associated panic attacks

- car accidents/motor vehicles accidents (past)

- descriptions of fatphobia in dating and society

- family trauma (infidelity, divorce)

- references to traumatic accidents and medical care (Madi is a nurse)

- explicit language

- mentions of foster care

- implied suicidal ideation (past)

If these themes relate to personal triggers you might have, please proceed with caution. Your mental health matters to me, and I'd rather you put the book down or DNF than expose yourself to any harm. I've worked hard to handle these topics as sensitively as possible.

This book will also be reserved for the 18+ crowd as there is sexual content consistent with the adult romance genre. For a full breakdown of the scenes or kinks/acts, please proceed to the dicktionary on the next page ;)

The Dicktionary

For those parties interested in either skipping, skimming, or searching for any smut scenes or tropes used, I've listed all of them below:

Smut Scenes and Kinks (by Chapter):

Chapter 2 contains blowjob, fingering, nipple play, dirty talk, praise, and penetrative sex

Chapter 7 contains texting as foreplay, dirty talk, toy use (vibrators), sexual overstimulation, nipple play, and penetrative sex

Chapter 13 contains dirty talk, nipple play, dry (or wet) humping, pool/jacuzzi sex, (female receiving) oral, fingering, and semi-public sex/exhibitionism

Chapter 19 contains car/limo sex, fingering, biting, praise, nipple play, semi-public sex/exhibitionism, and aftercare

Playlist

Each chapter had a different song I listened to while writing the scenes, befitting the vibes of the chapter or the characters at that point of the story.

1: Undercover by Selena Gomez
2: In My Head by Jason Derulo
3: Gambling Addiction by Leanna Firestone
4: I Want by One Direction
5: House Song by Searows
6: Something Big by Shawn Mendes
7: strings attached by gianni & kyle
8: trust issues by Jessica Biao
9: 10:15 by Leanna Firestone
10: LA Girls by Charlie Puth
11: Mutual by Shawn Mendes
12: blip by Olivia O'Brien
13: run for the hills by Tate McRae
14: Be Alright by Ariana Grande
15: Just My Type by Taylor Bickett
16: one before the one by Haiden Henderson
17: Please Cheat on Me by Precious Pepala
18: The Tree by Maren Morris
19: positions by Ariana Grande
20: Water Fall Out of Love by Victoria Monet
21: seeing you with other girls by Natalie Jane
22: me by Kelly Clarkson

Chapter 1
Madi

As Madison Caldwell passed the last corner standing between her and the nurse's station, the promise of her lunch break ran its victory lap around the halls of New Horizons Medical Center. Yes, she loved working in pediatrics, but even the best nurses needed time to rest.

Besides, everyone knew the New Year's Eve shift brought unpredictable cases through the automatic doors of New Horizon, which was *severely* understaffed on all major holidays.

"Alright, I'm heading out to lunch." Madi smiled at Kiara, her direct supervisor and the much-beloved charge nurse of the peds unit, before sliding over her charts. "Is there anything you need before I go?"

Kiara shook her head. That day, she slicked her gorgeous chestnut curls into a neat little bun, complete with a satin scrunchie in the muted cherry blossom pink reserved for the peds staff.

"If you finished your rotation, then go enjoy your lunch! But if you pass by Wilshire Wellness, could you check if they still have those BLAST energy drinks? The evening nurses will be cranky without them." Kiara grabbed Madi's charts off the counter, beaming with her million-dollar smile.

Kiara would've been a supermodel in another lifetime—with willowy limbs and an almost otherworldly glow to her sepia-toned skin.

"Absolutely! See you in a bit." Madi flounced for the door, waving to Kiara and the other nurses before grabbing her tote bag. The white canvas with a painted strawberry print pulled her whole outfit together, balancing her role as a nurse with her cozy, feminine style.

In a few quick strides, she escaped the waiting room without an emergency pulling her back in. The dull bounce of her tote bag against her hip followed each step down the hallway until Madi caught the elevator doors rolling open. Several smiling faces dressed in different-colored scrubs entered her sight.

"Get in, Sunshine!" Sonia squealed, throwing her hand out to hold the door. "I swear you have a sixth sense or something."

When Madi began working at New Horizons, she made friends with several other nurses from different departments. They had all been new to the hospital and clung to one another for support; the quad became infamously known as "JAMS."

If there were ever a quintessential mom friend, Sonia Morales would be her. Already being a mom to two rescue cats taught her the 'disapproving mom stare' with her pretty fawn eyes. She moved with precision throughout her life, which made her perfect for the position in radiology. She never left the house without a pack of hair ties for her shiny black curls, her favorite brown lipliner, and little packets of powder electrolytes crammed into her mini backpack whenever the girls hit a bar or club.

"I'm blessed with divine timing for my girls." Madi slid into the elevator, finding herself quickly wrapped in the bone-crushing hug of Alaina, the third member of JAMS.

No one embraced a lust for life quite like Alaina Robles. 'Social butterfly' barely covered all her bases, but Alaina would label herself a chatterbox. Her friendliness and perfect smile endeared her to the stressed impending mothers she assisted in labor and delivery. Alaina could come straight from delivering a baby into the world, yet she'd still look like Miss Philippines with her sun-kissed skin and perpetual glow.

"Lucky for us. If I missed out on the last quinoa salad to some college kid, I would be fighting someone in the parking lot." As the elevator doors closed, Janet's head lifted from her phone screen long enough to flash a tight smile and adjust her powder blue scrubs.

Rounding out their little quartet, Janet Coleman embodied the effortless cool girl—the opposite of Madi's loud lover girl. That calmness made her the go-to perioperative nurse in all of New Horizons. Petite and ashy blonde, Janet had a face made for cameras, which she applied to amass followers on social media.

"No fighting will be happening," Sonia chided, but everyone knew her tone to be teasing. The elevator slowed with a chime, flashing the lobby number on the screen. "And that's us!"

All four scrambled from the elevator carriage before the doors opened, rushing from the building in a fit of giggles. The December afternoon brought an overcast gloom to the downtown skyline that was cool to the touch.

Madi tucked into the back of the group, linking arms with Sonia while Janet and Alaina's strides carried them to the front. The sidewalk was crowded with the lunchtime rush, shuffling strangers across the intersection's crosswalk. Madi jogged to keep up with everyone else when her girls sprinted at the blinking red numbers.

But the second they popped onto the opposing curb, the girls stared at the bright blue sign of Wilshire Wellness, a trendy organic grocery store with an in-house food court. Madi and her girls made the one-block walk to the market every week. Without fail, they spent their lunch gossiping over overpriced health smoothies and whatever they ordered at the food court.

Air conditioning bellowed when the automatic doors rolled open, revealing the towers made of produce and the brightly colored interior of the food court off to the left. Even with the cooler weather outside, the store's glacial air hit Madi like a double shot of espresso straight to the head.

Just the wake-up call she needed.

Madi tucked her hands into the pockets of her scrubs, ducking inside behind her eager friends. Laughter tickled at the back of her throat when she saw Janet sprinting toward the salad shop like an Olympic track star. She took her salad game *seriously*.

She strolled toward the Mongolian BBQ place as Sonia and Alaina materialized at her side, smiling hard.

"You've got the right idea, Mads. BBQ sounds so good right now, especially before I go out tonight." Alaina gasped as the three fell into line, a few people away from ordering.

"Yeah?" Madi crinkled her nose, smiling nonetheless. "Don't you have an early shift tomorrow?"

"Unfortunately. I'll try to cut back on the drinks and avoid staying out too late. It's not New Year's Eve if I'm not a little messy, downing shots and dancing with a hot stranger, but I'll make it work." Alaina proudly flexed her nails, newly done from the shine of the red.

Sonia playfully rolled her eyes. "I'm too old for that shit. If I stay out past ten, my knees ache so hard that my ancestors probably feel it. I'm barely on the verge of thirty."

Madi snickered while Alaina full-out cackled; at social functions, Sonia spent more time ensuring everyone else stayed safe rather than enjoying herself. Clubbing on New Year's would be her nightmare.

"What do you and Val have planned for the evening?" Madi asked.

"We're currently on our binge of cheesy reality shows, so we're going to order some takeout before it gets too late and cuddle on the couch. Val says they think all the shows are ridiculous, but I know they're invested. They can't fool me—I've seen them watching telenovelas with my abuela."

"That sounds amazing." Madi nudged Sonia as the line crawled forward, bringing them closer to the steaming table. "I'll probably be home, ignoring the fireworks all night. I'm sure I'll find something to do."

Much like Sonia, Madi wasn't much for clubs. She went when all her girls got together, but a night at home where she indulged the rest she desperately needed sounded like a necessary reset for the new year.

As the line shuffled forward, Janet raced over with a plastic salad container held over her head. Icy blue eyes gleamed victoriously while she rattled the quinoa salad in the air. "I'm a winner!"

"Clearly," Sonia snorted. "So, what are you doing tonight?"

"Alaina and I are going clubbing. I got an invite to Cobalt and Neon, that trendy club downtown, and they're throwing a New Year's bash. I hear a bunch of celebrities are going to be there." Janet smirked, tossing her ponytail over her shoulder as Alaina squealed.

"It's going to be amazing!" She clapped, but her eyes flickered to Madi. "Mads, you should come with us! The three of us will look so good on the dance floor."

"Ah, I don't know—" Madi began, unable to get the words out before she found herself at the mercy of Alaina's puppy dog eyes. Her friend clasped her hands together, begging.

"Please? It'll be so much fun to dance and get all dressed up," Alaina pleaded, fixing her eyes firmly on Madi. When Madi looked at Janet, she shrugged noncommittally—not intervening one way or the other.

Turning down Alaina was hard enough already.

"Maybe I'll come out for a little while." Madi sighed, even while Alaina pretended to run a victory lap, her hands thrown into the air. "I'm sure I have a dress to wear."

"People suggest picking out something metallic or chrome since it's a club-specific thing," Janet mused, slipping into line with them.

Madi nodded, calculating the options in her closet from there. She had something in mind already. Besides, one to two shots and some dancing definitely sounded more exciting than channel surfing from her couch, watching the rest of the world have fun ringing in the new year.

The late December night nipped at Madi's bare arms with every car speeding past the packed downtown Los Angeles sidewalk. She probably should've brought a jacket, but she expected inside the club to be hot from all the bodies packed in the dark corners.

Behind her, a million and one conversations overlapped with the rabid, excited energy perfect for the celebration.

As promised, Madi joined Alaina and Janet at Cobalt and Neon for a night of drinks, dancing, and delighting in the new year. She pulled out her current ensemble—a shimmering, golden cocktail dress—from deep within her closet. Miraculously, the dress fit like a glove to her curves, outlining the soft slopes of her hips and stomach with shiny fabric.

Best of all, though? The dress didn't scratch Madi's skin, proving a comfortable choice to match her block-heeled boots. She and the girls sat at the front of the line but had been there for close to an hour.

Janet's social media side hustle brought her some extra recognition as a "microcelebrity," or whatever that meant. Without it, Madi assumed they'd be at the back of the line stretching around the block corner.

One of the bouncers leaned over after admitting a couple into the club, reading over the tablet in his hands. "You said it was three, right?"

"That's correct, sir." Janet pushed to the front of their little trio, pressed up against the velvet rope. She batted her lashes at him, smiling coyly. "Is it our turn?"

"Sure is. . . Step out of line, ladies. And hold your left wrist out," he instructed. Madi followed Janet and Alaina's leads, lifting her left wrist. One of the other bouncers approached with a stamper and marked hands.

Madi studied the stamp—the club's logo in faint purple—but quickly forgot about it when Janet and Alaina grabbed her arms.

Alaina exclaimed, "Shots are calling our names! Let's go!" She grinned, the smile stretched from ear to ear, and the two dragged Madi into Cobalt and Neon's dark tunnel.

Madi squinted hard, searching through the hazy dark until the first touches of the neon-colored inside pierced through. All at once, she stumbled headfirst into a world of color blossoming across the four walls and floor of the club.

Bodies packed into the open space, flitting about with reckless abandon, and rings of glow sticks looped around arms and necks. Music thrummed at an ear-splitting volume as the bass rocked the room, matching the flashes of the lights from the dance floor. Light and color flowed freely, blurring into a rainbow before Madi's vision.

She blinked, startled out of her trance, when something loose fell around her neck. Her eyes dropped to find two glowstick necklaces sitting at the base of her throat, matching her golden dress with their startling yellow.

Madi's head turned enough to catch a woman with glowstick bangles lining along both arms racing away, carrying more glowsticks. She raised her voice, "Anyone else get decorated already?"

"What?" Janet yelled back, but she sported a pink and green set around her neck.

"The glowsticks! Looks like they got you too!"

"They gave me blue!" Alaina squealed, pointing to her double-blue necklace. "We have glowsticks, and now, we need shots!" She had a one-track mind, and shots claimed top billing for the evening.

Madi didn't protest as Alaina dragged her along to the nearest server. Even among the light show, the floating trays with neon-colored shots stood out, sparkling bright.

Janet and Alaina grabbed enough shots for the two of them to double-fist. Madi, however, took one to pace herself and not spiral so early in the evening. She held her drink into the air and smiled.

"To us, and the new year!" Madi cried over the bass. Alaina and Janet chorused her toast before all three downed the unspecified liquor. Madi choked on it, taken aback by the burn and a vaguely cinnamon-flavored aftertaste, but she shook it off fast, spurned from lingering when her friends beelined for their next target: the dance floor.

Madi closed her eyes when diving into the sea of bodies, illuminated by the light under their feet in a vivid orange. She jostled around and bumped into a few people, but the swaying throng parted enough to swallow her whole. Alaina and Janet carved out a little alcove among all the dancing for the three of them, catching a pocket of strobe light like a spotlight.

"Don't just stand there! Let's dance!" Janet whooped loudly, loosening up with two shots in her system. She wound her hips up in a circle, running her hands over her body to the slowed music.

So, underneath the golden strobe, Madi danced. She never considered herself a trained dancer but knew how to roll her hips and feel the groove in her bones. With everyone else around her focused on themselves, she could let loose.

Alaina and Janet stayed close as the three girls danced together. Their hands often linked up to spin one another, earning laughter and squealing louder than the base. They moved as one, perfectly in sync, until a man emerged from the crowd.

The stranger, a tall hunk with a perfect face and body glitter smeared all down his exposed chest, shimmied toward them. His eyes locked on Janet, who spun into his orbit and wrapped her arms around his shoulders. She rocked her hips with his and forgot about the others.

Madi shook her head and Alaina giggled, watching their friend be snatched up by the first hot guy they stumbled across. Janet and her dance partner vanished into the crowd as the music changed. With the beat, the lights deepened to a dark pink stretching around the room. The bass thumped against the wall insistently, demanding all the attention.

Madi grasped Alaina's hands and danced with her like before. The two couldn't stop laughing as they pretended to grind on one another. Cheeky smiles and unrestrained laughter derailed any pretense of sexily dancing under the pink glow.

Then, like with Janet, a man emerged from the crowd with his eyes focused on the new duo. Madi traced the line of his vision straight to Alaina, who exaggeratedly thrust her hips into the air like a terrible Elvis impression, biting her lip to stifle her laughter.

"Looks like someone wants to dance with you!" Madi shouted over the DJ's high-energy house mix, turning Alaina enough to see the gentleman eyeing her up. For a split second, her friend's face brightened until her shy smile brought out her dimples. "You should go!"

"But wait, you'll be alone!" Alaina snapped to her senses quickly, staring at Madi with wide eyes. The pink glow illuminated her features, perfectly encapsulating the turmoil from her realization.

"Don't worry about me! I'll be fine!"

"We can go together! Maybe the guy won't mind having two hot girls to dance with?"

"Alaina, listen to me—" Madi squished her cheeks before Alaina flung herself into a full-blown tangent on the dance floor. *She knew how to handle herself alone on the floor.* It would be fine. "You deserve to have fun. Mr. Right might be waiting."

"You're the best." Alaina squeezed her hard before taking off in her heels with the stranger. She waved to Madi as her new beau guided her into a darker corner of the room.

And then, there was *one*.

Madi glanced around the crowd for any eyes watching her, curious if the universe also slipped her a little eye candy for the night. But with no one jumping out from the crowd, she accepted her quiet shimmy off the floor.

The crowd bounced Madi around while she wiggled through the cracks of space, riding out the energy until she reached the edge of the floor. She barely exhaled before someone knocked into her. She righted herself quickly and glanced at a guy, three drinks past tipsy, holding an empty shot glass.

"Woah! Sorry, pretty lady." His words were slurred, run-on sentences, strung together with a hiccupping laugh. He reached his hands toward Madi but seemed to get lost along the way. "Let me buy you a drink," he said.

"Oh, it's okay—" Madi assured. Yet her words didn't dent the poor guy's resolve. His hand planted on her shoulder and steered her to the bar.

"I insist!" he exclaimed. "I'm a gentleman!" The loud, gargled burp following that statement truly sealed the deal for Madi, who grimaced politely. She let the stranger usher her into a bar stool and lean onto the counter, signaling for the bartender.

A blue-haired woman sidled over to them, sighing. "Buddy, I thought I told you ease back on the drinks."

"Not for me." The guy shook his head, pointing at Madi. "I'm adding her to my tab. Whatever the lady likes."

The bartender shifted her gaze to Madi, brow raised. Yet, a quick scan of her expression changed her whole posture, and she smirked. "Sure thing. What can I get for you, doll?"

"Um," Madi glanced at the guy, now face down on the bar, but he popped up long enough to flash her an affirming thumbs up and a toothy grin, "I'll take a Cosmo, thanks."

"One Cosmo coming right up." The bartender winked, sauntering down the line to help another customer. Madi's eyes followed her until a pair of eyes intently watching her landed in her view. She froze, meeting a pair of intense green irises.

It was like all the club's noise melted into nothing, muting in the background as Madi admired the gentleman sitting several bar stools down from her and the drunk guy buying her a drink. She came to one easy conclusion within moments—he was the *finest* man she ever saw.

His features were sharp, perfectly demonstrated by a classic Roman nose and a more oblong shape to his face. His medium brown crew cut appeared darker until flashes from the strobe lights revealed its actual color, but the subtle twitches of his lips and the intent stare of his eyes kept Madi's focus.

He nursed a cocktail with dark liquor, loosely swirling his drink with those big hands. Madi watched him bring the glass to his lips and drink, unable to tear her eyes from his visage.

Shit, she was thirsty.

Beside her, she heard the drunk guy start rambling about something, but between his slurred words and her attention elsewhere, comprehending him was nearly impossible. Maybe a well-placed "uh-huh" slipped from her, or a quiet smile encouraged his rambling.

However, Madi couldn't care less, not when her eyes refused to leave the stranger for a damn moment.

Chapter 2
Cal

WHEN HE STEPPED INTO Cobalt and Neon, Cal promised himself two drinks at most before he called a ride home. He should've known his sensible rules would fuck off into the evening. He felt it in the air.

Dark purple liquor dribbled down the curve of his lips when Cal pulled the highball glass away, but he ignored it. He couldn't be bothered to care, not when his eyes clung to the goddess in the golden dress sitting across the bar from him.

For the New Year's celebrations, plenty of people went all out for the occasion. Somehow, he missed the memo about the dress code because the shining sea of chrome reflected the ever-changing colors inside the club. But that's why among the silver, the buxom redhead glittered like a damned spotlight.

Poking at a Cosmopolitan sitting untouched on the bar, she appeared mentally somewhere else while her companion blabbed at her. His drunken sway knocked his chest against the bar every other minute, yet he seemed oblivious. Cal knew he wouldn't be much better with a gorgeous woman in his line of sight.

The goddess in gold finally sipped at her drink, taking her companion's eager conversation in stride, but her gaze leaped off the bar's top back to him.

She was ready for another round of eye tag across the bar.

Since he first saw her, the stunning stranger played a rather coy game with her attention. She'd shy her eyes away after staring for too long, usually mumbling a few words to her male companion. She never strayed away for too long, though. Eventually, Cal pulled her back in while they pretended to be unaware of the other person's unspoken interest.

A night like tonight reminded Cal of the old him, who *perfected* the thrill of the chase.

As he set his drink down on the bar, having his fill of liquor, he caught his lucky break—seeing the woman's companion yell something incoherent to her before racing into the crowd. Once alone, her shoulders relaxed, and she shook out her soft-toned red hair, bouncing in beachy waves. Color flooded her cheeks, turning her vibrant against the dark backdrop.

Before Cal could consult his better judgment, his legs propelled him out of his stool at the bar. He promised to be on his best behavior for more than that night. That promise of *no more girls—hookups, flings, or otherwise* sauntered out the front doors when he settled his eyes on the goddess in gold.

His eighteen-month streak would be ending with the new year.

Cal weaved through incoming patrons heading for the bar; his eyes focused on the golden cocktail dress beckoning him like a beacon. A few people bumped into him, earning disgruntled shouts or a few stares before Cal left them in the dust. Right then, he was a man on a mission.

He reached for the empty chair—abandoned by the guy who had been talking the woman's ear off—and slid onto it. He bit back a smile, especially when the object of his desire turned her face.

She quickly did a double take, lips parted wide like she hadn't expected to see him there. "Hi."

"Hey." Cal cleared his throat, leaning his elbow on the bar. He rested his chin against his knuckles, freeing his smirk. "There must be something wrong with my eyes. . . I can't seem to take them off you."

He paused for the punchline to hit. The delivery felt smooth, as effortless as when he knocked a home run over the stadium walls to the crowd's roar. And when the goddess's face brightened, a flashing red point added to his personal scoreboard.

Nice going, Lambert.

The woman laughed, her hand clamping over her pouty lips to muffle the sound. "Has that line ever worked on anyone?" she asked, but the crinkle at the corner of her eyes seemed to say that Cal nailed the opener.

"I've never used it on anyone else, so you tell me, beautiful. I thought opening up with a laugh might land better than being aggressively blunt about how attractive you are."

"I don't know. Being blunt never rubbed me the wrong way. Still, I appreciate the originality." The woman dropped her hand from her mouth, flashing Cal a smile that was utterly devastating when paired with her pink lips. "But you're in luck. I'm a nurse, so I'd happily stare deeply into your pretty green eyes."

It was Cal's turn to laugh, taken off-guard by how fast she flipped the tables on him. While a rarer occurrence, flirting with someone who shamelessly flirted back always aroused his interest.

The goddess in gold had a sense of humor. . . He liked that.

"Alright, I'm convinced. I'm Callum, but everyone calls me Cal. Any chance I could get your name?" Cal sat taller on his stool. Confidence was sexy, so the pretty nurse had him like putty in her hands.

"Madison. But you can call me Madi." She smiled. Her hands pushed the unfinished Cosmo further down the bar, kicking the last reminder of her prior admirer to the curb.

Cal's tongue swiped over his teeth, holding a chuckle in. Instead, he ran the name along his tongue, "Madi, huh? Pretty name for an even prettier girl."

"I see we've jumped straight into the blunt flirting stage. I like this better." Madi's hands brushed down the hem of her golden dress, not stopping until they trailed down her exposed thighs. Soft, fair skin pressed flush against the bar stool, and Cal's eyes wandered down, obediently following the path her hands had made.

Oh, she knew how to play the game.

"What can I say? When someone tells me what they want, I like to listen." Cal scooted closer to her despite already being perched along the edge of his stool. If he needed to stand, so be it. Being closer to Madi was the goal—close enough to hear the hitches in her breath when he laid the charm on thick or caught the scent of her perfume.

Somehow, he sensed Madi smelled sweet but *tasted* even sweeter.

Madi's eyes widened for a second before fluttering closed. She tugged her lower lip between her teeth, fighting against her smile and losing the entire time, but her strength didn't stop a giggle from escaping her.

And with one, a whole avalanche of laughter tumbled from her lips. Cal listened to the full-bodied sound—resonant from the depth of her chest with its mirth—unable to stop himself from joining in. Maybe a passersby would see them laughing about nothing and fix them with a weird look.

Ah, but who cared? Cal was having fun.

The slight hitch in his chest left his breathing a little wheezy. Cal chased after it while he tried to compose himself, even as Madi could barely contain her giggles. Alcohol must make her the giggly type.

However, when Madi's eyes darted past Cal's shoulder, she perked up with her expression stone-cold sober. A nervous glance jumped between him and whatever caught her eye over his shoulder.

Cal's lips parted to ask until a firm hand clamped down on his shoulder, pushing harder than necessary. Hot, alcohol-heavy breath brushed against his ear. "I was sitting there!"

Cal winced; a drunken fool shouting in his ear wasn't ideal, but he did try to steal his girl. Hopefully, they weren't there together, or he might've gotten into more trouble than he intended.

So, he spun around on the bar stool, hands raised into the surrender position. "Sorry about that, man. I was trying to talk to Madi."

But when Cal came face-to-face with the stranger, prepared for an argument or a punch, the guy's face lit up. He gawked, jaw dropped wide open, pointing directly at Cal while spluttering. His noises scrambled together incoherently but were nowhere near words.

"You! You're. . . Oh my god!" The stranger's hands waved wildly through the air, flapping like a bird attempting to take flight. His excitement garnered attention from others seated at the bar and those mingling around the open space, craning their necks to see. "I'm a huge fan, bro!"

"Thanks. Much appreciated." Cal stiffened when the stranger threw his arms around him, squeezing him into a hug. Awkwardly, he patted the guy's back until he let him go.

Although he still freaked out, his volume drastically dropped, thankfully catching the unspoken memo to cool down. He shook his head, almost as if he couldn't believe Cal stood before his eyes.

The stranger peered around Cal to Madi, pointing his finger right in Cal's face. "Do you know who this is?"

"Um, should I?" Madi blinked when Cal glanced over his shoulder, features flushed in confusion. *She had no clue who he was. . . That was the best possible thing Cal heard all night.* Her eyes searched his for how to proceed.

"Nah." Cal shook his head, quickly pushing the stranger's hand away from his face. "Sorry for taking your chair, man. I didn't interrupt anything with you and Madi, right?"

"Her name's Madi?" the stranger asked, promptly cut off by a nasty burp that wafted the scent of stale beer and something garlic into Cal's face. Guess he wasn't her boyfriend, then?

"Yeah. You two aren't dating, right?"

Madi snorted, shaking her head. "Nope. Just met this guy like twenty minutes ago when he nicely bought me a drink." She nudged at her unfinished Cosmo, which she gleefully abandoned not too long ago.

"Then, my good man here won't mind if I steal you for a dance or two," Cal remarked—not asked—when offering his hand to Madi. One half-finished drink hardly meant a thing compared to the potential sparking between him and Madi. But it was her choice if she wanted to take the risk.

She, to no one's surprise, linked their hands together and slid off her stool, moving so fluidly and gracefully despite the curve-hugging tightness of her dress. "I would love a dance."

"Great." Cal flashed her a wolfish grin, escorting her around the drunken stranger. He tipped his head to him, watching the guy wave with a wide grin and a spacey look between his eyes. He wouldn't remember anything tomorrow, especially not a famous athlete swooping in and stealing the girl he wanted.

Cal and Madi, still grasping hands, wandered toward the dance floor where the crowd gathered. Bodies rocked to the rhythm of the thumping base, loud enough to rattle the walls. The floor and walls pulsated in a warm red light, eliciting a darker feel from the crowd. People's bodies tangled together, connected at the mouth or the jumble of their limbs running over silhouettes.

Cal guided Madi to a small pocket of space among all the action. His hand slid down to her wrist, and within seconds, he pulled her in by her hips. Surprise flashed across her face but vanished behind a vixen's smile.

Madi's hips swayed to the beat, hitting every mark. Her whole body glided with such fluid movements—it was hypnotic, entrancing. She grooved closer to Cal until their chests brushed together, leaving no room between their bodies. The subtle thrust of her hips nudged against the rapidly blossoming warmth circling his stomach.

She struck the match, starting the inferno. The question was if she'd let Cal take her home tonight, ready to let the fire consume him whole.

Madi's hands ran along Cal's back in opposite directions. One curled a fistful of his bomber jacket into her grip while the other dipped into the back pocket of his jeans. If Cal focused on anything besides the intoxicating gleam in her eyes, he might've known for sure if she copped a feel of his ass.

Yeah, he wanted her. *Badly.*

He leaned in close, brushing his mouth against her cheek while they moved together. "So, what are your intentions with me tonight? You seem to know exactly where you want me."

To her credit, Madi gave the proposition some thought. She paused for a moment, still rolling her body against his to the infuriating tightness below the belt. She squeezed his ass again. "How about we play it by ear? I'm open to wherever the night goes."

"Sounds good to me," Cal hummed. "Let's dance. The night is still young."

While they huddled together in the backseat of his chauffeured car, the urge to pull Madi into a bruising kiss without regard for the consequences had Cal on the edge of his seat. Three was a crowd—him, Madi, and the growing anticipation—but possibility tinged the air with its sweetness.

For all their talk about playing it by ear, Cal managed to last an hour before he had Madi pinned to the club wall as her hand toyed with his jeans. So, they agreed on a quick getaway, and Cal's hotel room was closer.

Except for when Madi went to grab her purse from her friend's car, Cal hadn't let her from his sight. He memorized the little details about her, from how the shimmery gold fabric clung to her curvaceous figure, to the tiny quirk of her lips whenever their eyes met through the dark. She shined, even without the pulsing lights and neon wash.

"We should be at the hotel momentarily," he whispered against Madi's cheek. "You still want to come back with me, right?"

"Yes, I do. Let me send a quick text first. . ." Madi didn't hesitate to answer. If any nervousness lingered in his body since their rushed departure, it jumped out of the car without a second to spare.

Cal nodded; he watched her fumble with her purse until she grabbed her phone, hesitating over the unread messages. She glanced over to him, thick lashes framing fawn brown eyes. "What's the name of the hotel?"

"The Obelisk." Cal averted his gaze while she tapped at her screen, not the guy to read people's text messages over their shoulder. For all his faults, nosiness wasn't one of them. He found that being invasive invited more trouble than strictly necessary and never the good kind. "If you need the address, I can grab it."

"Don't worry, I've got it!" Madi assured, typing at the speed of light. He knew why she needed it. More importantly, he understood; his best friend, Claire, used to text him her location when she went on dates until she met her husband in college.

Besides, he was a virtual stranger taking her back to his hotel room.

Cal moved fast when the car rolled to a perfect stop at the hotel's parking lot. He stripped off the black bomber he wore, wrapping it around Madi's shoulders as Tommy, his chauffeur, stepped out to open the doors. They'd have to run fast for the distance between them and elevators.

Cal never knew when paparazzi hung around, waiting for the opportune moment to strike. The last thing either he or Madi needed would be pictures of her to end up in the morning paper, her life blown up because the world chose to pry.

"You ready?" he asked, flipping the hood over her head. A few strands of hair stuck out, but the remainder of Madi's beautiful face hid in the jacket's shadow.

Madi laughed, tightening the hood and her grip on his hand. "So ready."

Cal grabbed her purse. When the door opened, he guided Madi from the backseat. She bounded after him, nimble, wearing the jacket to cover herself.

Fireworks boomed overhead while the two raced inside the Oblisk, finding their laughter buried underneath the reverberating explosions of color across the skies. Glittering light trails streaked and fizzled out, hardly comparable to the thrill rushing through Cal's veins.

The same thrill he used to get on the diamond, winding up his arm to strike a runner out.

With midnight fast approaching, no one hung out in the lobby beyond a few stragglers and the employees behind the front desk. Their heads turned when Cal and Madi sprinted past, but those two left them in their wake.

The nearest elevator's doors slid open, and a few people stumbling out, drunk and laughing, did not pay Cal or Madi a second glance. Cal thanked his luck and slammed the button for his floor until the doors closed.

"This belongs to you," Madi said, curling her hands around the bomber jacket and peeling it away from her skin, but Cal stopped her, flashing a wolfish smirk that he caught in the mirror's reflection.

He said, "Keep it on for now. It'll be on my floor soon enough."

Instead of a response, Madi's hands abandoned the bomber jacket for a fistful of Cal's shirt, tugging him close. Their lips collided, bridging the gap with a rough, bruising embrace, devolving into laughter laced between each kiss.

Cal's tongue flicked across Madi's lower lip, finding entrance into her mouth. She rewarded his boldness with open access and her nails raking down his back. Even through the fabric of his t-shirt, the blissful sting burned a path into his skin. Madi's hands never stopped at the waistband of his jeans, however.

Just as her fingers ghosted over his ass, the elevator chimed. Its doors swung open, and the two didn't waste another moment trapped by the chrome walls. Cal guided them down the empty hallway, head on a swivel for cameras or prying eyes. They were so close to home base, where his guard would lower.

He dug into his pocket for his key while Madi fumbled with her purse. Their clumsiness seemed contagious as they struggled to breach the final barrier between them and their clothes being kicked to the floor. Eventually, Cal shouldered the door open after a pitiful click from the electronic key.

Cal stumbled backward into the dark, and Madi followed him, lunging forward. His arms snaked around her waist as their lips met in the middle, spurred on by the click of the door's lock.

As promised, Cal promptly shoved his bomber jacket from Madi's body and dropped her purse with it. They stepped around the rumpled pile, which quickly grew from how Madi's skillful hands hoisted Cal's shirt off. Her mouth moved against his while her fingers mapped out the broad, muscular expanse of his chest.

Cal laid his hands over hers, pausing their exploration to find her gaze through the dark. The glow of fireworks exploding in the Los Angeles skies filtered through the window, illuminating Madi in a beautiful haze of colors.

"Woah, girl," he panted, catching his breath. Madi paused despite the hungering gleam in her eyes, the one threatening to knock Cal to his knees. "Can't wait to take my clothes off, huh?"

"What can I say? You're charming, and I've been thinking about how nice my name will sound when you moan it loud enough for the rooms next door to hear," Madi replied, batting her lashes innocently.

Cal's jaw dropped, taking in the seemingly delicate expression compared to the wicked smirk stretching over her pouty lips.

What a dirty fucking girl.

"Oh, and how do you plan to do that?"

Madi's smirk didn't waver. Instead, she guided their hands over the firm ridges of his abs, past the tiny sliver of his v-line, and pressed her palm against the bulge in his jeans. If he hadn't already been hard, the weight of her hand rubbing his cock through his jeans and boxers would've gotten him.

She inched closer, pushing onto her tiptoes to whisper against his cheek, "Why don't you lose the rest of the clothes and let me show you?"

"Yes, ma'am." Cal whistled. His fingers wrestled with his belt and the button to his jeans, rushing through the motions. He watched Madi's every move, admiring her slow strip as the golden fabric of her dress loosened. He caught a peek of flesh-toned lace as he kicked off the last of his clothes and she abandoned her boots.

Madi's hand gently pushed him backward onto the bed while she stepped out of her dress. The bodysuit she wore underneath clung to her curves like a second skin, enticing Cal to search for where the garment ended, and she began. He'd find out soon enough.

Madi crawled onto the edge of the bed as the fireworks painted the room in a shower of golden light. Cal laid back, head short of the pillows, propping onto his elbows to watch Madi move closer.

She stopped when her hands brushed against his waist, curling into the sheets. She hunched back onto her knees, eyes dropping to his hardened length pressed against his stomach. His cock stood at attention, flushed pink with a need for her attention and her touch.

Madi leaned down, arching her perky ass upward and rolling her hips for Cal's attention. She pushed some loose hair away from her face before her fingers curled around his cock, fingertips barely grazing. She winked as her tongue flicked out to run down the slit.

Cal's breath hitched, holding still when Madi's pouty lips wrapped around the head of his cock. Warmth rushed straight down the length, pooling throughout Cal's hips. His hands darted forward, gathering Madi's loose hair into a ponytail in his fist.

His jaw clenched, straining against the urge to moan her name. "Fuck me. Such a pretty girl with my cock in her mouth. Can you take more of me?"

Madi nodded, accidentally bobbing a little to his stuttered breathing. She took another inch of him down her throat but didn't stop with one. Instead, she pushed as far as possible, stopping shy of the base and its small cropping of dark curls.

Soft moans, muffled by her full mouth, accompanied the medium-fast pace that Madi's wicked tongue set. She swirled around the head of Cal's cock while she sucked him off.

Cal tightened his grip on her ponytail, body tense from pleasure. A thin bead of drool ran down from Madi's lips, tracing down the length of his cock in a slow, tantalizing vision. He stared, mesmerized by the sight of Madi.

He let the pleasure carry him away, fading in and out of the moment. He buzzed hot from the last touches of alcohol running through him, fueling the arousal like gasoline on a fire. Madi's hands gently scraping up his scarred thighs sent electricity shooting through him, causing his hips to buck out of surprise and pleasure.

Madi's eyes widened as she gagged softly before lifting her head. Spit connected in a thin thread from her puffy lips, broken by a shy sweep of her tongue.

"Are you okay? I'm sorry—" Cal sat up, dropping his hands to cup her face. His thumb caressed over her cheek, and Madi nodded.

Madi smiled, laughing a little when Cal cleaned spit off her lips with his thumb. "I'm good, promise—" But a startled gasp escaped her when Cal's mouth crashed into hers, kissing her for a taste.

Madi wrapped her hands around his shoulders while he lifted, bringing her to straddle his hips. Cal didn't balk at the taste of him in her mouth. Salt and sweet liquor tangled in a heady harmony, awakened when Cal's tongue brushed over Madi's.

He pulled back enough to whisper, "I can taste me still, and it's driving me crazy."

"Oh yeah?" Madi panted hard, chest heaving for breath. "How crazy?"

Green illuminated the room, followed closely by blue and pink from the night sky. In the cacophony of color, Cal's desire materialized. So, he hooked his leg around Madi's and flipped the world on its head.

Madi's back crashed into the duvet with Cal hovering over her. His fingers curled around the neckline, tugging it down to expose more of her breasts. "Crazy enough that I can't wait. My turn."

Madi's lips parted, but she nodded fervently. "I have a condom in my purse if you need it. I carry extra when my friends and I go out—"

"Don't worry, I'll get to it. . . in due time." Cal's hands peeled the bodysuit off her shoulders, rolling the garment to her waist. His eyes traced over her hardened, rosy nipples, not hesitating before wrapping his lips around one. His fingers tweaked at the other, pinching hard enough to elicit a shiver from Madi.

She moaned, arching her back to push her breasts harder against his mouth. Cal obliged her with a cheeky bite and smoothed it over with his tongue in the same breath.

He switched to the other nipple, sucking hard. Madi couldn't hold her facial expressions back; her eyes rolled back while her mouth struggled around pleading whimpers. Madi's little noises went straight to his cock, twitching against his stomach.

Cal reached out, pressing his thumb against her lower lip to Madi's shocked gasp. He pulled his finger back while she stared, but her pupils dilated when he ran the same thumb over her clit. He stroked over the bodysuit, yet Madi rocked against him all the same.

His lips detached from her breast with a wet pop. "Where's the condom?" he asked.

Madi blinked, voice trembling, "The pocket. It's in the pocket."

Cal slid off the bed, snatching up Madi's purse. He heard the rumple of fabric while he rifled through her bag in search of the condom. As his fingers snagged the foil, the feel of Madi's bodysuit smacking against his legs drew his attention back to the bed.

Now completely naked, Madi stretched out for him, glowing in a deep purple from the fireworks. She crooked her fingers, beckoning Cal to dive back into her with what little self-control he had left.

Cal tore the package open and slid the condom over his throbbing cock, lunging toward the bed. His momentum carried him onto the bed, mattress dipping under his weight when he scooped up Madi's thighs. His legs tucked underneath Madi's bent ones, looming over Madi's sprawled-out body.

She stared up at him, biting down on her lip. Gold illuminated the room as Cal lined his and Madi's hips together, hands lingering there. His cock nudged up against her entrance, rubbing along her pussy.

Madi squirmed, hips grinding down and face contorted into a silent plea for more. Cal met her eyes, grinning. "Ask me for it. I want to hear you say it."

"Please fuck me, Cal. . . I've been waiting," Madi whispered. She moaned when he rocked their hips together, striking more friction. "I can't take more waiting—"

A loud moan interrupted her sentence when Cal pushed into her. Her pussy eagerly accepted every inch of him, greedily squeezing around his cock with a tightness that might finish him off.

Cal leaned forward, anchoring himself with his fists gripping at the sheets. His hips thrust to his own accord while the room filled with the sound of slapping skin, accentuated by Madi's high-pitched moaning. His hair fell into his eyes while he admired Madi taking his cock in stride.

In the light of the fireworks, nothing else in the world outshone Madi. Cal stared at her, rocking her hips with each thrust into her, awestruck. The golden goddess from the bar lay in his sheets, drawing him further into her spell. The fireworks could crash outside, and the world could celebrate the passage into the new year, but Cal couldn't take his eyes off Madi.

For the night, she had him entranced.

Chapter 3
Madi

WARMTH BRUSHING AGAINST HER face brought Madi out of her tentative sleep, but the press of something *firm* against her inner thigh snapped her wide awake. The blurry vision faded after a few blinks, revealing the dawn's first light filling the spacious hotel room. Warm brown walls lengthened the space, lightened by the brightness of the rising sun. Everything popped with white or light wood accents. Somehow, with her cursory examination of the space, every inch screamed quiet luxury.

But if she shifted her gaze even half an inch, Madi would find the peaceful expression of a sleeping Cal.

She spent the night. . . Most guys never asked her to stay over.

Even while lying on his side, the duvet they shared rippled with the rise and fall of his chest. He didn't snore or move much, otherwise, she would've been wide awake as a pitifully light sleeper. Yet, she hadn't felt the weight of his muscular leg settled atop hers.

His body pinned her to the undeniably intimate position of staring at Cal's perfect face as he slept, blissfully unaware of her gaze. Cal's cock rested against her thigh, inspiring flashbacks to their late-night activities from mere hours ago. *Thank goodness neither chose to get dressed afterward.* Madi chewed on her lower lip while admiring Cal's toned chest. *Fuck, he was so damn pretty.*

Madi could've stayed there for *an hour. . . a day. . . the rest of her life* if it included staring at Cal's face. However, the hospital would hardly understand with patients to oversee and emergencies to remedy. Ringing in the new year with a handsome stranger ended right there. A pity, really.

So, Madi quietly sucked in a breath and leaned backward, testing the sturdiness of Cal's hold on her. The bed squeaked a little, confessing her runaway intent to the silent room, but not enough to stir Cal. He didn't even murmur or move from his sleep, deep in the land of dreams and drooling ever so slightly on his pillow.

Nice to know that such a perfect-looking guy wasn't devoid of being a human.

She tried another lean, wiggling a little more than the first attempt. Slowly, she applied more force to the gesture as her legs and hips began sliding free from their tangle with Cal's. The more she moved, the less of his warmth washed over her body like the return of the tide. She'd miss the simmering touch of his skin against hers.

Eventually, with a final push, Madi rolled free of Cal's arms without falling off the side of the bed. She sprung out of bed, moving fast to snatch her dress from its puddle on the floor. The fabric rumpled while she peeled it over her body, forgoing the bodysuit she paired with it last night.

The walk of shame would be interesting that morning. Madi needed to call a ride and keep her head down until she returned to her apartment.

Through it all, Madi snuck a few glances at the still-sleeping Cal. *So, he could sleep through a damn earthquake.* He hadn't moved or made a single noise since she'd awakened. A peaceful morning after added a cherry on top of the already great sex.

The dimmed light accentuated the fading pink and white lines crossing over his legs and hips, standing out from the untouched skin. Madi would recognize scars in her sleep after years in the medical field. She hadn't paid them notice the night before but couldn't take her eyes off them now. Her fingers twitched, still holding her dress, stricken by the sudden urge to trace her fingers over the scars adorning Cal's body.

That would certainly wake him up, though.

"Thanks for the fun," Madi murmured to Cal, snatching her purse off the floor and grabbing her boots. She jogged for the door and stuffed her bodysuit into her bag, ready to dash.

She closed the door to the room behind her, hearing the lock click before she fled down the hallway. No one else loitered around to see Madi's walk, or rather *sprint* of shame to the elevators.

Madi tapped the *down* button before sliding her boots back on. She smoothed over her disheveled appearance in the elevator's chrome doors—frizzy hair and the rumpled fit of her dress over her rolls and curves.

She caught the time on the screen of her nearly dead phone—5:45 AM—much to her relief. Her shift at the hospital began at seven. That should be enough time for a fast shower, quick breakfast, and recovering from last night's high as long as traffic wasn't bad.

The elevator opened to Madi, and she holed up inside the empty carriage, leaning against the wall despite the room. She closed her eyes and let the elevator take her to the lobby. Quiet accompanied her, devoid of the curious stares and judgment of strangers.

When she stepped out, Madi intended to march straight for the door and call a ride outside. If she was desperate, there should be a metro stop a few blocks from her with a line close to her apartment. Public transport should be more robust, but Angelenos made do.

However, Madi barely made it halfway through the lobby before a voice stopped her. Someone called to her with soft insistence, "Miss!"

Madi slowed, glancing around the empty lobby. She spun around, searching for the source of the voice. . . and locked eyes with the woman behind the front desk.

"Me?" Madi mouthed, pointing to herself instead of drawing more attention from those in the lobby.

The woman nodded, waving her over to the front desk. Even while her heart screamed in her ears, she strolled over, pretending to have all the nonchalance behind her. Madi ignored the hem of her dress riding up her thighs, sticking to her skin. She leaned against the desk, smiling awkwardly at the desk worker. There was no way she landed herself in trouble.

The desk worker smiled back, glancing around before she spoke, "So sorry to spook you, miss. But is your name Madison?"

"Um. . . yes." Madi swore sweat beaded along the column of her neck. "How'd you know that?"

"The guest in Room 1602 called us last night and mentioned that a woman named Madison in a golden dress would be coming down in the morning. He instructed us to have his driver on standby to escort you home. He wished for discretion for his guest," the desk worker remarked, punching some numbers into the phone. The knowing glint of her smile spoke volumes.

Relief fluttered through Madi's chest like someone tipped a basket of butterflies loose among her ribcage. Cal slept upstairs, unaware she snuck out without a note, while she leaned on his generosity. Maybe she could wait for him to wake up–

The suggestion fell apart at the seams when someone stepped beside her, appearing as a dark shadow in Madi's peripheral. She turned enough to see the tall, blond gentleman in a pristine black suit and dark sunglasses settled atop his head. His hands tucked into the pockets of his suit trousers, showcasing a peek of a wrist tattoo. *The driver from last night!*

"Miss Madison?" He cleared his throat. "Are you ready to go home?"

"Yes, thank you. . ." Madi tightened her grip on her purse. She watched the desk worker set the phone back down. She waved goodbye, darting away to focus on another task behind the desk.

"You can call me Tommy," he said, perfectly monotone. He guided Madi through the lobby and out the glass doors. Tommy parked the car—a dark, non-descript SUV—in one of the closest parking spots to the doors.

Tommy held open the door for her, and Madi nearly dove into the backseat. She curled up in the back, head laid against the cool glass of the tinted windows.

She heard the driver's side open, buckling herself in as Tommy turned the engine. "Where to, Miss Madison?"

"3487 W Olympic Boulevard. I live at The Sunset Palms Apartments," Madi replied. A yawn ripped through the middle of her sentence, interrupting her to the quiet, amused hum from Tommy. "Thank you."

"Driving is what the boss pays me for." Within a few smooth moves, Tommy pulled onto the open road, speeding across the intersection as the light flashed yellow. The little window between the front and the backseat rolled up after the first street, plunging Madi into silence.

After the chaos of the night before, the spontaneous whirlwind of excitement known as Cal, Madi needed the break.

She leaned closer to the window, knees tucking into her chest. She rifled through her purse for her keys and phone, counting the streets that passed. She wasn't far from home, including the morning rush hour traffic. Soon, she'd have a little time to decompress before her shift and return to the mundane routine.

No matter how hard she tried, she suspected Cal would find a way to worm his way into her thoughts. Those green eyes might haunt her dreams for the next few weeks alone.

Her phone screen weakly flashed, and her battery was near dead. Madi dropped it back into her purse, wrapped in her discarded bodysuit.

Was it better that she left without a word? Without exchanging numbers?

She and Cal never made any promises about what would come next or how their night together would shake out. Long ago, she stopped waiting for the casual dismissal from the men she encountered and took the initiative to walk out, finding the fallout less than marginal.

Yet, this time felt different, too much to put her finger on.

Before she could stop herself, Madi's hands dove back into her purse and rifled around until she pulled out something paper-like and something that felt like a pen. Granted, the items were an eyeliner pencil and a crumpled receipt from the chain gas station by her house. But those worked for the moment.

Madi scribbled her number onto the blank back of the receipt with the eyeliner. The black glitter sparkled, pulling a smile out of her. However, the uncertainty left her to her own devices.

What's the harm in leaving her number behind? Should she hand it to Tommy? What if he throws it away? What if Cal did? What if he kept it?

The question stood while the streets began to look familiar to Madi's tired eyes. Did her and Cal's fateful encounter, which turned into a night of incredible passion, mean nothing more than harmless fun?

No matter what she chose, she'd live with the decision. Focusing on the regrets of her life was never Madi's way.

Madi messed up. *Big time.*

The minute Tommy dropped her off outside her apartment and wished her a good day, Madi stumbled inside and headed straight for the shower. She let the warm water cascade over her until she felt like a new person, smelling of cherry and chia milk soap or touches of tea tree shampoo.

She had planned on indulging in a quick but filling breakfast before she jumped into her beat-up car and headed to work. Keyword: *planned*.

That suggestion went up in smoke when she stepped out of the steamy shower and damp bathroom, finding herself with less than ten minutes to head out the door. So, her leisurely morning turned into a scramble to get dressed, scarf down some meal prep she luckily saved, and make a mad dash to the hospital.

With five minutes to spare and still-damp hair, she sped into the hospital parking lot for staff. Her eyes scanned through the crowded lot for any possible parking spot; she had nightmares about that exact scenario in the past, but living it far exceeded any anxiety in her dreams.

"Come on, come on, please," Madi begged the universe not to drop her after such a high. Being late to work and thrown off for the rest of her day would be the worst start to the new year. She would consider that a bad omen for the rest of the 364 days left. "There has to be one spot left."

As it happened, those words must've summoned one out of thin air from how fast one caught her attention. Sandwiched between two other cars, the spot would be a tight fit, but it would get the job done. Future Madi could worry about backing out when she crawled to that bridge after a long shift.

Madi rushed from her car, jogging toward the front of the hospital with her work bag and coffee. She passed patients on the sidewalk, flashing them with bright smiles to match her soft pink scrubs. Not even a bad start to the morning could damper her cheeriness in the face of patients.

Around her friends, however? That was an entirely different story.

When Madi hopped onto the curve outside the doors, she spotted the huddle of Alaina, Janet, and Sonia gathered just short of the doors. All three scrunched around one of their phones, giggling and gossiping about *something*. Whatever it was, they appeared to be wholly entranced and oblivious to her approach.

She chugged her coffee, powering through the heat burning down her throat, hoping she might feel more awake. She cleared her throat as she reached her friends. "What's got you three so excited today?"

Sonia's head snapped up, eyes wide and bright after a probably restful night. "There she is! How was your night last night? I heard you headed out early with some. . .*company*."

"Yeah, I did," Madi hummed, drawing Alaina and Janet's attention to her. "What? You two knew that."

"We did! But I want to know all the dirty details about it, so you will be spilling your guts later," said Alaina, more of a demand than anything else.

Madi tried not to laugh at her eagerness. Janet and Alaina usually shared the juicy tidbits of their dating lives without hesitation about getting into the dirty details. On the other hand, Madi usually kept the spicy bits to herself.

"Sure thing. Now, what's got you three all giggly?"

"Oh!" Alaina pointed at the phone. "Have you read up on any of the hot news from Hollywood Star Observer?"

"Madi doesn't read gossip magazines. She's too good for tabloids," Janet interjected, snorting. She took the phone from Sonia's hand, scrolling back up. "Apparently, there were some notable celebrities at Cobalt and Neon last night, including this super-hot baseball player."

"Imagine if one of us ended up dancing with him instead. That would've been insane!" Alaina fanned her face, taken by the fantasy of a famous paramour more than anything.

"Yeah, that would be cool. . . but this guy is allegedly trouble. The tabloids say he's supposedly a known player, never settling down while he hops from fling to fling. A shame because he's sexy."

Janet finally shoved the phone into Madi's hand, allowing her to see the photos. When Madi lifted the phone, she caught a clear sight of the images—a little grainy, but they told a straightforward story.

The guy in the photos stood tall, wearing dark clothes and ushering someone into a dark SUV. But the shimmering yet blurry glimpse of a golden dress ducking into the back of the SUV stopped Madi cold.

She swiped to the next image, breath instantly fading out of her chest. Despite the graininess of the previous shots, the last one captured an unmistakable visual of the man's face. The same face that she admired while he fucked her into the mattress last night, painted in the colors of the fireworks.

Cal.

Madi swiped through the photos until her finger threatened to cramp up, analyzing the frames. Besides the small strip of dress in the second photo, which was not enough to identify her, the photographer never caught her on film. But Cal's face was immortalized in their midnight retreat to his hotel room.

She searched for the accompanying paragraph attached to those photos, struck by the title: **PLAYBOY BASEBALL PLAYER SCORES BIG ON NYE.**

Avid fans of Major League Baseball might be on the edge of their seats at seeing Callum Lambert, 26, out for New Year's Eve with a mystery woman in

Los Angeles, California. The Foxhounds baseball player hasn't been seen in months since the end of the season. But it's been longer since he's been pictured out with a woman. Has Lambert returned to his player ways with all the questions surrounding his next moves?

Madi handed the phone back to Janet, at a loss for words, before the touch of it burned her. The headline and the commentary from whatever snarky celebrity gossip writer penned the article flashed across her vision. Thankfully, Madi hadn't eaten much, or she might have thrown up on the sidewalk.

She left the club with a famous baseball player last night. She *fucked* a star athlete!

"Mads, you okay?" Sonia's voice prodded through the rush of nausea clouding her thoughts, prompting a rush of nods from her. She might have made it through the day if she hadn't thought about it.

"All good. We should go inside for our shift," Madi lied, but no one checked her on it. The girls continued their gossip about what celebrities showed up at the club last night, starstruck by their proximity to the Hollywood elite. Yet Madi mulled over the night before with the new information.

She narrowly avoided a scandal that would've turned her whole world upside down. A close call if she ever had one.

Chapter 4

Cal

GROGGILY LIFTING HIS HEAD from the mountain of pillows, Cal acknowledged the insistent knocking with a middle finger. Never in his life had he considered himself a morning person. The dull headache throbbing between his temples hardly helped.

Cal's hand swept over the rumpled sheets beside him, anticipating the feel of a second body sharing the space. But when his hand ran unobstructed, his eyes snapped wide open despite the sleep crusting at the corners. The empty spot where Madi should've been greeted him instead.

Cal sat up, glancing around the room. The rational instinct would've been to guess she went to the bathroom. . . except her clothes weren't on the floor where they left them. *Did she leave? He usually was the one who left in the morning. . . not the other way around.*

The knocking continued, raising another decibel. The whole row of hotel rooms might be able to hear it. Cal, not in the mood for noise complaints, rolled out of bed despite the sharp ache in his left leg matching the inside of his head.

He snatched his discarded boxers off the floor, hoping into them while he tumbled toward the door. Cal bumped into the wall before he flung the door open, fixing the waistband of his boxers over his hips.

Tommy's hand recoiled, raising a brow at his undressed state. "Morning." The thin lines of his lips twitched, fighting back a smile.

"Morning." Cal rubbed at his face, shifting his weight off his left side. "I assume that Madi already left?"

"She did. But that's not why I'm here. Desmond's been calling me for the last twenty minutes because you haven't answered his calls. He sent me to make sure you weren't dead in a ditch somewhere."

Cal cursed under his breath. *Shit. Missing calls from his agent would earn him an ass-reaming later.* He stumbled toward the bed on unsteady legs, searching for his phone among the discarded pile of clothes.

Tommy let himself in and stood guard at the door, observing Cal. He leaned against the door and tapped at his phone. "He'll probably be calling you right about. . . now." As soon as he said that a muted buzz shouted from somewhere underneath the pile of clothes.

Cal ignored Tommy's chuckle while tearing through the clothing. He raised the phone into the air victoriously, flashing the screen with the almost dead battery begging for a charger. The unflattering photo he assigned to Desmond Dellbrook, his agent, took up the whole screen.

He answered the call, prepared to plead his case for forgiveness and brush it under the rug in one go. "How's my favorite agent doing—?"

"First of all, kid, glad you aren't dead or worse. Second, stop the nice bullshit before I punch you through the phone." With his voice gruff like a chain-smoker's, Desmond croaked on the other side of the call with annoyance on par with a coffee drinker deprived of their morning cup, "We clear?"

"Yeah, yeah, you old bastard. I was out late and needed to sleep in. Sue me," Cal replied.

Desmond scoffed, "Evidently—"

"What's that supposed to mean?" Cal couldn't stop himself from pulling a face. He met Desmond at the start of his college baseball career, needing a mentor to give him guidance. Desmond stepped into the fatherly role he craved without hesitation; his loyalty to Cal was why he signed with Desmond after he got drafted. So, much like family, the two loved and argued in equal measure.

He ambled to the dresser drawers, half-stuffed with his clothing for the warmer California weather. He grabbed a pair of linen trousers from the pile, not hesitating to change. Tommy would look away, and he spent years naked in front of other guys as a hazard of the job.

"I saw it on several gossip sites that got emailed to me, kid. Apparently, someone recognized you at some club in Los Angeles last night and snapped pictures of you getting into a car with some girl!" Desmond snapped.

Cal froze, swearing the phone nearly slipped from his grasp. He stumbled when putting on his pants before gripping the phone so firm his knuckles ached. He thought he'd been so careful, especially with her.

"What did they see?" Cal swallowed. He leaned against the dresser, hit by the headache and the familiar bitterness called "guilt" meshing together in one "fuck-you" from the universe.

"Of the girl? Not much. The only photo caught a grainy shot of her dress as she entered the car. I'll say she should've picked a less obvious color than gold," Desmond remarked, but Cal overlooked the snark of that last part. His agent never proved himself a fashion-forward guy to be talking such a big game. Relief came as the remedy to the suddenness of his worry, smoothing everything over. "But you? Your face is as clear as day in those images, and now everyone is running with headlines about the playboy returning. The first time you've been seen in months, and it's at some club. People are going to ask questions about the accident—"

Cal cut him off, "Got it. I assume you have everything under control with 'no comment,' and the team manager already knows?"

"I've been doing this since you were in diapers. I have it under control." Cal could see Desmond in his head, waving him off like he asked a stupid question. The secondary reason why he trusted Desmond: he was a mean, old son of a bitch. He worked like an attack dog; he needed that aggression in a cutthroat industry filled with people who sought to use and extort to land on top.

"Okay then, so you don't need me." Cal rifled around for a t-shirt to wear. He grabbed a light one to match the linen pants and prepare for the Californian heat. "I'll check in later for updates. I've got that meeting with the realtor in Los Feliz to close on escrow."

Cal didn't wait for an affirmative response or for Desmond to chew him out over all the missed calls. He ended the call and passed his phone over to Tommy, who would charge it for him on the ride to Los Feliz. It wouldn't be the first time a late-night bender of his needed assistance from Tommy the following day. It's why he paid a *hefty* bonus for his discretion and assistance.

He grabbed his wallet and room key, leaving everything else behind. He could get through the day, one thing at a time, starting with buying the house of his dreams.

He'd still miss Virginia Beach, though. Los Angeles was his first home, but Virginia left its mark in his memories.

Tommy and Cal strode down the hallway in total silence until the elevator, never needing to chatter aimlessly to fill the space. But when the elevator doors closed, Tommy flashed a crumpled piece of paper in his vision.

"What's this?" Cal asked, accepting the paper. "It looks like a receipt. . ."

"It is, but Miss Madison scribbled her number on the back in eyeliner for you. She dropped it in the back of the car, accidentally or intentionally. I figured you'd want to know that she wrote her number out," Tommy said with the most nonchalant hum.

Cal scrambled to turn over the receipt. As Tommy said, a phone number written in sparkly eyeliner by a shaky hand stared back at him. The sight of Madi's phone number—however messy and rushed through—tugged at the tension in his chest. She left without a goodbye to him, but her true thoughts sat on the receipt. She was open to seeing him again.

So, he wouldn't miss the opportunity. . . as long as the run-in with the paparazzi didn't send her running for the hills. She would be the first girl in a long time who was put off by his fame. He hoped that she'd give him a shot despite it.

"I need to borrow your phone in the car," Cal begged while he and Tommy strode across the lobby, non-stop since the elevator dropped them off. People stared as he passed, a few with recognition lighting up their faces. When he passed, a few guys in suits stopped their conversations to gawk at him.

"Sure thing, boss." Tommy chuckled while the two made a beeline for the car. Cal scowled at his driver; he was so glad that his slight desperation to chase after his most recent one-night stand amused Tommy so much. "I'll give you space, so you don't get performance anxiety when trying to woo Miss Madison back."

"Asshole." Cal rolled his eyes while he climbed into the backseat. The door shutting cut off any laughter from Tommy while he headed for the driver's side. He tossed his phone to Cal and rolled up the window without further teasing, giving him the space he promised.

Cal stared at Madi's number. He typed the number in the phone twice, double-checking the screen. He hadn't realized how clammy his hands became, growing hot from the phone in his grip. His thumb slid over the call button twice, and each pass brought a reconsideration.

If Madi dropped the paper, did she mean for him to have it? What if she changed her mind, and calling would be a mistake?

The what-ifs battled it out in his mind, swinging hard punches and knocking into one another. Sure, he could call Madi and look like an idiot with a bruised ego if she turned him down. But he'd never know unless he tried.

Cal's leg bounced in perfect sync with the ringing. The first few rings passed without any sign of Madi returning his call. She might've decided not to see him again, or maybe the unknown number deterred her from picking up the call.

But just as the phone would head to voicemail, the other line picked up with a polite, borderline timid "Hello?" Madi's voice was unmistakable, even when softer spoken.

"Madi, hi. . . It's Cal," he paused, waiting to see if she hung up on him. Luckily, the other line went quiet beyond the small huffs of her breathing. "Listen, I heard about the photos going viral, and my driver found the number you left behind in the car. I wanted to check if you're doing alright."

"I am now. I was a little shaken up before when my friends were gossiping about who possibly went home with the famous baseball player from the club last night. Speaking of. . . that was a shock to learn after the fact." Madi sighed, teetering on the edge between disappointed and eerily calm.

Cal winced. "I know. I should've told you sooner, but I thought we had been careful enough last night. I apologize for causing you stress." He hated the thought of making people's lives harder because of their proximity to him and his proximity to fame. There was a reason he lost most of the people in his life before all the fame.

"It's okay. You did your best. I should've guessed there was more to the story after we ran into that guy at the bar." Madi's voice curved, invoking the image of her shrugging her shoulders, clad in scrubs. Cal imagined them in a powder blue or maybe a soft pink. After she mentioned it last night, he hadn't asked what kind of nursing she did.

He shook his head, shunning the thoughts to the side momentarily. He should focus on what mattered if he wanted to keep things smooth. He'd been out of the dating game for so long that he became rusty, huh?

"Still, I knew better. In apology for my carelessness, I owe you a nice dinner where we can talk and get to know one another," Cal remarked. A soft noise of protest sounded from Madi, but a hum from him dissuaded her from a full-blown retort. "I insist. I know a place where no amateur paparazzi can find us. . . The food's pretty alright too."

He held his breath, giving Madi the space to accept or deny. Regardless of the answer, he gave it his all. The choice would be hers.

Madi took a moment before laughing. "That sounds great. So should I call you back after work, or will you call me back?"

"I'm borrowing Tommy's phone since mine is almost dead. I forgot to charge it after last night. So, I'll call you tonight to set up plans." Immediately, a to-do list of what he needed to make a solid evening flashed in his mind.

"I look forward to hearing from you." Madi's voice softened as the background noise around her grew louder, echoing with footsteps and conversations of other people. "Bye, Cal."

"Bye." Grinning like a madman, Cal rolled the window down and leaned through it for Tommy. "Switch phones. I need to bother a friend for a favor."

Tommy snorted but did as Cal requested, swapping his phone for Cal's barely charged one. Twenty percent worked enough for a short phone call to a good friend with plenty of strings in the City of Angels.

Cal hit the familiar contact and rolled up the window. Unlike before, he clicked on speakerphone and relaxed while the phone rang. He didn't have to wait for an answer as long as with Madison since the phone picked up after the second ring.

"Cal, there is no way you're calling me this early," the groggy, sleep-heavy voice of one Jensen Ramsey filled the backseat of his car. "Is it an emergency?"

"Good morning to you, Sunshine. I'm calling for a favor that's a little time-sensitive." Cal slumped back in his seat. He heard some inaudible noises and braced for Jensen to cuss him out before getting to business.

"Make it quick," Jensen grumbled, more exasperated than anything. I have important business to attend to." His seemingly serious demeanor crumbled when Cal overheard the rumple of blankets and distinctly feminine laughter just beyond the phone.

Ah, so that was Daisy's new nickname. Important business.

Cal waggled his brows, knowing Jensen couldn't see the shit-eating grin he likely wore. "Say hi to the missus for me."

"Your favor, Lambert?" Jensen interjected with his perfected *don't flirt with my wife, that's my job* tone.

"I need a recommendation for a private car service willing to drive from downtown to the Ridge and last-minute dinner reservations for two sometime this week."

Cal heard Jensen sigh, some background noise from one Daisy Ramsey, and then the eventual, "Alright. I'll call you back later with your request. Now, if you'll excuse me. . ."

"You're the best." Cal refrained from a snarky comment after Jensen's generosity for such an early morning. He knew when to push the boundaries with his friends, but he wouldn't ruin his hard work either—not when he needed things to go smoothly.

Like a miracle worker—or the owner of the most sought-after luxury resort in Southern California, The Royal Ridge—Jensen managed to scrounge up a reservation for two at Abalone at the end of the week.

Cal organized everything in the few days between the first call and dinner. He secured a car to Madi's place, ensured he got the dress code right, and handled all the security passes for her so the night would be stress-free.

Sitting at a table bordering the wall, Cal listened to the ample, ambient conversations swirling overhead. He drowned himself in the presence of the packed restaurant, finding it better than checking his smartwatch every other minute in a panic that Madi decided to change her mind.

He opened a bottle of wine, but the half-filled glass remained untouched. With enough wine, he'd grow hot under the collar of his pristine white dress shirt. For once, he took his outfit choice seriously. . . and consulted the wise minds of Claire and Daisy for some brutally honest fashion advice.

He got more than he bargained for, but Cal left his new house looking better than any outfit he picked out on his own.

Cal's leg bounced underneath the table while he counted the seconds under his breath. Without baseball, a natural jitteriness settled into his body for moments like this, ready to run wild at the worst possible times. He flipped over his phone, searching for a text from Madi. Instead, he closed the screen on a "you feeling okay?" text from Claire, who might've sensed the distance in his texts.

His impatience whistled in his veins, wondering what might happen by the end of the night. Cal couldn't remember the last time he went on an actual date, let alone with someone who didn't look at him and see the famed baseball player. Everything would be okay as long as–

"Cal?" Madi's voice punched straight through his hectic thoughts. His head whipped toward her, too late to smooth over a spooked reaction. However, seeing her in a black dress clinging to her body and layered necklaces dangling into the tasteful cleavage she displayed put all the buzzing on mute.

"Madi, hi!" he scrambled onto his feet, screeching the chair a little too loud. A few tables turned their way to stare but quickly returned to their business. Cal swallowed back the nerves. "You look amazing."

"Thank you. You look great, too, by the way." Madi smiled. The two leaned toward her chair, grazing their arms in awkward laughter. But Madi stepped back enough for Cal to drag out her chair.

The two sat across from one another, hands reaching for their drinks and napkins neatly folded in the corner of the table. Cal swirled his wine, and Madi rattled her water to the twinkling chimes when the ice knocked against the glass. Neither spoke up, at least not at first.

But when Madi cleared her throat, the tension in the air abated as if the mere touch of her voice pierced through its underbelly. The soft flutter of her lashes while she studied him drew Cal in, bringing him to scoot his chair closer to the table.

She cocked her head to the side. "So, I know the photos came as a shock to both of us. . . but I've finally managed to drop the worry that something bad's about to come. I don't think anyone knows it was me."

"More photos would've surfaced by now if people had them," Cal agreed. "Considering my expertise in these things, you're in the clear."

"Being seen with me—or my dress—didn't get you into trouble, right? I haven't told anyone about the other night. I wouldn't—" asked Madi.

Cal shook his head. "You're fine. I didn't get into trouble besides my agent's crabby call. He's used to me by now."

"Apparently, you have a bit of a reputation," Madi hummed between sips of her water. Although, she eyed the wine in his hands with a graceful once-over, broadcasting the hunger through a single look. "Is it true? That you're known as a womanizer, a playboy who jumps from girl to girl?"

"The old me. I was a little fast and loose with my flings, and the media loved every second of it. I made for good content. But it's been years since I acted like that... only they've never let it go." Admitting that lifted a small weight off his chest, but the remainder sat on Cal.

Being a playboy might've been a *blip* of time in his life. However, reputations lived on forever once the press sank their claws into it. His old ways hung over his head, broadcasting his greatest shame whenever someone ran a headline or generated some new think piece on him.

Madi nodded. She didn't rush to respond, chewing on his explanation until the silence needled at Cal. Thankfully, she broke the tension with a hum. "I understand. For what it's worth, I enjoyed spending time with you the other night... a lot. The playboy thing doesn't scare me off."

"It doesn't?" Cal could've kicked himself under the table for how incredulous he sounded. He forced himself to breathe before he shoved his whole foot into his mouth, knowing Madi opened the door for a chance. "Would that mean you'd want to see me again?"

"Absolutely. But how about you, superstar?"

"It's been a while since I've actively considered dating. However, I'm willing to give this thing—*our thing*—an honest try. My life trajectory has shifted majorly in the last few years, and I would love to spend my frequent free time with someone. You seem like just the girl for the job." Cal grinned.

He finally set down his wine, taking Madi's hand in his. His thumb traced over the ridges of her knuckles, sparking up heat in the wake of his fingertip. Their eyes locked from across the table, a much shorter distance than their first glance at the nightclub bar. The rest of the world ceased to exist, at least for that moment.

"Then, I think we should see each other again. . . so long as tonight goes well," Madi said, lips curled into a picture-perfect smile. Her cheeks downright glowed under the restaurant's lights. Compared to the neutral black dress, each piece of Madi loudly stamped its bold mark on the world. The goddess in gold became the goddess in black, still radiant.

Cal chuckled when the waiter quietly dropped a basket of bread and oil at the table's edge and dashed away without interruption. He squeezed Madi's hand and said, "This is officially a do-over date. No clothes will be lost this time."

"Maybe. The night's still young." Madi laughed, head leaning back. She grasped his hand nice and tight, shaking it. "Hi there. I'm Madison."

"Hey, Madison. I'm Cal," he whispered back, letting the moment savor. He liked the sound of a do-over date. Tonight could be the start of something. . . *good*, as long as they kept the rest of the world out.

Chapter 5

Madi

JANUARY ALWAYS DRAGGED BY so slowly after the excitement of the new year, making one week feel like a whole lot longer than seven sunrises and sunsets. It was in that "eternity" that Madi began texting Cal. She dropped the first text after their date, half-expecting him to respond every few hours like most men she had dated before.

Instead, she barely set her phone down once she hit send before it buzzed with Cal's response. Eager, excited responses chased after hers within minutes. Cal never left her messages unread for an hour, leagues ahead of the rest of the dating pool.

It was the difference between the major league and little league, turning their week-long acquaintanceship into something more profound. Madi felt like she'd known Cal all her life instead of several measly days.

His responses—filled with humor and plenty of tongue-in-cheek sass—kept her skipping down the hospital halls. She felt the looks of her colleagues whenever she passed by, smiling after reading something Cal sent her. She earned her fair share of curious questions and gentle prying from coworkers and patients alike, all wondering what made her so smiley—or more smiley than usual.

That morning wasn't an exception. Madi had an evening shift at the hospital, usually the worst possible shift for her. All her friends clocked out the night before and headed off to one of the nearby haunts popular with all the hospital staff. She should've been bummed to be alone. Yet, Cal's grin lingered in her thoughts whenever she checked her phone for some new text.

He revived the pep in her step while she ran through her final rotation, having seen the sunrise when she should've been buried face-first in her bed. Despite craving coffee, she needed a few hours of sleep before tomorrow's shift.

Madi clicked her pen as she crossed into the last room on her rotation, the final barrier between her and her bed, smiling. "Morning, Robby. How are you feeling?"

In the hospital bed, a boy no older than sixteen shook out his hair when the textured fringe fell into his eyes but offered a polite smile. The poor thing had a rough recovery after a car hit him while he was skateboarding, landing him in the hospital with a dislocated pelvis and other injuries. But the kid took everything in stride with a sarcastic comment at the ready. He was Madi's favorite patient.

"Eh, feels like I got hit by a car," he snorted when Madi approached his side of the bed. He didn't fuss when handing his uninjured arm over for a vitals check, used to her poking and prodding by now. "At least I'm getting visitors today. I've run out of books to read."

"Oh? Who's coming to visit?" Madi ran down her checklist when assessing Robby's vitals, falling into muscle memory. Caring for people… That acted as second nature to her dead, tired brain.

"Chel decided to bring a whole army of people today with some breakfast. No offense, but hospital food sucks," Robby remarked. A smirk brightened the freckles splattered across his cheekbones. His nose scrunched, further accentuating the *very valid* observation that hospital food sucked.

"Sounds exciting. Are you excited?"

"Yeah. My sister told me several friends—Amy, Yasmin, and Mo—asked to see me. However, I'm hoping that my girlfriend comes with them. I'm overdue a face-to-face visit instead of a video chat." The mention of his girlfriend softened Robby's features even more. Madi had met her once or twice at the start, recalling the pretty blonde who sat at his bedside for visiting hours.

"Well, I hope she comes. You're always smiling for hours after she leaves, even with that busted hip," Madi teased while noting his blood pressure for her notes. "If you need any pain medication, now's the time."

"I'm okay for now. I want to eat first, spend some time with everyone." Robby shook his head. Yeah, that kid was a trooper.

Madi slotted her clipboard under her arm. "Well, I'll see you for the late shift this evening. Have a good visit. I'm sure they'll be as happy to see you as I am every shift." She patted the edge of the bed, sharing a grin with Robby.

She headed for the door, but his voice stopped her before she got too far. "Before you go, could you change the channel? I'd prefer sports or news," Robby asked, awkwardly lying in bed with his compression stocking and the baggy shorts loose around his thighs.

Madi smiled. "Of course! Let me get that for you." She snatched the remote off the nearby chair. She flipped through the channels to the flashes of game show re-runs and morning talk shows on celebrity news.

But when she landed on the sports channel, Cal's face plastered on the screen stuck Madi to her spot. She stared at his headshot, one with him in his baseball jersey and the gray colored ball cap, stranded somewhere between the border of fear and anticipation. *Oh no.*

Madi unmuted the television, catching the tail-end of whatever comment the talking head in the camera's focus said, ". . .I've got to be honest, Joe. I don't think Lambert is coming back next season."

"What makes you say that?" Several panel members asked follow-up questions, but one stood out above the rest.

"By this point in the post-season, we should've heard about his recovery. The Foxhounds are hoping for a miracle and that he can return from the impossible. Unfortunately, we all saw pictures of that damn crash and heard a small extent of his injuries. I don't think he's returning to baseball—next season or ever—and the Foxhounds are waiting to release the news," the commentator replied, shrugging so nonchalantly as if he hadn't predicted the end of a man's career.

Madi soaked in every word, jaw dropped. She vaguely felt herself handing the remote off to Robby in the bed beside her. *Crash? Was Cal in an accident? When? Not today, right—?*

She had been texting him not long ago but couldn't remember the hour of their last contact. At first, something cold spread across her chest with all its prickling, naming itself once the sensation climbed into her throat. *Panic.* Every nerve within her legs screamed for her to run for her phone and call him, proving that he was okay, but her eyes were glued to the television screen.

"As succinct as your analysis is, Phil, Lambert can beat the odds. The kid has been a star since his college days for anyone versed in his stats. No news can mean that his months of recovering since the accident are going well. People have seen him out and about after all."

Madi swallowed hard, shoving the panic into the bottom of her stomach. *Not today. . . Months ago. Thank goodness.* The relief came in, but confusion slipped through the opened door alongside it.

During their chats, Cal mentioned the trajectory of his life shifting recently, but she never questioned it too hard. She had assumed other things—maybe he was traded to a team in Los Angeles or something benign. She never considered forced retirement, which added another reason to keep them out of the limelight.

Heat stung at the back of her eyes while she admired Cal's smiling face on the screen. His eyes used to be much brighter, sparkling with mischief. Had he lost the light in the accident, or did that come after the fallout?

"Always rooting for the underdog, huh Joe? Only time will tell whether Cal Lambert's career has crashed and burned and what will become of the Foxhounds without their star player. Their finish to the season—missing the playoffs—ended up rocky, and the future doesn't look so optimistic for future returns to the World Series."

All further discussion ended with a segue from an unnamed panel member to a commercial break. An ad for an anti-depressant filled the room, playing the cheesy commercial of smiling people and dancing trees on the tiny, cramped screen. Yet, Madi stared into it like the abyss while her head rattled through all the chaos.

"Uh, I'm heading out... See you later, Robby." Madi cleared her throat, trying to shake off any lingering weirdness. She should've gone by now but gawked at the television, ready to keel over.

She didn't hear his response while she strode down the hallway. She dropped her chart at the nurses' station when she passed, not stopping long enough to get lost in conversation. Mustering a smile came harder than she ever expected, tossed about her thoughts harder than a ship on troubled waters.

What hadn't Cal told her? How much information was she missing?

She shut herself into the locker room, comforted by the empty space. Madi dodged around any items out of place from their respective lockers while picking out hers from the crowded cluster.

Madi grabbed her bag and her phone out of her locker. She dropped the bag at the foot of the bench and settled in front of the rows of lockers. She sat down, turning her phone on. Messages poured in, all demanding her attention for something.

The JAMS text chat had a dozen unread messages, several email notifications cluttered her screen, and her last listened-to playlist popped up for her focus. But she searched for her text chain with Cal among all the notifications.

> **CAL: Okay, my turn**

> **CAL: if it was an ideal day off work, what would you make for breakfast?**

> **CAL: I feel like this says a lot about a person**

His last text, so harmless and straightforward compared to the rush of emotions Madi sat with in the empty locker room, almost pulled a laugh out of her. Whether in relief or over the lingering confusion of it all, it didn't matter. A few minutes before, Cal sat on the other line and sent the question, probably smiling to himself.

Madi didn't hesitate to answer, nor did she play coy. She knew all the dating advice of her friends would suggest she let him simmer in the wait before she responded. Don't be desperate, she heard in Janet's disapproving drawl.

But if Janet had a guy like Cal on the other end of the line, Madi doubted her "rules" would still apply.

> MADI: I love a good pastry in the morning. I always have eggs and protein at home, but I like something sweet with it. So, I adore this bakery in Santa Monica—Buttery Bites—that makes THE BEST chocolate stuffed croissants.

> MADI: That, paired with some scrambled eggs, chicken sausage, and iced coffee, makes the best possible start to my day.

Madi relaxed when she tapped that send button. During their date at the Royal Ridge—a place she still hadn't gotten over—Cal proposed an innocent game of questions. They needed to get to know one another since they had busy schedules, and neither hated icebreakers that much. So, they made it into a game, sharing answers and swapping turns on questions. None of the questions got too deep, only one week into the exploration.

Yet, Madi learned small crumbs about Cal with each response she got back. Cal, the Los Angeles native who packed up everything for the other side of the country when he got drafted into the MLB. Cal, the guy who loved early mornings when he could watch the sunrise while on a walk. Cal, the loud and proud dog person who knew dozens of fun facts about various dog breeds in preparation for the day he finally got a dog. Each piece built a better vision of the complete picture, making the man named Callum Lambert.

She had seen him without clothes, so the "getting to know" piece seemed logical. Should it have been the first step? Probably. But there was something fun in the unconventional adventure their relationship took. *Whirlwind* suited its description perfectly.

Madi cleared the rest of the notifications with quick responses and cursory glances over emails. Nothing grabbed her attention, not with urgency nipping at her sneakered heels.

Exhaustion from the end of the shift finally set in, seizing her by the shoulders. She should head out before she fell asleep behind the wheel. Her bed called her for the next few hours.

Madi trudged out of the locker room with her bag slung over her shoulders. She plastered on a smile, more for the comfort of her coworkers, as she headed for the elevators. She blinked heavily, lost in her own world despite the shuffling of her aching feet.

On autopilot, she walked into the sunny Los Angeles morning in the blink of an eye, swearing she just stepped onto the elevator. Blinded by the light, her eyes squinted shut as she searched for her car. However, it didn't take long to find its bright yellow exterior standing out among white, black, and silver.

She jogged the rest of the way, rushing to get home sooner. But as she tossed her bag into the backseat with a soft *thud*, her phone buzzed in her hands and caught her attention.

Madi checked her screen, catching sight of Cal's name:

> **CAL: Wait, that sounds amazing. You'll need to cook for me sometime… or at least give me the directions to that bakery.**

> **CAL: I believe it's your turn**

Immediately, flashes of the commentary panel from the hospital room played through her head. Once confident, her hands typed a question, and she stared at the screen. *When you said your life trajectory has changed, why is that?*

Shame burned her palms until they sweat, turning her fingers slippery. Faster than she typed her question, she deleted it. Something told her to keep the question to herself, not to scare Cal away by coming on too strong or too accusatory.

It was none of her business. . . It was none of her business, right?

Madi slid into the driver's seat of her hatchback and closed herself in, welcomed by the faint aroma of the cherry car freshener hanging from her rearview mirror. The slight clutter in the backseat collected light specks of lint and a few discarded cardigans she wore on the colder days before her shifts. This place brought unspoken comfort, rich in memories.

She held onto her phone, sending Cal the spare question. She hoped he found *what reality television show do you think you could win and why?* favorable, blissfully unaware of her growing curiosity about his life before her.

She stared at the screen. The next thing Madi knew, she opened an internet browser tab and entered his name and 'accident' into the search bar. Guilt could eat her alive, but the curiosity might get the job done faster.

Madi watched the screen load, chewing her lip while the news articles appeared. Headlines in bold blue exploded across the screen, but she didn't click on them.

Instead, she switched over to images. Madi assumed her years in the medical field could keep her calm, but she thought so wrong. The sight of metal shrapnel on a dark road and a mangled motorcycle turned her stomach upside down.

Madi closed the tab, exiting without a second thought about the photos. She closed her eyes, shaking her head. "I can't. . . I shouldn't look without his permission."

Cal told her the other night that the paparazzi ran with their narratives, whichever story got them the clicks and the money. They had their side to the story, but not the correct or full one. Cal knew his story better.

But she couldn't ask him, at least not right then. And if she couldn't muster the courage to ask him face-to-face or through a measly text, then she wasn't ready to know the truth of whatever happened in that accident.

Some things were better left in the dark until they needed to come into the light. Her curiosity could starve; Madi wasn't interested in the fullness of guilt instead.

Chapter 6
Cal

CHOCOLATE MELTING ON HIS tongue, and the crunch from the buttery, flakey crust of the croissant immediately woke Cal up. He hadn't even taken a sip of iced coffee from *the* Buttery Bites—just as Madi described—but he knew it would be a million times better than he imagined.

Madi had great taste. . . Evident by her choice of food *and* men.

The more he got to know her, the more Cal liked Miss Madison Caldwell. His phone buzzed constantly with texts from Madi on her days off, always equipped with a funny or flirty response to any of his questions. Even on her work shifts, she never left him hanging for too long without an answer. A woman held Cal's undivided attention for the first time in a long time.

As he sat in Desmond's office, primed with a perfect view of Melrose Ave and the roads winding through the heart of Hollywood, Madi kept him company with his choice of breakfast. *Her favorite breakfast.* He could almost hear her voice echoing in his head, laughing at the pleased expressions he probably pulled. Without Desmond sitting across from him while he loudly barked on his phone, the office became the perfect space for an already hectic morning.

If he were back in Virginia Beach, he'd probably be running with his guys in the air-conditioned facilities of the Foxhound gym. Despite the itch the move burrowed under his skin, Cal tried to embrace the warm morning and the hint of possibility in the air. A man stranded between two lives and two homes, neither fit quite right anymore.

He could blame the exhaustion, sure. He hadn't been sleeping much these days, spending nights roaming through his brand-new bachelor pad. But whenever the groan of an engine sped past the quiet neighborhood street, every nerve inside him flared. It would be better to do something than lay there in his new bed, running through the same old nightmares.

Cal reached for his iced coffee once he devoured the last bites of the croissant, cleaning all the crumbs stuck on his bottom lip with a swipe of his tongue. Before he dove in, the door swung open behind him. Desmond's heavy steps in his boots announced his presence loud and proud, almost as if his demeanor screamed his arrival through a megaphone.

However, additional footsteps followed behind Desmond's, spinning Cal's head around on his shoulders. Several strangers in suits shuffled into the office space, lining up against the back wall without so much as a word. Yet all of their eyes landed on him, quiet in their assessment.

He knew the look all too well, used to people sizing him up on and off the field.

Somehow, he didn't think Desmond's surprise opportunity for his post-baseball life included an emotionless wall of suits watching him. Although he could never predict his agent's next moves with perfect certainty, Desmond always likened himself to a human curveball, relishing in the surprises that came from him being a wild card.

Cal cocked his head, shooting silent questions with his eyes to a beaming Desmond. *What did that old bastard have up his sleeve?* But then Desmond stepped to the side, revealing the last person to step into the office.

Cal wished he had kept himself together when his gaze landed on Joe Avery, one of the greatest ballplayers of the last few decades, Hall of Famer, and beloved baseball commentator. However, the little kid in him took one look at good old Joe with all the flashbacks to the poster he stuck on his bedroom wall. Where most guys he knew lined their walls with swimsuit models or cars, he collected baseball players. It came to the shock of no one when Cal chased his baseball dreams to the biggest diamonds in the league.

His slack jaw elicited a chuckle from Joe Avery, who fixed his bolo tie. Texas radiated off him in the worn boots and denim jeans, missing only a pristine cowboy perched atop his thinned-out, wheat-colored hair. His sun-touched tan didn't hide the ruddiness of his cheeks or the blinding glint of his open-mouthed grin. Although older and a little more wrinkled in the face, the titan of sports television looked like he stepped straight off one of Cal's old posters.

"You weren't lying, Des," Joe bellowed as Desmond shut the door behind him, clapping his hands together. He grinned at Cal, gesturing to all of him. "This guy would make for amazing television. He should be on every magazine cover with a face like his."

Desmond's grin broadened when he shot a discreet wink at Cal, whose body appeared stuck to the chair. His phone buzzing in his hand, chirping over new notifications, dragged him straight through the paralysis of staring his childhood hero in the eye. "I never lie about good deals. So, it's my honor to introduce you to my star client, Callum Lambert. Cal, I don't think Joe needs an introduction."

"No, he doesn't. It's a pleasure to meet you, sir." Cal broke free of the emotions weighing him down to the chair. In a split second, any heaviness dissipated into the air as Cal offered his hand to Joe. "Longtime fan."

"Nice to meet you, Cal. I've seen your work. You're arguably one of the best players to join the league in the last few years." Joe grasped his hand, giving a firm shake. Cal hoped his palms weren't half as clammy as he thought. In the face of meeting his childhood idol, he had the demeanor of a teen boy meeting his girlfriend's dad for the first time.

Desmond poked his head into view, interrupting, "Alright, now that we've all met, let's discuss business."

"Of course." Joe reached for the spare chair beside Cal's. He and Cal sat across the desk from Desmond, who lounged in his leather chair and clasped his hands together. If Cal didn't know him as well as he did, the sight evoked the posture of an action-movie villain. "As I'm sure Cal knows, *Beyond the Bases* is one of the more popular talk shows for baseball during the annual season and playoffs. We routinely pull in massive viewership numbers, but the panel of three is looking to expand full time. . . and we want him to join us."

Cal wished he would've taken a sip of his iced coffee because then he'd have an excuse for the startled choking noise rattling in his throat. Instead, he masked it as a cough, burying his face into his elbow to avoid looking anyone in the eye. *This wasn't happening! He had to be dreaming or something—*

Desmond, not waiting for him to get ahold of himself, said, "Considering that Cal has a newly free schedule, and the press keeps asking questions about his return to baseball, we have the perfect opportunity to launch this next stage in his career. Baseball is what brings us all together. . . right, Cal?"

Cal wiped his mouth, catching his composure while everyone watched. "Absolutely. My schedule is wide open for the foreseeable future. The Foxhounds and I haven't officially announced my departure, but I'd like to figure out my next moves before I make the news public."

"Well, I've got two opportunities for you then. Like I told Des, I want you to be on my panel. According to people who've met you and your past post-game interviews in the last few years, you have the charisma necessary to be in front of a camera. Your knowledge of the sport shines through, too. So, we can either get you as a full-time commentator on *Beyond the Bases* or have you join us during playoff season as a guest. These things are up to your schedule, which Des has been coy about in our conversations," said Joe.

He looked at Desmond, who still steepled his hands and quietly smirked in his chair. Clearly, Des had been hard at work while Cal galivanted around Los Angeles and tried not to think about baseball.

"Truth be told, working with you is such a high honor for me. Baseball—as eloquently said—brings us all together. It's the one interest that stuck around throughout my life, and I won't let it go simply because I don't run the bases anymore. I'd love to join you full-time if you'll have me." Cal sat up in his seat.

He watched the faces around the room, how they perked up the further along he spoke. Cal focused his gaze on Joe and Desmond, the two people with the power to set this new vision into motion. Cal hoped his sincerity dripped off everything he said, but he wasn't sure how else he could convince them that he was perfect for the job.

If only the past version of himself could see the brighter future ahead. . . Knowing that the world wasn't unfathomably bleak in the wake of him losing baseball might've made the road to recovery a little less tedious.

Desmond's voice pulled Cal out of his quiet contemplation, reminding him that he wasn't the only one in the room. Something he said must've been a hit from how boisterous Joe's laughter pinged off the walls, encouraging echoes of chuckling from the suits gathered around them. What a shame that Cal missed it.

But when his agent leaned forward, he slapped something onto his desk before pushing it toward Cal. *His company credit card.* "Joe, your lawyers are waiting in the lobby. While we hammer all that boring contractual stuff out, Cal will take you to lunch on behalf of Farley, Walker, and Dellbrook. There are some fantastic restaurants nearby that would bend over backward to host two shining stars of baseball. Personally, I'm a huge fan of Sal's Slices, this Chicago deep dish pizzeria and sports bar three blocks away."

"You sure, Des? I'm not necessarily hurting for cash," Cal lowered his voice when scooting closer to the desk. He laid his hand over the corporate card, still flashing a smile for the sake of his audience.

"Nah, let the company take care of it," Des whispered back, matching Cal's smile. He nudged the card into Cal's open, sweaty palm. "We here at Farley, Walker, and Dellbrook are family. That means all our guests are treated like family."

"Ain't that nice. What say you, Lambert? Care to spend the next few hours or so with me over some cheap beer and greasy pizza?" asked Joe, swinging himself out of his chair to loom over the desk.

Cal wasn't dumb enough to hesitate. He rose from his chair, snatching up the crumbs of his breakfast in the crumpled pastry bag and the half-empty iced coffee with its partially melted ice cubes.

"Let's go. I could use the walk to Sal's." Cal grabbed the door for Joe, holding it long enough to shoot Desmond a look. More of a *please don't screw this up* in a teasing way that Des knew all too well. "When the papers are ready to sign, you'll call us back?"

"Of course. But don't worry your pretty little head about it, Cal. That's why you hired me." The room roared, amused by Desmond's tongue-in-cheek commentary. Cal rolled his eyes and shrugged it off when the door shut behind him.

He held the iced coffee after trashing the pastry bag on his way to the elevator. Joe walked beside him with his hands tucked into his pockets. Neither spoke when getting on the elevator or when the doors closed. Instead, Cal watched Joe take a call, facing the corner and talking in hushed tones.

Cal's hands swapped the company credit card for his phone, rushing straight for the unanswered texts from Madi.

> FIREFLY: Are we still on for tonight? You said you had a big meeting today, but I forgot to ask when!

> FIREFLY: *2 photo attachments*

One of the photos included a mirror selfie of Madi wearing pink scrubs and flashing a cheeky peace sign. The other showed off a full spread of seafood and pasta materials, causing drool to gather under his tongue. Oh, he would be eating good today. . . Dinner *and* dessert, if he was lucky.

> CAL: I'll be there. The meeting is ongoing, but I don't see it going past 5PM tonight.

His message barely delivered before the read receipt appeared at the bottom. Those three typing bubbles eagerly bounced in the corner of the text chain before Madi's reply sped into view.

> FIREFLY: great! I'll text when my shift ends around 7 so Tommy can bring you to mine!

Cal's throat bobbed when reading that last message over twice. He liked the message, knowing Madi spoke nothing but the truth. He still heard the rustling of the sheets, paired with the breathy moans rolling off Madi's glossy pink lips in his head. He barely hid his phone when the elevator spat him and Joe out at the lobby, garnering stares from people milling around the space.

No sooner than Cal and Joe exited the Farley, Walker, and Dellbrook building, Joe turned to him, cocking his head. He hummed, "Alright, Lambert. . . It's just you and I now. Let's get to the real test." The once affable smile muted while Joe's eyes darkened, studying Cal from head to toe.

"I thought I left pop quizzes back in high school," Cal joked, unsure how else to respond. He kept walking, dragging his pace until he fell into step with Joe, but managed fleeting eye contact. "Any chance I could ask what I'm in for?"

"I researched your life before and after baseball, but I know I shouldn't believe anything I read without scrutiny. I could ask Desmond all my questions, but I'll get more honesty from you. No offense to him because I admire his reputation as an attack dog, but his aggression flares fast and hard. It leaves little room for transparency. Got it?"

At that moment, Cal stared into the gaze of his childhood hero and didn't see the charismatic, beloved star. He saw a man, one just like him. Joe built a legitimate media empire; someone like him with *his baggage* might be a wild card. The last thing he ever wanted was to destroy someone else's life because of his bad rep.

So, Cal swallowed his pride and nodded. "Got it. Whatever you want to know, it's on the table. I'm not the guy the media wants me to be, I promise."

"That's what I like to hear." Joe relaxed, shaking off the gruffness while the two approached a red crosswalk. "I heard you're a California native?"

"Born and raised in the South Bay, yeah. I lived there until college, and only after I graduated did I leave the state for the last few years. Virginia Beach is great, but something about California is irreplaceable." Cal shrugged.

"I've heard the same from every Angeleno I know. According to your profile, you attended school in Santa Barbara, is that right?" The little walk sign flashed, coaxing Cal and Joe across the faded crosswalk and cracked asphalt stained with runaway tire treads from over the years.

"Go Gauchos. . . Yet I don't think that's what you wanted to know," Cal snorted, giving a half-hearted fist pump to his alma mater. Whenever people coming down the opposite side of the road stared, he tugged the baseball cap lower over his eyes. His dark hair brushed right into his vision, fixed by his calloused fingertips.

"I'm always a Bruin guy myself," Joe chuckled, all gruff and gravel in his throat like the Los Angeles smog, "but I assume you played baseball there, too?"

"Yes, sir. Baseball for all four years while I worked on grabbing my degree. . . in sports journalism."

"Isn't that a lucky choice? You'll put that degree to good use if you join *Beyond the Bases*."

"I suppose it works out. College had always been more about baseball than sitting in lecture halls for me, but I took my education seriously. My best friend, Claire, would've had my head if I blew my potential on a maybe." Cal's eyes wandered ahead of him and Joe while chatting. He caught sight of the pizza-shaped neon sign mounted on the exterior of a white, industrial-style building on the corner. *Sal's Slices.*

"Sounds like a good friend," Joe hummed in response. "How about your family? I assume they had strong feelings about the baseball gig as a long-term career path?"

"It's me and my parents, no siblings or other relatives. We don't really talk beyond the occasional phone call. There was never much to talk about anyway with my folks." Cal breezed past that response without a care. If it made him sound heartless or out of line, then that was a truth from which he couldn't run.

Putting it nicer would be misleading for the sake of comfort. . . and something told him that Joe wasn't the type to appreciate white lies for pleasantries.

Joe pursed his lips and nodded, saying nothing more on that subject. *As Cal had thought.* Honesty without fault might score him the gig after all. Desmond could scold him later for being crass or too comfortable ruining the careful image he and the rest of Cal's team pieced together. For the moment, the truth controlled every bit of information diving out of his mouth; *nothing* appeared off the table.

The two men slowed their leisurely pace to a standstill when they reached Sal's Slices, with its vibrant red windows and the classic maximalist décor of a dad sports bar shining through the glass. People flowed past them on their way, some hesitating when seeing them. Yet the world felt perched on the edge of the conversation with how Cal met Joe's eyes, finding the curiosity still not satiated.

"One last question from me, and then I promise we'll enjoy pizza and a pint." Joe reached for the door to Sal's. "How do you feel about leaving baseball? That was your dream since you were younger, and now it's sitting in the rearview mirror."

Cal froze. He had months to think about his new reality, accept the circumstances, and face his unanswered what-ifs. However, Cal avoided the discussion in the thick of physical therapy, blowing off anyone who broached the question. Clinging to the hope that he would return to the field and wear his uniform again got him through the physical, only for those hopes to be dashed.

He would *never* play again, not at the level of the professionals, and he needed to learn to accept that.

"I hated it. For months, I pretended like every doctor was wrong about me, desperate to prove them wrong. Then, I spent so much of my time angry because of how someone's senseless act could rob me of everything. But now, I'm coming to terms with it, slowly but surely." He might've stammered over himself once or twice, but Cal couldn't fault the execution when the words spoke volumes.

"You will. My wife always says. . . Used to say, sorry." Sadness glossed over Joe's eyes as he caught himself. Joe's wife and former high school sweetheart, Gretchen, had passed away a few months back due to cancer. Cal remembered the news in the haze of his days in the hospital; that news cycle had been ruthless. "She used to say to love something deeply is to embrace the pain if it ends. I never understood how right she was until I lost her."

"She was a wise woman," Cal whispered.

Joe grasped the door to Sal's. "She was. . . and she would've taken one look at you and know that you're a stand-up man, Cal. Once the lawyers get everything sorted out contractually, I look forward to having you on the show. Everything from here on out is your second chance. Use it to set up the foundation for the next stage of your life and all the good things coming your way," he remarked, letting Cal stew on his words before he pulled open the door.

Joe didn't know how right he was.

Chapter 7

Madi

AMY WINEHOUSE'S *B*ACK *TO Black* spun on the floral turntable in the corner of Madi's living room, adding a pop of jazz to an already smooth evening. Leaning against the kitchen counter, Madi soaked in the warmth from her steamy shower, a nice contrast to the late January evening right outside her apartment's walls. The cool air filled the space, accenting the icy mocktail in her glass. She tightened the collar of her fuzzy pink bathrobe, wrapping herself into the plush.

Madi scrolled through her options for food delivery, emboldened to go all out after a particularly long, trying shift. With dozens of restaurants at her fingertips in the heart of Los Angeles, the world quite literally was her oyster.

"...I can't lie. Thai would be so good right now." Madi chewed on her inner cheek. Her mouth watered at the mere suggestion of savory, spicy Thai food while sprawled across her couch. She might channel surf until she found something for background noise so she could fall asleep.

Her thumb hovered over the nearest Thai restaurant on the list. Tonight would be a lesson in convenience: no cooking, no cleaning, and no other chores allowed until tomorrow. She finished the last rotation of her shifts for the week, finally hitting her break to do errands and basic life upkeep.

She ran through her order, adding everything to the cart for checkout. Before Madi hit send, her phone chimed with a new text from Mr. Callum Lambert.

CAL: hey firefly

CAL: saving the world one patient at a time? ;)

She hadn't heard from Cal since that morning, wishing each other sweet goodbyes at the start of her shift. Out of all the guys she met and chatted up with, the literal superstar had the most patience. Madi cringed when thinking about her dating life pre-Cal; she remembered the tantrums of talking stages when she didn't answer fast enough, didn't put out on the first date, and when her photo didn't showcase her size "accurately."

Compared to all of that, Cal was a breath of fresh air. Fame be damned, he was the best boyfriend she'd ever had.

MADI: I'm finally off for the week. So, I'm about to let my hair down and get my foodie on.

CAL: You too? I'm stuffing my face with sushi.

MADI: Thai food here.

CAL: fuck, that sounds good.

MADI: it's about to be even better in my cute PJs that arrived this morning ;)

Madi giggled as she sent the message. She left her drink in the kitchen and sauntered to her bedroom, where the two-piece awaited on her neat bed. Among the pastel dandelion sheets, the lacy camisole top and matching shorts in the color of wine lay, ready to be worn.

Her phone buzzed just as Madi's hand hovered over the loose knot of her bathrobe. She loosened the robe first, then dove back into the text chain, confident that she had enticed Cal's attention.

She had been hooked on the memory of their New Year's celebration for the last few days. *Toy time didn't match the sensation all the way.*

CAL: you're teasing me.

MADI: I'm serious! I've been waiting a few weeks for this cute little number.

CAL: Can I see?

MADI: If you ask nicely... maybe.

Madi watched the eloquent, oh-so-casual stream of "please please please" from Cal roll in, biting on her lip. Laughter tickled at her ribs, begging to be let out while Cal put on the best show. *Guess he asked nicely.*

So, Madi snapped a picture of the PJ set on her bed. She sent the photo to Cal and tossed her phone onto the bed, ignoring the rush of buzzing from new text messages filtering in. Instead, Madi slipped the cotton shorts over her bare hips, delighted by the gentle caress of the fabric. The hints of lace grazing her skin sparked a low, sweltering heat gathering in the pit of her stomach.

Catching sight of herself in the mirror, Madi studied her reflection with one thought. She was fucking hot. . . *Good gracious.*

She struck a few poses, popping out her hips and chest. Each move appeared to accentuate her body in the best way as the fabric molded to her skin, flattering the faint flush of her skin with its deep, sultry wine color. The lace pattern added something extra, chic and classic.

Madi plucked her phone off the bed sheets, ready to check Cal's messages after letting him squirm. With him, unlike the rest who came before, he took the chase in stride.

CAL: fuck me.

CAL: I think some drool dropped into my lap.

MADI: it looks even better on me

CAL: now you're being evil... picture?

MADI: how about you come over and see it in person? Pictures don't do it justice.

CAL: I'm grabbing the check. I'll be there in under fifteen.

MADI: drive safely or else, honey. I kind of like having you in my life.

Sauntering around her room after sending *that* text, Madi couldn't stop herself from diving toward the warm wood end table beside her bed. She switched on the flower lamp before rustling blindly through the top drawer. Even with extra light, Madi knew what she needed by touch alone.

Madi lifted two things from the drawer before making a beeline for the living room. Forgetting all about the mocktail on the kitchen counter with its melting ice cubes and the fuzzy bathrobe discarded on her bedroom floor, Madi crashed onto her couch. She laid out, stretched from one end to the other while she stared at the secrets between her fingers—a baby blue vibrator wand *and* a bottle of lube.

"I think I have a few minutes before Cal gets here," Madi mumbled, words half-mumbled under her breath while juggling her occupied hands. A tiny droplet of lube smeared across the broad head of the wand right as the low buzz filled the air.

Madi dropped everything but the vibrator onto the coffee table, not sparing a second glance at where anything landed. Instead, she hooked the waistband of her shorts around two crooked fingers, lifting them up. A faint cold from the lube along the vibrator prickled against the sensitive skin of her pelvis, but Madi pushed further despite it.

When the head of the vibrator slid over Madi's clit, pressure and vibration collided together in pure pleasure. A low moan bubbled up on Madi's tongue, and her head slumped back into the creaky old couch cushions. Her hand adjusted the angle of the vibrator, pressing down onto her clit until she hit the right angle to make her toes curl.

Her hand flexed, lifting some of the weight for a brief moment before she returned to the position. Beyond being *incredible sex*, Madi's first time with Cal stood as a shining exception to most of her semi-active sex life. Most guys she'd been with didn't get her to finish, even with their sincere efforts. It was no one's fault per se, but Madi liked feeling the rush of her orgasm turn her entire body into jelly.

It meant that she sometimes required a little extra warm-up at the end. She never imposed on her partners to do the extra work for her when she knew a toy or two suited the job.

Madi's hips arched off the dilapidated couch cushions, caving inward underneath the subtle motion of her bucking hips. She bit down on her lower lip *hard* when soft, pleading whimpers rattled off the walls, growing in their insistence and volume. But when she rolled the vibrator around her clit, summoning an almost primal scream of pleasure, something different slipped out.

"Cal—oh *fuck* I didn't—" Madi gasped through trembling breaths, too focused on the slight movements of her wrist to realize what she said at first. Heat stained her cheeks and chest, tinging her with its domineering presence. "If the neighbors ask me about that, I might die on the spot."

Madi screwed her eyes shut and gripped the body of the vibrator until her knuckles ached, probably ghastly white. Her hips rolled against the friction with little rhyme or reason, chasing the sweet taste of the high. She was so lost in the rush that she almost missed the static cry of the buzzer to the intercom until her phone began buzzing.

Madi fumbled around the coffee table for her phone, slowing the pace with which she circled around her clit. Decreasing friction didn't bring her closer to the edge, yet Madi held herself together until she answered the call. "Hello?"

"Hey, I'm outside. I needed to make a pit stop at the convenience store—" Cal's heaving breaths matched hers, almost as if he ran the entire way to her place. The thought sent a tingling wave throughout her body, humming low, like the vibrator between her legs. "Is something buzzing in the background?"

"No," Madi panted, but the tiny cracks in her voice gave away any possible deniability. She paused long enough for the vibrator to yell its presence over the phone.

". . .if that's what I think it is, you're actually going to tease me to death. Madison Caldwell, please let me up," Cal's voice dropped to a whisper, sultry and rumbling. The mere switch-up of his tone turned Madi's feeble resistance into rubble.

"Okay. . . I'm coming," Madi promised, ending the call to get off the couch. She abandoned her faithful vibrator and stumbled toward the front door on shaky legs. She leaned against the wall, hitting the button to let Cal in.

Not even two minutes later, frantic knocking at her door called out to her until she tugged the door open. She stared into Cal with his blown-out pupils and darkened green eyes. His chest heaved, and his whole body leaned forward.

There were no hellos or greetings before Cal surged forward, crushing his lips against Madi's like she suddenly became the air he needed to breathe. Madi heard the door shut behind them, but her body bumping into the wall had her rapt attention.

Cal pulled back long enough to lock the door, licking his lips without shame. He rocked the casual look—a simple white t-shirt and some dark jeans—but the backward baseball cap hiding his dark hair turned her nerves haywire. *Cal was so damn handsome.* And if he kept looking at her like she was his next meal, she'd fold before a single plea crossed his lips.

"Hey, Firefly," Cal rasped into the parted opening of her mouth, caressing the curve of her bottom lip when he tugged it between his teeth. The fleeting, teasing bite pried Madi's legs wide open, enough for Cal to slot one of his knees between.

"You look so good in this little number that I almost don't want to take it off. . . *almost.*"

"I was hoping you'd say that—" Madi panted, cutting herself off when Cal's mouth smashed against hers. His reckless tongue drove the momentum forward while his muscular body pinned Madi against the wall. He cupped the back of her neck while he kissed the living daylights out of her.

Madi grasped his other hand, the one seated at the juncture of her hip, and dragged it to her chest. Cal's fingers brushed over her breasts without much provocation otherwise. His touch alone teased her nipples to harden into stiff peaks, poking through her clothes despite the layers of fabric.

Cal's lips released Madi's from their intoxicating spell long enough for him to dip his head and drag her neckline down between his teeth. The flat of his tongue flicked over one of her nipples, leaving it shiny from his spit. Heat lapped at her thighs, nestling hard between them with the dull throbbing from her toy time.

His hands guided Madi off the wall as the two made a beeline for the couch. Along the way, his and her tops found their way onto the floor in a trail from the front door. Madi's knees knocked into the couch, but not before Cal's hand slid down the front of her shorts.

She shivered when his fingers brushed past her clit, rubbing two against her throbbing, wet pussy. He leaned in, mouth parted to suck in a breath. "Looks like I have that toy on the table to thank."

"You're the first guy in a while that isn't intimidated by me using a vibrator first," Madi moaned when one of his fingers circled her entrance, playing a dangerous game. She almost considered grinding against his fingers, even if it made her look desperate. "I love it."

"What can I say? I'm used to being a team player." A crooked grin stretched across his face while his eyes jumped between her face and the coffee table. "In fact, let's keep the fun going. Take those little shorts off and get on the couch."

Madi didn't wait long after Cal's hand pulled out of her shorts. She pushed them off her hips and soaked in the leftover heat, kissing her bare skin. Madi climbed onto the couch, knees settled on one of the cushions with her hands holding the arm closest to her.

She glanced at Cal, whose jeans puddled around his knees, trying not to laugh at the wrapped condom gripped between his teeth and her vibrator in his hand. Madi's eyes tentatively traced over the scars around his hips and thighs, more visible than the last time they got naked, careful not to stare too hard. Instead, she watched him undress the rest of the way, still holding onto the condom and the vibrator.

When he said he was a team player, this wasn't what she had in mind.

Yet the glint in his perfectly fern-colored eyes lit the fire lying dormant in her stomach, tossing aside all her reservations. Cal approached her side, nudging her thighs open more. He switched the vibrator back on, hovering the head over her stomach. "Hold onto this for me? Put it where you like it."

As he instructed, Madi traced the head of the vibrator over her stomach and hips until it hit her clit. Trembling thighs greeted the embrace, and shaking breaths caused Madi to grip the couch's arm with her free hand. She repeated the same circular motion in search of the sweet spot.

Her search, however, derailed when Cal's firm chest, with all its hardened ridges, pressed into her back. . . and his rock-hard length nudged against her parted thighs. She felt him guide the head of his cock to her entrance stopping right at the edge.

"Cal. . . please," Madi blurted out, voice shaking when the vibrator slipped down and touched a sensitive spot. One single slip awakened all the nerves and electrified her to her core. "You can just push in—!"

"I wanted your permission first." Cal's hot breath preceded him pushing inside of her, not slow or particularly delicate. But she loved it, rough around the edges and frantic with impatient need. She took every inch of his cock he offered, too busy to protest when Cal's hand grabbed the vibrator. "Here, let me."

One of his arms wrapped around her chest while the other traced the vibrator over her pussy, keen to explore. Madi's freed hands latched onto the arm of the couch, not able to do much else when Cal began to thrust.

His resonant chuckle hit her ears, but the sound delayed, fighting through the molasses of her thoughts. Cal's cock was deep inside her, and the buzz of the vibrator on the medium-high setting turned her brain into useless mush, stuck on the overwhelming pleasure. He could've been talking to her about anything—baseball, taxes, wanting to break up—and she wouldn't hear any bit of it.

Madi's eyes fluttered closed while she arched her back further into Cal, leaving no space between them. Consequently, the angle of his thrusts pushed deeper. He could rearrange her guts at that point, and she'd be down.

Overwhelmed by it all, especially when Cal found the right spot with the vibrator as he rocked his hips into her, Madi's grip on the couch tightened, and she cried out, not caring who heard. "Right there! Oh, fuck!"

"Atta girl," Cal replied, but his voice strained under arousal. Labored breathing, more like grunts, slid down the column of her neck with a few sloppy, eager kisses peppered in by Cal. "Keep doing so good for me. I can feel you getting close."

Hearing the praise from Cal's mouth went straight to her head. *Who needed alcohol when his words left her buzzing?* Madi squeezed harder, letting the climax blindside her.

Madi cried out—a pathetic, wanton sound—when she crashed into her orgasm. Cal didn't slow down or stop, coaxing her through the looping, dizzying high. Her body shook and took everything he gave her until exhaustion was all she had left.

Her body slumped forward, leaning on the arm of the couch. She felt the vibrator leave her skin, but Cal's thrusts became a little more sloppy, more frantic while he chased his end.

She listened to the deepening of Cal's breaths against her neck while her pulse thundered in her ears. A guttural grunt buried into her hair met the final thrust of his hips. Warmth tickled her inner thigh, but Cal's breathless chuckle into her ear spread the flush across her body.

"I fear you've ruined other men for me," Madi mumbled under her breath, still leaning on the arm of the couch.

"What's that?" Cal asked, between heaving breaths when he settled his hand onto the couch's arm. But before she could repeat herself, a loud *crack* and the arm curved inward. Both jumped back, retracting their weight from the broken part of the couch. "Oh shit."

"We actually fucked so hard we broke my couch... Granted it was old," Madi gasped, breaking into giggles at the end. "That's a new one."

"Same here." Cal chuckled, burying his face into her shoulder. "I'll buy you a new one, don't worry."

"I'll hold you to it." Madi nestled further into his arms, catching her breath from all the excitement. She needed dinner soon unless she wanted to collapse once all the adrenaline ran out.

Opening the door with a smile plastered on, Madi accepted the plastic bag from the teenage delivery driver standing in the hallway. Her nose crinkled, hit by the mouth-watering smell of her Thai takeout. "Thanks! Here's a tip."

"Thanks, Miss!" The girl beamed at the fifteen dollars tucked into her palm, speeding down the hall. "Have a good night!"

"You too." Madi watched her vanish around the corner before shutting the door. She locked up behind her and carried her takeout to the bedroom on shaky legs. She hadn't fully recovered from round two—Cal decided to prop her on her table and eat her out for his dessert since she "interrupted dinner."

She pushed open her bedroom door and saw Cal lounging shirtless in her bed. He scrolled on her ancient tablet, clothed in a sunflower patterned case. Focus painted his features in a softer light than the harsh glow from the screen's blue hue.

Madi climbed onto the bed on her favorite side, drawing Cal's eyes away from her tablet. She grabbed her food. "Any couches catching your eye?"

"A few. I've bookmarked them in the cart so you can sift through the options and pick whichever ones you like. I'll pay extra since I broke your other one." Cal tipped the screen toward her.

Madi nodded, too busy tearing into her takeout. She snuggled closer, offering him a bite to start—*only a few, though. She'd been dreaming of Thai food since work.*

Cal declined but fed her instead. He grinned as he said, "Alright, we'll handle couch shopping in a bit. How about some television?"

"A great idea. The remote's closer to you, in the drawer." Madi scarfed down her takeout while Cal searched for the remote. They'd been on a few official dates but nothing as simple and *domestic* as post-sex cuddles with television and food. Madi wasn't complaining, though. She liked spending time with Cal.

After a moment, Cal passed her the remote, and channel surfing began. Between every bite, Madi jumped across different offerings for the semi-late hour. *Reality TV? No. Cooking shows? Pass. Evening news. Bore. Crime or medical dramas? Not right now.*

As she crossed from the TV shows to the movies, Madi snuck a glance at the man beside her. Cal's attention jumped between the tablet and the screen, bouncing with perfect precision whenever she changed the channel to something new. His mouth rested into the ghost of a smile. *Maybe he enjoyed the silent, comfortable moments?*

The movies went from in color to classic black and white, bringing Madi's pace to a much slower stroll. She sifted through the familiar and unknown until one channel showed the end credits of another movie. . .and the preview of the next one.

"Oh my god! *Singin' in the Rain*!" Madi gasped, nearly spilling her damn takeout from how fast she sat up. Her body screeched with all its aches, and Cal's reflexes caught her Styrofoam container before it fell to the wayside. "How do you feel about black-and-white movie musicals? This is important."

"Okay, I wasn't prepared for dealbreaker questions already. . . I've never watched *Singin' in the Rain*, but I've heard good things?" Cal paused, visibly bracing while watching her expression.

Madi gasped, but not in affront or upset. In *shock* would be a more apt description. In her humble opinion, although no one asked, everyone should watch the following three classic Hollywood films in their lifetime: *Singin' in the Rain, Funny Girl,* and *Pretty Woman.*

"That settles it. We're watching it!" Madi cranked up the volume and scooted into Cal's arm. She grinned hard at his raised brow, coaxing him into submission as the opening scenes began to play. Cal's arm curled around her shoulder, and the two settled in for the long haul.

Chapter 8

Cal

THE END OF JANUARY came slowly. Yet the days rolled by faster whenever Cal was away from Madi's company. Spending time with her managed to stop the world, if only for a moment.

In the aftermath of the accident, the world continued to spin while he lay paralyzed in the wreckage of his life as he knew it. When the world moved on where he hadn't, Cal festered in his anger, wondering how everyone else managed to get by when he couldn't. But then there was Madi, whose presence softened the jagged edges piercing the wounds of what he hadn't let go. She plucked the shrapnel out with gentle hands, never invasive or pushy for the details.

It's why she lived in his thoughts, occupying the quiet moments with the sweetness of her laughter and those doe eyes that could turn seductive on a dime.

Cal's hands stayed busy while she dominated his thoughts, knowing all too well how fast he'd text her just to see *Firefly* brighten his screen. She had him wrapped around her finger in a way no other girl had before.

Knocking so hard that it rattled the doorframe of his brand-new home interrupted his daily daydreaming about Madi, announcing the arrival of the merry band of knuckleheads. Cal nearly dropped the stack of red solo cups onto the floor in his rush to stop his idiot friends before one of them accidentally broke his door.

This was the same group of fools that unleashed chaos on Vegas with enough drinks in their system. He wasn't trying to maul his new house so soon into his ownership of the place.

As he jogged into view, the warped glass of his front doors distorted the grinning faces of Gage, Mason, Jordan, Diego, and the ever-exhausted Coach Rodgers. He counted a few boxes stacked between Gage and Diego and the unmistakable cases of his favorite IPA in Mason's firm grip.

Cal opened the door, leaning in the frame. "Welcome to the new and improved House Lambert, boys. It's an upgrade from the beachside bachelor pad." He smirked.

Immediately, his closest friends since joining the Foxhounds years ago engulfed him in a swarming hug. Cal didn't fight them off or swat them away like the old him might've, shrugging off any kind of affection in casual dismissal. Instead, he became the center of the embrace, soaking it all in. Those hospital visits shifted his perspective.

Over their shoulders, he spotted Coach Rodgers's worn face soften with a rare, closed-mouth smile. Although the expression became all mustache with the bushy, chevron-shaped facial hair he'd rocked since the literal 80s. Despite sitting comfortably past middle age, his hair rocked a suspicious lack of gray and white streaks, boasting a muted and light brown instead. Prominent crow's feet gathered in the corners of his eyes, perfectly split between green and brown to create the purest shade of hazel. If Desmond was a fatherly figure to him, then Coach Rodgers took up the same mantle in stride.

"You look good, bro." Mason clapped his shoulder, nearly throwing Cal's shoulder out. Cal swallowed his grimace for the sake of the guys. "The post-season hasn't been the same without you. All the trouble we've gotten into hasn't been as fun."

Lighthearted snickers erupted from the guys when Cal arched a brow. He caught a glimpse of Coach Rodgers, who pinched at the bridge of his nose, expecting more fatherly frustration. At that point, he shouldn't be surprised at their antics.

When Coach noticed Cal's stare, he rolled his eyes with a scoff. "It's nothing I don't already know. You lot are worse than a herd of excited kittens." He waved Gage and Jordan out of the way so he could take his turn for hugs. "Will Desmond be joining us today?"

"Not today. Des has. . . some paperwork to finalize for press releases. So, everyone's here for the grand tour and housewarming." Cal ushered everyone inside, checking past the iron gates separating his property from the quiet public. Even when hidden away from the world, he couldn't trust paparazzi or fans not to be lurking outside of his place. *He couldn't pretend to believe anything else.*

His former teammates and Coach Rodgers shuffled inside, quickly dropping off the pizza on the counter and the beer in the fridge. They tucked into a single file line behind Cal, all eyes on him.

"Alright, let's get you the condensed tour. All the bedrooms are upstairs. You can crash at mine if you're ever in the city. But all the fun is downstairs." Cal wandered through the kitchen and dining room, an open space without the walls to hide everything. He didn't stop at the living room while he let the others examine the space with all their verbalized awe. The massive sectional and wide-screen television mounted on the wall would make for perfect movie nights when he invited people over.

He led them to the long, wide hallway hidden underneath the stairs to the second story, where all the bedrooms were, taking door by door. "And here, we have my personal gym with all the machines and a shower room, my at-home bar and pool table, a study for any professional meetings with its very own award case." He opened each door for his teammates and coach to admire the room.

Cal stacked several machines in the gym across the room, yet none took more space than the sound system for music. He wouldn't be training for the baseball season, but his recovery relied on steady physical training. Upon receiving doctor's clearance, Cal bought a treadmill, a punching bag, several racks of weights, a Jacob's ladder, and a stationary bike. For the moment, he stayed in the realm of long walks and stretching.

The rich, brown walls gave the home bar the elegant vibes of a vintage speakeasy, matching the fancy glass bar top and shelves of internationally sourced liquor. Although wealth oozed off the furniture choices—like the dark wood pool table with its neat green trim and pristine polish—the posters of famed rock legends and records added a modern twist. Evenings of entertaining guests would pass through his fingers if he introduced them to the bar and pool table.

According to the realtor, the study used a more subtle color palette, blending muted blues and warm wooden accents. The room focused on comfort and functionality above everything else. Bookshelves of books he'd meant to read lined both walls, flanking the large writing desk and leather armchair. Yet Cal's favorite part was the glass case, where he stored every trophy, achievement, and medal bestowed upon him. A small slice of his personal space housed his achievements, while the rest would be for the public to see.

"Holy shit," Gage whistled once Cal shut the door to his office, summarizing the grins and wide-eyed expressions from the whole group. He brushed the shaggy blond hair away from his eyes, draping over his face. "This place is amazing."

"You haven't even seen the best part. . . The backyard. It's got a pool, an attached hot tub, a deck, and the best grilling set up with plenty of room for a lawn in case I finally decide to get a dog." Cal gathered everyone and brought them to the sliding glass doors leading to the scenic backyard.

As promised, the house boasted an open space with manicured grass and the best view of Los Angeles in the distance. Out of every place Cal toured while back in the city, this one stood head and shoulders above the rest for the backyard. Everything about it screamed the modern American Dream, ditching white picket fences for luxury and the high life.

Glittering blue waters lazily sloshed against the tiled walls and rim of the swimming pool. The babbling trickle of water through the little slit of the attached hot tub garnered a few audible gasps from the guys.

"It's nice, isn't it?" asked Cal, glancing over his shoulder to see Mason and Diego sprinting inside. They returned momentarily with the stack of pizza boxes and the beer hauled between them.

"Nice? You better get ready for a few of us to move in," Diego cackled. Under the sunlight, his deep tan caught the light for a coppery glow, and his mini ponytail of dark curls jostled as he rushed to the outside dinner table.

"Same!" Jordan and Gage cackled, raising their hands.

"None of you idiots are moving in here," Cal snorted. He nudged them toward the deck, shutting the door to keep the heat out. He loved his teammates, of course. But they had their lives back in Virginia, and he would resume on the opposite side of the country. "I cleaned off the table, so break out the beers and pizza."

Everyone moved to the table on its raised deck, shielded from the sun by a few thin layers of shimmery tan canopy. Two overhead lanterns swayed in the residual breeze. They laid out the pizza boxes and cracked open the beers, chasing aimless chatter while hands around the table reached for what they wanted.

Even then, they still worked like a team—in perfect sync.

Cal cracked open his bottle, accepting a plate piled with a few slices of Margherita pizza. Before he could take a bite, Mason stood from his chair. His friend raised his drink, whistling until all the side conversations petered out.

"I raise a toast for Cal, our fearless leader and the best damn center fielder in the league. We joke that things aren't the same without him in Virginia. There's a lot of truth there. Cal brings this extra edge to our game, which we consider friendly competitiveness. He strives to always be the best at what he does, which rubbed off on us all. So, while we hope you're returning for the next season, you deserve the best, Cal. So, cheers to your return or your retirement."

The table applauded Mason's speech, whistling and rattling the table rather excitedly. Their hoots and hollers pulled a smile out of Cal, even though the thoughts of retirement still spun through his chest, turbulent as the unpredictable, untamed sea. Mason's almost feral grin—emphasized by sharper canines—urged Cal to rise from his seat.

He clinked his beer against Mason's. "Before any of you drink, I figure that was the perfect segue for an announcement of my own. However, what I'm about to tell you is absolutely top secret. I won't force you into an NDA, but Desmond would have all of our heads if his press release were spoiled by a leak."

Attention flocked to him as everyone's gazes peeled away from Mason. Well, everyone except Coach Rodgers. He already knew about Cal's forced retirement as soon as the papers arrived. They hadn't talked about it one-on-one, which was a conversation Cal dreaded.

"I've been waiting to announce this for the last few months, sitting on all the things I've been dying to say. I loved every moment I spent as a member of the Foxhounds—a member of your team—but that time is ending. Doctors don't think I'll ever play baseball at the highest level again, even after regaining mobility. So, I'll be declaring my retirement within the next few weeks," said Cal, hit with the sudden shift in the atmosphere. Crestfallen expressions from his close friends carved the metaphorical knife between the ribs. "But I'm not leaving baseball for good. I've accepted a commentator slot on *Beyond the Bases* with Joe Avery."

The second shift in the mood induced whiplash from how swiftly everyone's expressions changed. Two sentences made all the difference, pulling a verbal U-turn on everyone at the table. Cal meant everyone *that* time; Coach Rodgers hadn't learned about his next moves until the words left his mouth.

At first, no one spoke while a fury of silent glances tossed across the table like one of their practice exercises ensued. But after a second—and *likely* the realization that Cal *wasn't* playing some elaborate prank on them—the guys began to jump out of their seats.

"You're joking! No!"

"Are you for real?"

"Cal, you are THE MAN!"

"I can't believe we'll see those pearly whites on television *every* night!"

Jordan, Gage, Mason, and Diego scrambled from their frantic celebration with one another to engulf Cal in a crushing hug. They squeezed the life out of him, jumping up and down like a gaggle of excited teen girls.

Cal chuckled, head lolling back. "Yeah, you guys won't get rid of me that easily. Besides, the damn degree that Santa Barbara paid for might actually get some use. It collects dust in the last of my boxes to unpack."

He jostled his friends back, who continued with their excitement until Diego jumped into the pool with his shoes still on. He emerged from the waters, shaking his damp hair, still grinning like a madman.

Gage and Jordan leaned over to help him out of the waters, shaking their heads while biting back their laughter. From the table, Coach Rodgers snorted, which happened to be a telltale sign of him holding back laughter. Despite all their antics, Coach had a sense of humor.

"Alright, knuckleheads! The pizza will get cold, and the beer will be hot if you keep messing around. I'm sure there will be enough time for swimming later on."

Everyone knew Coach's word equaled the law, so no one protested. Cal followed his friends to the greasy pizza and cold IPA. He slid onto the edge of the bench but quickly found himself squished into the middle between Mason and Jordan. Eager hands dished out pizza, stained by grease and half-melted cheese against its flimsy paper surface. The clinking of IPA bottles meshed with the faint interjecting of conversation, intertwining with the celebration laced in the air.

Maybe now he could close the door on that chapter of his life. The future seemed. . . kind of alright.

Shouts followed the sound of a striped ball sinking into a pocket after a clean shot echoed off the walls. Cal's head turned away from the bar, where he poured himself a finger of bourbon. He saw Gage pretending to flex his muscles while Jordan and Mason scowled, leaning on their pool cues.

The guys decided on a couple rounds of pool, which Cal welcomed wholeheartedly. He provided casual commentary from the sidelines, enjoying snacks and alcohol from the cozy leather couch tucked into the corner. None of the guys seemed to mind.

Cal swirled his neat bourbon, letting it sit before sipping. "Go easy on them, Gage. You might hustle them out of all their money soon."

"That's the plan," Gage snickered. He dodged around a shove from Jordan, who leaned over the table to swat at him. Gage rounded the opposite corner, eyes narrowed while analyzing his possible shots. As he set up, a phone rang out, drawing his eyes up. "Not mine. I'm always on mute."

The rest of the room reached for their phones, checking for the buzzing. But Cal knew from the vibrating sensation tucked into the back pocket of his jeans that it was his. He checked the screen and was confronted by an incoming video chat: *Incoming Call from Firefly. . .*

"Oh shit." Cal almost dropped his bourbon with how fast he spun on his heel and turned toward the exit. He snatched up his glass, feeling eyes on him, and laughed it off. "I need to take this. Don't wait up for me."

Before anyone could prod further, Cal had one foot out the door already. He hopped a few doors down and ducked into his study. One of the best perks about his home office? The former owner soundproofed it.

Cal accepted the video call as he crashed into the comfortable chair at the desk. He propped the phone up while his camera adjusted, seeing the gorgeous and *very exhausted* face of his firefly. Madi appeared intensely focused on something outside the camera's view as the phone tilted awkwardly.

But when Cal cleared his throat, her head snapped toward him, brightening. Life jumped back into her face, now flushed a soft peach in the cheeks instead of the almost lifeless ashen color she had been. "Cal!"

"Hey, gorgeous." He winked, only to see her mouth twitch with a smile. "How was your shift today?"

"Eh, it was one of those days," she mumbled, both an answer and an evasion of the question. As she spoke, her eyes fluttered a little, looking ready to close then and there. "How about you?"

"I spent some time with my friends and broke the news about the retirement thing." Cal leaned back. He observed Madi's eyes continue to droop and her efforts to force them back open, blinking heavily after each time. She leaned against her kitchen counter—a familiar sight to Cal—to fix the messy bun she twirled her hair into.

Madi yawned hard, trying to cover her mouth with a hand. She spun the camera around, flashing her fridge when she opened the door. "Oh? How'd they take it?"

"They were happy for me, which was a relief. . . What're you making?" Cal saw Madi pause, standing at the open fridge with heavy eyes. She blinked twice, shaking her head.

"Uh, probably leftovers."

Cal hummed, "Leftovers are great. But maybe you should take a nap first. You're falling asleep standing up, Madi." At his words, Madi's eyes snapped open from their heavy-lidded stare.

"I—" She went to protest but faltered when Cal pulled a face. He tried his best interpretation of Coach Rodgers when any of the hijinks of the team got a little out of hand. Madi sighed. "You're right. I barely made it home, and I'm not that hungry. I'll make something later."

"Good girl. Get some rest, okay? You can call me if you get up to make dinner since all the guys should head back to their hotel before then." Madi's face tinged a soft red, glistening with a thin sweat dotting her cheeks and forehead. Her eyes dodged for a split second from his, playing a coy game of tag. Cal wasn't oblivious to what he said. In fact, he liked it when Madi blushed. . . a lot.

Damn, she was such a cutie.

"Goodnight, Cal," Madi whispered. In the background, traffic cried into the darkened skies, and Cal imagined the busy intersections. He studied the quiet smile on Madi's tired face, watching exhaustion slip through. "See you soon."

"Sweet dreams, Firefly. You had a long day of saving the world, one patient at a time," Cal whispered before the call ended. Silence slithered back into the room, evoking the image of Madi trudging off to her bedroom in her scrubs. Something about that apartment induced comfort, found in the crevices of the thrifted couch they broke or tucked under the pastel sheets of her bed. Her place felt like a home, well-loved and lived in.

Cal stretched out of his chair, intent on spending the rest of the night with his friends and some good drinks. However, someone else pulled it open when he reached for the door. He came face-to-face with Coach Rodgers, who offered a sheepish chuckle.

"I promise I wasn't snooping, son. The others told me you took a call and stepped out." Coach held up his hands. "I was hoping to talk to you before I rounded everyone up. We have an early flight back to Virginia tomorrow."

"Of course. Please come in," Cal offered, but Coach shook his head.

"I'm alright standing. I hope you know how proud everyone is that you've taken the raw hand, turning it into something golden. Most pros retire with their sights set on a whole lot of nothing. You chased after something new yet so familiar. I can't wait to see you on television, Cal."

Those words barreled straight into Cal, hitting with the force of a freight train. Desmond always poised himself as the first person to believe in Cal, the first father figure, and the first. . . everything in his career. But Cal could count on one hand the number of times he recalled Desmond voicing his pride. Those praises came rare and so unexpected from everyone in his life.

"Thanks, Coach," he managed, swallowing back the sudden heat coiling around his Adam's apple. Its presence weighed hard on his tongue, making him pause. He stuttered, "I'll miss being on your team."

Coach Rodgers waved him off. "You're always on my team, even without you being on the field. Cal, you've outgrown the twenty-two-year-old troublemaker you were when I first met you. I've watched you change and grow in the nearly five years we've known each other. You've figured out how to become the better version of yourself without much guidance from me, so I have one more lesson to impart to you."

"Oh yeah? What's that?" Cal asked.

"You've closed the door to what used to be. Now, you have the perfect opportunity to embrace possibility. The world gets a brand new you, enjoying a brand new start. . . so don't stop yourself from redefining who Callum Lambert is." Coach Rodgers tipped his head, yet his gaze met Cal's. As if he knew something Cal didn't, his eyes twinkled with the kind of wisdom only acquired by time.

The conversation ended there, interrupted by the door to the bar swinging open. The Foxhounds filtered out, laughing. Cal stood in the doorway, watching the reminders of his past gather their belongings to leave. It was like Coach said—a new him with his new life.

So, what would he do with it?

Chapter 9
Madi

THE STRING OF LIGHTS hanging overhead and twined around the bushes fencing in *Blues Brews*, a beer garden and live music venue, cast a delicate glow of possibility over the bargoers. The February chill had the heat lamps out in full force, stationed at the head of every wooden table. With its location a few blocks from the hospital, most of its patrons were the nursing and doctoral staff from New Horizons. People often came after work to unwind with a pint of the house brew, a game or two of darts, and the occasional indie performers cutting their teeth on starter gigs.

Madi loved the place as a meeting ground for her, Alaina, Janet, and Sonia to gossip over good drinks and even better bar food. The mozzarella sticks and honey mustard chicken wings were to die for, which made for a nice distraction when Janet and Alaina got into one of their 'friendly competitions' about their dating lives.

She and Sonia always sat those conversations out, content to witness the imaginary scoreboard flash with every story, one-upping the one that came before it. Tonight, however, was no different, considering Valentine's Day lurked around the corner.

". . .and that's when he suggested we get away for Valentine's Day weekend! I can't get time off to cover a trip out of the country. Ugh, sunbathing in Ibiza would've been the highlight of my year. I'd probably get a million DMs from followers about the trip." Janet snatched her wine off the table—never a beer drinker by her own admission—and swirled the red around her lipstick-stained glass. Her ponytail bobbed with the faintest shake of her head, bright like spun gold underneath the twinkling string lights.

She raised her brow at Alaina, whose teeth sank into the tender honey mustard chicken wing right as Janet finished talking. Such a gesture conveyed a silent challenge: the passing of the baton for Alaina to top the outlandish and jaw-dropping lengths to which a man would go to make Janet Coleman their girl.

Madi found solace in her drink—a beer cocktail she had already forgotten the name of—while sneaking glances at Sonia across the table. Sonia met her eyes in the middle of the table, over all the appetizers the table ordered. Neither Madi nor Sonia spoke a word to interject, too busy minding their business at the bottom of their drinks.

Alaina knew how to handle herself.

Clearing her throat, Alaina scooted closer to the table, grasping her drink in perfectly manicured hands. She offered a coy smile, thriving on the competitive air surrounding them. It didn't storm often in the city, but something brewed on the cusp of unpleasantness, and no, it wasn't the beer.

She hummed. "Ibiza is nice, if not a little chaotic with the party scene. For Valentine's Day, Mr. Big Apple is flying me out for the weekend. He's taking me to New York for a weekend of shopping, fine dining, and two tickets to Broadway. It'll be perfect; I've already cleared the time off with my department."

Alaina giggled while raising her beer cocktail, brushing her dark hair back from her face. She showed up to work rocking a new cut of curtain bangs. Madi wished she looked half as good with bangs. Then again, she DIY-ed hers as a pre-teen, courtesy of scissors she snatched from the group home's kitchen.

Alaina scrunched her nose. "Alright, we need a small intermission from the roster talk. Sonia, what do you and Val have planned for the evening? They probably have some romantic shit planned, straight out of a novella."

Somehow, the bluntness diffused the tension—or was it a 'competitive spirit—from the air as all eyes flickered to Sonia. Madi planned to pay attention to this one, always one to swoon over the sheer romance of Val when it came to their woman; Val and Sonia modeled everything she wanted in her future partner.

Yet the flash of her phone screen with Cal's name dragged her out of the conversation, tossing her into a rush of heat slithering down her spine.

She picked up her phone, rushing over to her unread messages as Sonia laughed. "Okay, this is quite the story. So, I noticed Val being cagey whenever I brought up Valentine's Day plans, and this is year seven of being together. So—"

The world faded into mute when Madi dove headfirst back into Cal's texts, a long string of jokes, flirting, and an endless sea of tongue-in-cheek humor. Cal had a way with words, namely in how he committed himself to finding ways to make her blush. She lost count of the instances in the last week she had dropped her phone into her lap, cheeks burning at some innuendo that Cal sent.

One thing was sure: Cal added a new criterion to her list of "must-haves" in her future man. *Must have a good sense of humor because she couldn't be the only one making the laughs flow.*

CAL: nothing in the world beats a post-gym shower

CAL: *1 photo attachment*

Madi stared at the image, swearing drool dribbled down her chin at the sight of a shirtless, post-shower Cal. Her gaze traced lazy circles around his bare torso—abs, abs, and *more* abs—and his muscular, somewhat veiny arms flexed in the fogged-up mirror. His dark hair fell wild around his face, still damp from the shower as it coiled into loose curls. His broad shoulders and the hardened ridges of his chest summoned a slew of memories lost between the haze of her bedsheets.

This man is a troublemaker.

Madi gulped down a greedy taste of her drink while staring at his body, a stunning amalgamation of years of athletic training. However, more notable than that, Cal hid his face behind the baseball cap he wore. He tipped the bill of the cap further down, casting shadows over his face to obscure his identity. As far as she knew, Cal didn't have any identifying tattoos or marks in case her phone fell into the wrong hands. *But oh, she needed more of it.*

She flipped her phone over for a second, tuning back into the conversation barreling full steam ahead without her.

"—and after dinner at Guadalupe's, Val said we'll enjoy an evening at the movies. They rented a theater to play a double feature of *Shakespeare in Love* and *Titanic*," Sonia gushed.

A collective "awwwww" erupted from the group, which Madi joined in on despite missing most of the conversation until then. But, knowing Val, they planned something ridiculously unique that no other partner in the group could top. It wasn't even a competition at that point; Val had a seven-year head start on any potential forever partner.

"Oh my god!" Alaina squealed. Kicking her feet under the table, she grasped Sonia by the shoulders and shook her. "How does it feel to live my damn dream? Give me the link to buy a Val and customize them."

Sonia rolled her eyes at Alaina's antics, swatting her away so she could devour another wing. "They're one of a kind, I fear. I lucked out, but I can ask them if their cousins are single. Their abuela taught them well in the ways of romancing."

Madi's lips parted, ready to reply with a joke of her own, when her phone pinged in her hand. She flipped off the ringer in a blink. Heat crawled along the back of her neck, causing every hair to rise along her skin. Goosebumps marked her body with their telltale warning, foreshadowing the anticipation of a new Cal text.

She retreated back into her phone. Madi lingered an extra second on the perfect visage of Cal's shirtless selfie. Her teeth chewed on the straw floating around her cocktail, tasting the faint traces of beer watered down by the melted ice at the bottom. Without it, she might tell the world about the finest man in all of Los Angeles.

CAL: is that so?

CAL: You're free to come over whenever you want. My bed will always be waiting for you to bless it.

MADI: if I didn't have a shift tomorrow morning, I would already be driving over.

CAL: Then I should plan so you can spend days at mine. I'll be taking advantage of uninterrupted Madi time.

Sweat gathered along the column of her neck, born from the heat rushing through her veins. The mere thought of days spent in Cal's bed, uninterrupted by work or the rest of the outside world, elicited dozens of scenarios of how to spend their time. Almost all of them were dirty.

The other night, Cal turned her meager queen-sized mattress into an acrobatic show from the positions he contorted her body into. She bent like a pretzel while he showered her in a never-ending parade of praise. If he managed to do all that with three hours constantly interjected with calls from his agent, Madi couldn't fathom what he had up his sleeves for days' worth of time. Well, she assumed it included her forgetting how to walk straight.

Madi let out a wistful sigh, muffled by the straw clenched between her teeth. Any more daydreaming about Callum Lambert, and she might go against her better judgment and drive straight to his place.

A fluttering, insistent heat blossomed across her stomach, caressing the peaks of her hips with its exploration. There, Madi sat between flashes of warmth rumbling throughout her body and an endless desire for the man who inspired a new sort of hunger—one that couldn't be satiated by the delicious and plentiful appetizers collected on the table.

"Madi? Still with us?" A gentle whistle from Sonia yanked Madi out of her little world and tossed her back into the real world. "You seem. . . awfully smiley at your phone tonight."

Janet snorted. "More than *just* tonight," she mused into her wine, nearing the bottom of her glass. "Something's got her distracted."

Sonia shot Janet a look that screamed *behave*, all tightly pursed lips and narrowed eyes with furrowed brows to go along with it. Yet Janet wasn't wrong. In the dynamics of JAMS, Madi usually took a backseat in the romance conversation unless she had something to contribute, which never happened as frequently as Alaina or Janet. She did, however, provide thoughtful insights or at least active listening when the subject came up; she dubbed herself a 'hopeless and helpless' romantic since her college years.

Alaina nudged Janet, fixing a smile. "Do you have any plans for Valentine's Day, Mads? We could find you some other lonely heart for a night out if you have nothing planned. Oh, maybe we could double date!"

Despite her good intentions, the 'other lonely heart' earned her a scathing look from Sonia—the second one of the evening. Alaina barely masked her wince when the words came out, knowing she stumbled right into that one.

But Madi shook her head. "I don't know yet. I'll pass on the double date, though. Thanks," she lied. Okay, maybe it wasn't technically a lie since her Valentine's Day plans were to be announced. However, she wouldn't be alone or a lonely heart that night, not if Cal had anything to say about it.

Distracted, Madi failed to notice Janet leaning over her shoulder and peering at her phone. She heard the, "Who's Cal?" before Janet snatched the phone out of her hand. Gasps echoed around the table but Madi? She panicked.

"No one!" Madi yelped, lunging for her phone while still seated. Janet leaned her arm out of reach of Madi, not reading the screen when playing keep-away. So Madi lunged again, worried about them recognizing Cal from the grainy tabloid photos on New Year's or some old magazine cover he'd been on. "Give me that back."

"Only if you tell us who Cal is!" Janet refused. Her voice pitching higher caught the attention of the nearby tables, whose heads swiveled away from their drinks and meals for some free entertainment. *No fucking thanks.*

"Fine! I'll tell you, but give me my phone back or else," Madi threatened. Like a trail of dominos, enough of a push knocked over the feeble resistance. Janet handed Madi back her phone and sat back down. The girls glanced at Madi.

So, she sighed, "Cal and I are. . . seeing each other."

A gasp escaped Alaina. "You've been holding out on us? Madi, I'm shocked. . . but not disappointed if you give us the full dirt on this guy!" She leaned forward on the table, hands clasped together. Batting her lashes hard in a pleading stare, she was eager to gossip about this new, mysterious beau.

Madi almost wanted to die. She calculated the most evasive responses to the question in her head without outing herself or Cal. She never searched for his name after that one night in the dark of her car. However, her friends occasionally ranted about pop culture and celebrity gossip. . . and Cal's news headlines might've caught their interest in the past. Regardless of the reason, she didn't want herself and Cal discovered, not like this.

"We met in January. We've gone on a few dates since then, and I like him." Madi shrugged. "I guess you could call him my boyfriend, but neither of us has rushed to put a label on anything."

"Why didn't you tell us before? This is exciting news!" Unlike Janet and Alaina's curiosity, Sonia had hearts in her eyes. She seemed taken by the news.

"Like I said before, it's relatively new. I don't want to speak before anything is certain, especially not with a guy like him."

"Any chance you have a photo of him or maybe a social media we could lightly stalk?" asked Alaina, who stumbled out of her stupor with a wide grin. One thing to know about her: she loved stalking all prospective suitors on social media and learning details about them. In another life, she would've made a frighteningly good federal agent.

But tonight, the photo was a no-go.

"Sorry, I don't. And if you'd all mind, I'm probably not comfortable sharing his photo," Madi remarked. Although disappointed, Alaina and Sonia nodded, pulling back.

But Janet didn't seem pleased with that answer. "What's wrong with him? Is he morbidly hideous or something?"

Sonia crossed her arms. "Janet, stop."

"No, I have to know. With how Madi's been smiling and skipping down the sidewalks for the last few weeks, it's apparent that he has something going for him. Maybe he's rich. Maybe they have great sex. Maybe he's funny or whatever else Madi considers good enough for her dating criteria. The no pictures thing is telling."

Madi inhaled, choosing that instead of a snarky comment. Janet didn't know how right she was. . . *and* how terribly wrong she was. Cal happened to be rich, funny and fucked her better than anyone else had before him. She *detested* the implication of his ugliness. Such a surface value analysis; Janet had her flaws like everyone at that table and judging was her main one.

She didn't need to prove Cal's beauty because the magazine covers he graced showed that. Madi knew better than to run her mouth. She shook her head. "He's beautiful. We're staying lowkey right now. I don't want to jinx anything while we're early in our relationship, okay?"

"Who suggested that?" Janet asked, not missing a single beat. Out of wine, she snatched up a greasy wing in the pause. "You or him? I would hate for him to be like one of those other guys who do it because they're ashamed."

The words lashed out, smacking Madi across the face with disrespect entrenched in every inch of her statement. *Ashamed? Cal wasn't ashamed of being with her!* She would've asked what compelled Janet to suggest that, but the entire table could figure out where that thought spawned.

Dating as a fat woman came with its damn problems, carried around like overflowing luggage, *always* on the verge of exploding open and souring the good vibes.

"I made the decision, actually. Cal accepted my choice and has been nothing short of a gentleman. He respects me a lot," Madi snapped. That respect line had a clear target but fuck it. The mood at the table rolled into solemn territory when Janet suggested what she had.

Alaina and Sonia, rightfully horrified given their wide eyes, hissed overlapping scolding. Madi made out a rogue "Janet!" and "What the hell?" from them before Janet threw her hands up.

"I'm not saying it to be mean. I'm only concerned about Madi," she defended. Her eyes darted around the table. Her posture screamed defensively, but the words struck the tone of assertiveness instead. No apology appeared in sight. "This guy sounds great, but Madi just met him. She's had so many guys in the past use her. She's put up with chubby chasers, gym bros who tried to change her, and that one finance dweeb who made her hide when his friends walked by their date."

Every recollection in her defense acted like a knife slotted between Madi's ribs, and Janet's grip held each one while she twisted it deeper. Her heart thundered in her ears while Janet continued to ramble in her own defense, staking her claim on the sure-fire stance that she did no wrong. *She couldn't listen to this—*

Madi pushed back her chair, greeted by stares and immediate protests from Alaina and Sonia. They tried to appease her with their pleading stares and the reach of their gentle hands toward her. But Madi refused to be touched, knowing her skin burned.

Disgust coiled low in her stomach like a snake in the grass, preparing to strike.

She needed to leave the conversation. Maybe the restaurant too.

Madi felt her lips mumble some excuse, half-hearted and dripping in disappointment. She rose from her seat and walked away, phone hot in her hand. Cal might've texted her back, but she had no interest in picking it up.

What once tasted so sweet became sour.

Chapter 10

Cal

THE BOW TIE OF his suit started to get on Cal's nerves after the first hour, but the promise of good liquor made black tie attire a little more bearable. Besides, as Desmond so *kindly* reminded him, wearing a stuffy suit wasn't that bad and to 'think of the children.' That nugget of profound wisdom wasn't incorrect as the two wandered through the packed charity gala.

Aim for Athletics, the charity in question, raised substantial scholarship funds for underprivileged kids who demonstrated great skill and love for athletics. Everyone loved to seem charitable, but Cal volunteered with AFA several times over the last few years. He believed in the mission, and so did his checkbook.

Desmond accompanied him as his plus-one for the night. In the past, he might've brought a beautiful woman as his date for the night, juggling arm candy and small talk with wealthy benefactors. But the woman he wanted to come with had a late shift at the hospital, covering for another nurse with a sick kid.

"And so, I said, I would rather hang from the Hollywood sign in nothing but my skivvies than ever eat there again. One time was enough. Plus, my health insurance wouldn't cover 'death by food poisoning,'" Desmond roared, giving an energetic fist pump to the raucous laughter of the small crowd circling around him.

Cal loitered on the outside with his dwindling drink. The French 75's bubbling flavor lingered on his tongue long after each sip, stronger than the artillery it was named after.

"You're always such a riot, Desmond. Goodness, I'm shocked you never considered an entertainment career." One of the women—whose name Cal had forgotten—patted at the corners of her eyes with her husband's bright pocket square. She probably meant to preserve her makeup from tears of laughter but ended up smudging her eyeliner like an emo band from the early aughts instead.

"Eh, I found my calling where I'm at. Besides, I'd like to think my comedic legacy lives on in my star client." Desmond gestured over several shoulders to Cal just as he finished his drink. The crowd turned, and heads swiveled to stare at him—the "star" as Desmond described him. Thrust under the spotlight, all eyes fell on Cal when he only wanted another drink.

Desmond's allusion wouldn't be lost on the crowd or a secret going over their heads. His retirement announcement and subsequent plans to join *Beyond the Bases* had been announced the other day to an outpouring of media attention. Fans, former and current players, and other commentator personalities weighed in with their opinions on the career changeup. The mass opinions crashed on top of Cal, burying him underneath the avalanche of input. He stood under the spotlight while the world waited for him to stick the landing.

He swallowed, awkwardly saluting the crowd. "I'm sure Desmond will be tuning in for the opening episodes. He always watched my games anyway, so his ancient DVR still has enough to keep it busy."

A few tittering laughs rustled in the crowd. However, more partygoers began visually picking at him. Their expectation became palpable, budging its presence into the room until Cal couldn't ignore it. Pressure pooled in his throat, teetering the thin line between anger and avoidance.

Desmond locked eyes with him, now tucked behind the crowd, with the center of attention on Cal's shoulders. He flashed a thumbs-up, winking in an unspoken conspiracy. *Charm them,* the gesture said. *Have them salivate his every word, ready to tune into the television every night of baseball season.*

"My husband and I were discussing the news on the way here," the woman from before remarked, voice devoid of discernable emotion. She could've been annoyed by his choice to speak or bored of the turn in the conversation. . . or any number of things really. "The accident was truly a tragedy for the sport."

Her husband nodded, jumping into the fray. "I thought the Foxhounds had another nearly undefeated season ahead of them before you got hurt. A shame that you missed out on your final season."

That sparked more conversation from the others, arising as a flurry of whispers quick to pick up steam. Their words collided, clumsy and eager to reach the surface. They were fast to derail, to unravel once the spotlight shone down on them for a brief moment.

Little did any of them know the monstrosity of memories they unleashed on Cal, paralyzed to his spot on the ballroom floor.

"Oh yes, such a horrible accident." *The taste of gasoline and blood invading his mouth, stuck behind a cracked motorcycle helmet while the odor of burnt rubber met the asphalt.*

"Can you believe the media ran with the photos from the scene? It was horrible with all that shrapnel—" *Said shrapnel cut up his skin in his hips and legs, digging its claws in while he lay on the highway, pinned underneath something heavy and hot.*

"It was everywhere for weeks! You poor thing, being laid in bed while the world talked about it." *Spending hours laid up in the hospital or at home, wishing the collision finished the job instead of leaving him in the wreckage of his dreams.*

"Did you realize then that your career was over, or did that come later? I assume you tried to recover enough to play again." *Phantom pains waking him up in the middle of the night, screaming into the dark of his bedroom until Claire or her husband came running in, bleary-eyed.*

"The accident may have ended the baseball thing, but that wasn't sustainable long term. This television gig will be good for your longevity as a star." *Frustration rose hot in his throat like bile while pushing himself through physical therapy, begging every force in the universe to give him another chance at baseball.*

With a tight smile plastered onto his face by sheer will, Cal ignored the distant echo of the world and the thundering pulse stranded in his ears. He shook his empty glass to the tiniest rattle. "I need another drink, excuse me."

They'd be horribly mistaken if someone expected him to wait for dismissal. He walked from the conversation, even when confused murmurs followed in his wake. *No charity felt worth reliving the worst six months of his life for the morbid curiosities of strangers he'd never speak to again.*

Cal ducked into the crowd, waiting until he disappeared from their view before he discarded his glass. He didn't need another drink, he needed some fresh air and quiet before he lashed out at the next idiot who mentioned the worst day of his life like a circus curiosity.

He made a beeline for the nearest exit, slipping past security. Cal moved precisely through the hallway, knowing the Ridge well enough to have a few hiding spots. Granted, he learned them from someone else, but he doubted Jensen minded if he borrowed one for the night.

Cal climbed the nearest staircase to the second story, ready to find a balcony and brood until Desmond came to drag him back. Shit, being around some people truly brought back the angsty teenager in him.

As he threw open the ornate doors to one of the balconies, he froze at seeing a couple already in the space. But with a long enough glance, he recognized the perfectly styled hair and fine suit imported from some foreign country. *Speak of the devil himself.*

"Surprise lovebirds." Cal smirked, leaning against the doorframe, when Jensen and Daisy jumped at the sound of his voice. Their heads whirled around, backlit by the last strands of gold in the sky. Sea salt air collided with the February evening in perfect concert as the distant waves crashed along the cliffs beyond the Ridge's property line. "Am I interrupting the conception of the next Ramsey heir or something?"

"Cal," Jensen and Daisy deadpanned in unison, only sparing a tiny glance at each other. The slight twitch of their lips didn't escape Cal's notice, which was so Daisy and Jensen of them.

Cal held up his hands, managing a smile. "I was just checking." His grin persisted when Daisy stepped forward, engulfing him in a warm embrace. He patted her back before they let go. "How are my second favorite married couple?"

"Still miffed that we aren't your first," Jensen snorted, taking his turn to give Cal a total bro hug. They even slapped each other's backs and laughed. When he left the embrace, Jensen's arm slithered around Daisy's waist to pull her back to his side. Their wedding bands glinted a final golden in the last hints of sunset painting the skies. "We heard you were coming to the charity event—"

"We planned to say hello, but Jensen and I wanted some time to talk. Last week's been hectic for both of us." Daisy sighed. Cal understood exhaustion when it crossed Daisy's cherry-red lips.

"She has it worse than me. I sit in an office all day, handling big business decisions that I always consult her about before I choose. She's out here, lecturing as a doctoral candidate and discovering the next scientific phenomenon. It's hard being married to the next Newton or Einstein," Jensen remarked. Pride exuded off him in waves, almost as palpable as the ones right behind them.

Daisy rolled her eyes, albeit more playful than annoyed, while staring at her husband. Jensen offered a cheesy smile in return, not retracting his bold proclamation. But honestly, if anyone would become the next major scientific icon, it would be Daisy. That woman was like a real-life Barbie with how many accolades and accomplishments she snatched up.

She turned back to Cal, remembering that he stood there too, and it wasn't her and Jensen alone. She and Jensen had the minor quirk of forgetting the world existed when they saw one another. *True love or whatever.*

"How're you doing tonight, Cal? I hope the refreshments downstairs and staff are as good as when I oversaw the details of this place," Daisy inquired, almost as if she smelled the lingering anger on him.

Daisy's killer instincts worked infuriatingly well, even when Cal swore he hid his emotions behind a blank face. She dodged his defenses without messing up one of her perfectly manicured nails. He didn't know how Jensen kept any secrets in their house.

"Eh, I'm doing alright," Cal tried to play it off. The sentence hadn't finished before the urge to wince washed over him. He sounded hollow, spinning the same old lies of a worn-down record. "Charity events are always good for the soul, right?"

"Right." Daisy nodded, eyes softening from their exacting shade of rich brown. "If you'll excuse me for a moment, I should grab something to drink. I promised him some drinks after fresh air."

Before Daisy moved toward the door, Jensen flexed his arm around her waist, pulling his wife to his chest. The two shared a quick but intimate kiss, leaving a small smudge of lip-gloss behind on Jensen's mouth. He watched his wife stride through the double doors in a blur of ruby satin, leaving the two men.

Cal approached the balcony's edge, leaned one hand against the railing, and sighed. "Am I that obvious?"

"To us? Yeah. Did you want to talk about it or are you looking for a companion to silently commiserate with you?" asked Jensen. The two faced the darkened Pacific waters lapping at the California shoreline, devoid of any boats or disturbances on the waves.

"I knew people might be nosy when I re-emerged from my self-imposed media isolation, but they cross the damn line too much with their questions. Everyone wants to know about the accident, asking me to relive the single worst thing to ever happen to me over and over. And whenever they ask, I'm back there, lying on the freeway while angry horns and revving engines sit mere feet away. I am *stuck* on that fucking asphalt, trapped as I listen to the distant cry of ambulance sirens. I didn't get the privilege of forgetting that night, but the rest of the world won't let me either."

Cal didn't mean to unload all that on Jensen. Yet the moment he started, he couldn't stop the collision of his scorn and the last remnants of grief not lost on that cursed stretch of highway. It haunted him still, even when the nightmares lessened than the first few months post-accident.

Jensen, although on the receiving end of his rant, didn't swoop in with some cheesy platitude about life or that his suffering would mean something at the end of the day. Instead, he grasped Cal's shoulder like a lifeline, tempering his frown into something softer. *Not pity*. Jensen knew him well enough to not fall into that trap.

"I'm sorry. People let their selfishness get in the way, and you don't owe anyone answers. You're not some freak attraction to gawk at. Baseball is a big part of your life and who you are, but you're still worth being around without it. Even if you never pick up a baseball bat again, you're still Callum Lambert. No accident can take that from you," said Jensen.

A chill ran down Cal's body, coalescing around his left leg. A metal plate lived underneath the skin as a reminder of the accident, aching after too much walking on the treadmill or when the weather dipped below a specific temperature. Change ravaged his body for the worse. Thus, he learned to adapt.

As Cal stared into the ocean, his mind revisited the past. The man standing next to him didn't give up on him, even when he considered quitting on himself. His coaches and teammates came to the hospital a few times while he recovered, busy with their season. Jensen and Daisy, the CEO of a multi-million-dollar hotel and resort company and a doctoral student in astrophysics, on the other hand? They showed up once a week despite their packed schedules.

Second only to his best friend and her husband, Claire and Alexander, Jensen and Daisy made time for him. He couldn't say that about many people, not his parents, his past romantic interests, or his fellow celebrities who claimed him as a 'friend.'

He nudged Jensen with his shoulder. "Thanks. I should probably go back out there once I finish brooding out here. Kids depend on me to make small talk so they can play sports. Pay it forward, right?"

Jensen snorted. "Eh, you don't need to subject yourself to more bullshit and awkward small talk. Leave a check and head out for the night. It essentially does the same. You know Daisy and I are guilty of Irish exits when one of us doesn't want to stay somewhere." He cracked a smile, and Cal couldn't hide his either.

"You're right," the breeze buffeted against Cal's cheeks as the night grew a little colder, lost without the sun's warmth hanging above the horizon, "I owe you."

"Not for this. For that emergency Abalone reservation the other week, maybe. It depends on whether you give me the details." Jensen whistled oh-so innocently. He rocked on his heels, but the shit-eating twist of his grin tempted Cal to roll his eyes. Yeah, he walked right into that one.

There was a point in time, in the distant past, where Cal used to rib Jensen about his lovestruck puppy act. In those days, he just started dating Daisy after years of being her work nemesis. Cal lived for every chance to teasingly flirt with the blonde bombshell while telling Jensen that he better not screw things up.

Now, the roles were reversed, with Cal being the one who was head over heels.

At first, Cal said nothing. It wasn't that he didn't trust Jensen and Daisy; he didn't trust himself not to ruin a good thing.

However, eventually, Cal relented. His hands squeezed around the balcony railing, picturing Madi. Her soft waves splayed out over one of her pillows, and the landscape of her curves and thick thighs hidden by the thin duvet cover of her bed. Her laugh flowed over the crashing waves.

"I'm seeing a woman, but we're taking it slow. Her name's Madison. She's a pediatric nurse in Los Angeles. We met on New Year's Eve at Cobalt and Neon," Cal confessed, whispering so no wandering ears might overhear. He would not be so careless with Madi.

He caught Jensen's raised brows, wiggling not unlike how he used to tease him about Daisy. It made him feel like a teenager telling his parents he was going steady with a girl.

But Jensen snapped out of it, patting his shoulder. "Hey, that's great. She must be something special to have you so tied up in knots about impressing her."

"She's so kind and funny. Not to mention, she's a total knockout. She could be a model if the industry wasn't so superficial. Her curves are everything, man," Cal groaned. Any heat tinging his cheeks a dark red competed with the sea breeze. "I really like her, so I don't want anything to ruin it. Knowing me, I'll probably fuck it up somehow."

Jensen cocked his head. "You or the media? The media loves to run with a story, and a girl like Madi would be a prime target for them being invasive."

"We've agreed to keep things on the low for now. I don't know how long we'll keep it there. It's not fair to ask Madi if she'd hide our relationship forever so I could be with her."

"Could I maybe offer some perspective?" Jensen asked. He let Cal's despair hang for a moment before interjecting, rushing in to save the day in true Ramsey fashion. His wife's "fix it" tendencies must've started to rub off on him.

"Please." Cal wasn't above pleading. The truth of the matter was undeniable: eventually, he'd need to confront the situation he backed him and Madi into. Going public suggested being in it for *the long haul* but fame posed its downsides. After a long line of women who saw his fame as the selling point, he had no idea what to do with a girl who saw him first.

"You like this Madi woman a lot. There's no denying that. Despite how the world sees you, the Cal I know will find a way to make the connection last instead of running when things get hard. You've outgrown all that, and the world needs to catch up," Jensen sighed, "so, I say that—for now—you should just *go for it.* Don't worry about what the press might think or their projections. They don't know shit. You never know where life will take you when you embrace the unexpected. Maybe life can still give you a good surprise."

Cal met his friend's gaze, finding earnestness in his bright blue eyes. If there was one thing about Jensen, he wouldn't spare someone's feelings with a lie when the truth served them better.

A lump formed in his throat, tying him up in knots. His words felt flat, utterly inconsequential compared to the kindness of Jensen's reality check. His friend verbally knocked him back to reality, freeing him from the spiral of anxiety left over. The accident marked his past, but he would be damned if he let the world ruin the best thing he had in the wake of his loss.

"Thanks, man." Cal laughed, hoping he sounded more relieved than on the strained cusp of tears. "You've gotten all wise with marriage and shit."

"I'd resent that suggestion, but I can't deny that it's given me some new perspectives on life. Marriage has been good for me. I'm not saying you and Miss Madison should rush into marriage and go for the white-picket-fence lifestyle, though. Mine and Daisy's marriage is far from traditional. Still, it works wonders for us—" Jensen started, but Daisy's voice behind them cut him off.

"—And if marriage is in the cards for you two, I'm happy to pass along our wedding planner. Audrey Wood is a once-in-a-lifetime opportunity," Daisy hummed.

She wormed under Jensen's arm, placing herself between the three. She held two glasses of whiskey and passed one to her husband, whose eyes brightened.

Daisy winked at Cal. "I already figured the call was about a lady favor, so your secret is safe with us. I'm sure that Madison is a lovely person. Maybe we can meet her one day."

"I should've known you would've figured it out. You should consider adding 'detective' to your mile-long list of skills behind former corporate executive and future astrophysicist," Cal joked, tucking his hands into his pockets when the urge to undo his bow tie buzzed in his fingers.

"Maybe. Besides, Jensen would've eventually spilled the beans with me. He's actually a little gossiper and will tell me all the work drama when he gets home," Daisy cackled. His wife's confession—or rather, snitching about his deep, dark secret—made Jensen's ears flush red. The color became noticeable, even through the darkening skies.

Yeah, those two were made for one another.

Jensen cleared his throat, quick to raise a glass. "To Cal. . . and his speedy escape from the paradise of the South Bay. May the roads be empty so he can get home faster and maybe spend time with his girl."

Cal's brows shot for the sky. He watched as Daisy held her whiskey up, mimicking Jensen's toast, winking. "Here, here! Shall we go inside and stir up the attention so no one will notice that he left?"

"That sounds like a fantastic idea." Jensen's grin widened when pulling Daisy closer to him by the curve of her waist. "If anyone asks, we didn't see him."

"Nope," Daisy agreed. They turned their gazes to Cal, all smiles and twinkling eyes. "You drive safe, you hear?"

"You two are the best." Cal shrugged off his suit jacket and tugged that damn bow tie off. The three shared a nod before ducking inside, headed in opposite directions. Cal fled into the night, knowing the Ramseys would cover his tracks long enough.

Besides, he wanted to see Madi tonight. He needed to see her.

As Cal pulled onto the last street before his home, the radio slipped onto a commercial break from the rock station. Occasional bursts of static interrupted the stream of ads, never leaving Cal alone with his thoughts long enough to digest the evening's events.

His and Jensen's conversation on the balcony buried the invasive questions from strangers whose faces he'd never see again, submerging the anger six feet under. With his rage diffused, all his attention circled around one specific thing: Madi.

Jensen's words echoed Coach Rodgers's sentiment, telling Cal to let go of his hesitations. Cal never considered himself the hesitant type, a guy who shied away from the risks and rewards of living life on the spontaneous side. But somewhere after the fame, parts of him walled themselves away.

He didn't know how he intended to bring down those walls, but maybe he could chip at them? Or maybe Madi might break through with a sledgehammer smile and the sweetest laughter, tasting smoother than honey on his tongue.

Cal craned his neck to the side while looking for another car in his driveway as he rolled up to his driveway. At first, he didn't see it just beyond the iron gates. But when he pulled in after typing his code, he spotted the yellow car on the far side of his driveway, shielded from the street by tall shrubs. Madi leaned against the hood of her car, pulling her cardigan tight over her body.

Their eyes met through the window of Cal's dark SUV as he parked in his usual spot. Cal barely waited for the engine to cut out before he slinked out of the driver's side.

He sped over to Madi, engulfing her in a crushing hug to the squeals she buried into the crook of his neck. He breathed against her hair, "Oh, I've missed you, Firefly."

"It's only been a few days." Madi giggled when she lifted her head enough for their mouths to graze each other. "But I missed you too. It feels weird not having unread texts from you."

"Well, that won't be an issue while you stay here tonight. Did you pack an overnight bag?" asked Cal. However, his question was quickly answered when Madi nudged something on the ground. So, Cal scooped the bag off the floor, keeping an arm wound tight around his girl's waist.

The two locked their cars, hustling for the front door like someone might catch them in Cal's driveway. Madi's hand threaded through Cal's, lacing their fingers while he fumbled with his keys. The touch felt. . . *warm.*

Cal ushered Madi inside, quickly locking up and moving her away from the windows. He took in her silent awe—starstruck with wide eyes—as she admired his place. Their worlds looked utterly different. He lived the picturesque Hollywood life while she lived modest but cozy means. Yet, standing on the open floor of his living room, their two worlds crashed together for the night in harmony.

"Would you like the tour first, or should I throw some dinner into the oven, Firefly?" Cal murmured, leaning forward to brush a stray strand of hair from Madi's face.

"Are you ever going to tell me why you call me that?" Madi crinkled her nose, scrunching her whole face too.

"Maybe." Cal grinned, stepping closer to her. She smelled of her favorite shampoo and the hint of something new—vaguely floral like a strong perfume—mixing the familiar and the foreign. "If you convince me."

"Oh, I can convince you." Madi sprung forward as she slammed her mouth against Cal's. His hands sought her waist to cup and squeeze, hoping for little gasps from her. Their mouths moved in a playful chase, often pulling away to be roped back in for more.

Cal wandered back toward the couch, knowing the tour and dinner could wait. *Madi must be something special to have him so tied up in knots about impressing her?*

Oh yes. She was.

Chapter 11
Madi

"YOU'RE ALL DONE, GORGEOUS. You're glowing!" A soothing chuckle ousted Madi from the clutches of sleep. She blinked through the warmth, sitting heavy on her chest until the haze cleared. Warm, eyeliner-lined eyes twinkled into hers before the lights brightened. The glow came gradually, illuminating her esthetician, Paloma's, silhouette.

"Mmm, thank you," Madi said with a throaty hum while she sat up from the bed. She accepted her robe from Paloma's hands. "You are an angel. I feel reborn."

"You'll be walking out of here like Venus emerging from the sea, dearest!" exclaimed Paloma. She assisted Madi off the table, into her sandals, and toward the door. Cold air caressed her damp cheeks and ran along her moisturized skin. During the facial, Madi asked a few questions about buying products, and Paloma offered to put them on her tab.

Paloma dropped her off at the women's changing rooms with a gentle farewell in her smile. Madi didn't waste time exchanging her robe and fuzzy cover-up for the dress she bought for the occasion. Watercolor-style fabric made a statement, but it was Valentine's Day. So what if eyes followed her around for the night?

She only cared about one person's eyes more than the rest of the world.

Madi smoothed her newly manicured hands—painted a soft creamsicle color by one of the Oceanview spa workers—over her glowing cheeks. She adjusted the poof of her messy updo, chasing less structure for the windswept romance of it all. The multicolored dress rippled in the mirror with every shift in Madi's stance; sunrise orange blended into the pops of magenta, fern, and cream to mirror the illusion of runny watercolors swirling over the canvas. Ruched satin shaped over her frame, accenting all her softer parts in the flowy fabric.

She almost didn't come tonight. Janet's words from their evening at Blues Brews the other week stuck with her. More accurately, the words burrowed under her skin and refused to leave her alone. Every text she received from Cal instigated the reminder of Janet's accusation. It didn't just hurt Madi to know her friend thought her incapable of picking a decent man, it burned her to believe that her friend saw any male interest in her as feigned or subject to ulterior motives.

However, Cal's soft-hearted plea to take her out and the small bouquet of daisies dropped off at her door won her over. Insecurity couldn't mess this up for Madi. She wouldn't allow it to either.

Madi grabbed the rest of her belongings after one last look in the mirror. Paloma had been right, she felt as beautiful as a goddess tonight.

She snuck through the winding halls of Oceanview Spa, a tad lost despite the tour given to her before by one of the other workers. Madi squinted to read the signs on the walls through the dimly lit hallways to maintain the vibe. Eventually, she ambled through the frosted glass doors to the empty receptionist desk and the narrow hallway leading her to the rest of the Ridge.

That was when she spotted Cal. He waited outside the spa, scrolling on his phone while holding another bouquet of flowers. Madi noted sunflowers, hydrangeas, and freesias in a dainty blue and sunny yellow palette.

Cal opted for a button-down in white, tucked into loose linen trousers in an equally pale shade of tan. He abstained from a baseball cap to free his dark hair but rocked the hints of a stubble shadow along his jawline. He layered two silver chains, visible because the top three buttons of his shirt were undone, along with an eyeful of toned chest. *What a treat.*

Madi caught her tongue running along her lower lip. *Damn, he looked fucking incredible.* She sped toward the door and threw it open. The sound of her wedge sandals on polished marble snatched Cal's attention from his phone.

His jaw dropped, but not before he wolf-whistled loud enough for the whole resort to hear him, "Wow. Madi, you. . . You're glowing," he stammered, tripping over himself, not unlike a teenage boy standing in front of his crush.

That made the dress worth the extra money she spent on it.

Madi smiled, spinning around in her dress to the flutter of her skirt. She giggled, "You like? I wanted to go a little bold."

Cal stepped forward. "I love it. . . Can you do another spin for me?" He bit down on his lip, reaching for her hips. So, Madi spun again, not dropping her eyes away from Cal's.

She giggled when Cal's hands grasped her hips, tugging her close to him until their lips hovered less than an inch from each other. Madi tipped her head back, opening a little more space, while Cal leaned forward.

"Don't tease me. I'm already regretting the full evening I have planned instead of figuring out how we can spend all night in bed," remarked Cal.

"Save it for later," said Madi. She ran her finger along the silky bow tying the bouquet together. "Is that for me?"

"It is. The sunflowers reminded me of you. . . but I realize now that these flowers can't compare to how stunning you look tonight." Cal handed her the bouquet. He traded it for her purse, slinging it over his shoulder without hesitation.

"You're so sweet! Thank you."

"Of course. Now, we have a reservation for dinner in the next ten minutes. I asked Jensen for another major favor."

Cal joked, all tongue-in-cheek again. Madi, however, still couldn't wrap her head around the fact that Cal knew the CEO who owned the entire resort and half of the luxury hotels in the Los Angeles area alone. The fact inspired awe, highlighting the vast difference between the world where Cal lived and the one Madi came from.

He was a star. She was an ordinary girl, borrowing time in his world for the night.

Cal's arm coiled around her waist, tucking her comfortably into his side while the two walked out of the main building of the Ridge. Pink and orange skies overhead set the scene for love in the air, buzzing with Valentine's Day spirit from all the well-dressed couples scattered in view. With all the activity ongoing, no one paid Madi and Cal any mind while they strolled down the paved walkways.

Palms swayed in the breeze, promising a temperate Del Mesa evening and total bliss. Madi let Cal lead her through the resort since he knew where to go; she leaned into his arms and went for the ride.

Cal escorted them past the pools, the plentiful bars, and luxury cars speeding past the roundabout in the center of it all. They ended up outside a gorgeous, two-story building, surrounded by looming palms and the clamor of conversations. The golden nameplate dubbing it the "Palm Building" outside its wooden double doors should've been an obvious choice to Madi.

"We'll be on the second floor," Cal said, opening the door for her. It reminded her that he knew how to be a gentleman as much as he pretended to be a smooth-talking, sharp-grinned rogue. They passed security with no issues, climbing the stairs to the restaurant on the second floor.

The inside of the restaurant gleamed from every surface—polished wood tables and gold-rimmed mirrors hoisted onto every wall they passed—but Cal didn't stop at any of the tables across the room. No, he made a beeline for one of the open balconies with a solo table prepared under the sunset skies.

Madi watched him pull out her chair before he lounged on his own, seated directly across from her so she could stare into his eyes all night. What a perfect sight! Oh, and the prime view of the Del Mesa coastline was nice, too.

A waitress in a pristine uniform jogged over. "Welcome to *Sage & Salt*, the newest addition to the Royal Ridge family. Mr. Ramsey told us to be expecting you. The kitchen staff are at your command, sir and ma'am." She handed two menus over to them. "We have a three-course meal planned for you to peruse."

"Thank you so much." Cal clinked his tongue, bringing a charming smile to match. He turned to Madi. "Are you a red, white, or cocktail kind of girl?"

"Any and all of the above. Tonight feels red." Madi ran her eyes over the menu. She spotted cheese croquettes, grilled salmon, and dark chocolate mousse cake—all complimentary to red wine. She trusted the staff to know pairings and brands better than her; the fanciest wine she knew came in a box. "Thank you."

"One bottle of red, coming up—" The waitress smiled, collecting the menus and vanishing into the empty restaurant. Others might be coming soon to enjoy their meals, but she'd take the alone time with Cal.

Speaking of Cal, his hand reached across the table to envelop hers, fingers laced and warm palm flush against hers. His eyes darted up and down, admiring her like art. He made her feel different than anyone before him; Madi wasn't a stranger to the sensation of a crush, having plenty in her time.

But Cal? He played for the major leagues of men instead of the guys she used to date, ones whose affections fizzled quicker than a year.

"Hi," Cal murmured while his thumb stroked along the sensitive back of her palm. Shivers popped off like her own brand of fireworks—something else she associated with Cal after the night they met—when pinned by his gaze. "How was the spa?"

"It was amazing, thank you. I'll have to go back later and see how much the products I asked about are," Madi giggled.

"One, don't even think about reaching for your wallet. If the spa hasn't charged my tab, I'll buy whatever you want. Two, I'm glad you liked the spa. Daisy swears by Oceanview like her life depended on it and helped me pick out the services, so I can't take credit."

Daisy Ramsey, as in the wife of the CEO and one of Cal's friends. *Cool. That fact might make her faint.* Daisy Ramsey had a resume most career women drooled over and looked like she belonged on magazine covers or movie screens.

"Oh wow. Remind me to send Daisy a thank you card. . ." Madi's joke was interrupted by the waitress returning with a bottle of wine that probably cost more than her monthly rent. She watched her fill their glasses with the seductive dark red to the three-quarters point.

"Your appetizers shall be out shortly!" the waitress declared but turned to Madi, head cocked. "Ma'am, would you like us to store those flowers in a vase with some water for you? It might be easier than holding them for your meal."

"Oh! Thank you!" Madi handed the flowers over without a second thought. She faced Cal once the waitress ducked back inside the restaurant. "Wow, this place is awesome. Can we come here for date night more often?"

"If you want. I have a membership. . . but I am fond of spending time at your place," Cal replied. He sounded sincere, pivoting away from the lighthearted teasing of their usual conversation. It made for a nice distinction for Madi.

Madi scoffed, albeit intended playfully, "Oh yeah? You're a fan of the pastel bed sheets, somewhat messy kitchen, and the empty couch spot awkwardly highlighting the mismatched décor in my living room?"

But Cal nodded, a wolfish grin on full display. "Hell yes! Your place looks like it has been lived in, while mine still belongs in some fancy real estate magazine. Besides, your house is where most of the fun happens. Breaking a couch mid-sex is still the peak of my achievements."

Cal rushed to rein himself in when the waitress returned to their balcony table carrying a giant plate. She dropped off the plate with delectable, fried croquettes stacked on the ceramic surface. With the food handed off, the waitress glided back into the kitchen, giving Cal and Madi privacy.

Both reached for the croquettes, bumping hands together to grab one. Laughter ensued, and Cal let Madi take the first pick of the plate. She snatched one off the top, and he went for one slightly toward the middle like a heathen.

They bumped them together as if they were their untouched glasses of wine before taking the first bite. Spices, ham, and hot cheese slid over Madi's tongue in a savory culinary experience, stealing any possible words off her mind. All she could manage was a throaty moan and the flutter of her eyes while she chewed on that first bite.

A second bite followed on its heels, where she pulled the croquette back to the distinct sensation of strings of cheese bridging the gap between the appetizer and her mouth. Madi's eyes flew open to see thin, cheesy strings drooping from the croquette and Cal's amused expression just beyond that.

Madi's tongue broke the cheese strings, and she hummed, "These are so amazing. I've never had anything like it."

"Yeah? That's great—" Cal appeared on the verge of cracking a wide, toothy grin at her, hiding it behind a strategic wipe of his napkin. "—By the way, you still have some cheese on your lips."

"Oh! Where?" Madi's hands flew to her lips, tracing her thumb over the curve of her lower lip. "Did I get it?" she asked.

Cal shook his head, so she continued searching for it. Yet, he quickly interrupted, "Here, let me get it for you. . ."

Madi paused and nodded. She half-expected him to lean across the table with his napkin to brush her lips clean, smudging her lipstick onto the soft sage cloth. Or maybe the pad of his thumb if he felt romantic.

Instead, Cal rose from his seat and leaned over the table, capturing her lips with his. She froze in her chair, stuck at the mercy of his borderline *ravenous* kiss. A surprised moan slipped into his mouth when Cal traced his tongue along her lower lip to clean the cheese off. There might not have been any cheese, and he used the excuse to kiss her.

The thought of the latter awoke every butterfly known on the planet to invade her stomach, leaving her a fluttery mess. Under the tablecloth, her thighs clenched at the hot, dull throb gasping between her thighs. *If Cal wanted to seduce her, it was working.*

Cal pulled back enough for their lips to part but not go very far so he could whisper straight into her puffy lips, "Thanks for spending Valentine's Day with me, Firefly. It's been ages since I've had someone to spend it with. . . correction, someone I like a lot."

"It's my honor to spend tonight with you. I've never been treated like this by any of my past Valentines. It's a massive step up from a card or a non-descript box of chocolates," Madi murmured. She resisted the urge to yank her man back in by the lapels of his unbuttoned button-down, ready to say, *"fuck the croquettes. . . and fuck me instead,"* without a care in the world.

Cal's brows shot up. "Those men are idiots. I'm glad that I could treat you like you deserve. I know my romancing skills are rusty—"

"If this is rusty, then you might as well bury me now. I might swoon to death. You're such a romantic." Madi gestured to the elegant setup. In what universe was a romantic, three-course dinner with a balcony view at a luxury resort restaurant anything but romantic? Madi knew her standards could be lower, but Cal set his bar so high.

Redness leaped across Cal's nose and cheeks, painting his face in the soft flush like a dusting of freckles. Even his ears tinged a lighter shade of pink at her compliment. *Guess Madi needed to compliment him more often; he looked so cute when he blushed.*

Cal slumped back in his chair, reaching for his wine and his half-eaten croquette, ignoring how its warm cheese stuck to the plate. He lifted the glass. "A toast then? To a successful Valentine's Day dinner."

"To an incredible dinner and whatever else the night brings." Madi tipped her glass to simulate the clink of them together. She and Cal took a measured sip of their wine, adding a new, bold flavor to the palette of the meal.

With the sky darkening and the croquettes cooling on the platter before her, Madi spared a glance at the empty restaurant, so glad to have the time alone with Cal. At the Ridge, she never needed to glance over her shoulder and double-check that no one studied them too closely. No one gave them the stares of being mismatched, too busy in their own world. For once, her heart knew peace.

Madi sipped at her wine, finishing her first croquette from the stacked plate. "I wonder when everyone else is coming. There's no way a restaurant like this is virtually empty tonight of all nights!"

The sunset backlit Cal's silhouette in its golden threads of light, yet none of them compared to the brightness of his smile when he sipped at his wine. He winked over the rim as he said, "Oh, who knows?"

As it turned out, no one else showed up because Cal rented the entire restaurant for the night. Madi's jaw hit the floor when that little fact slipped out, which conveniently happened when her beau generously tipped the waitress and kitchen staff for their time.

Sage & Salt hadn't opened to the general public yet—not for a few weeks.

Madi hadn't shaken off the shock from the never-ending stream of events that evening when Cal suggested a walk along the nearby beaches. That was how she ended up shoeless and strolling along the cooling sands, hand-in-hand with Cal.

In the near distance, the lights lining the hiking trail back to the Ridge twinkled faintly with their amber hues. However, none compared to the silvery haze of the moonlight beaming down on the darkened ocean or the once-bright sands, now shadows compared to their state in the daytime.

Madi gripped her wedges in her crowded hands, fighting for space with her bouquet and the cardigan she picked out of her tote bag. February nights along the shore promised cold to kiss along her exposed skin, leaving its mark in goosebumps and a muted red. She didn't want it yet, not when Cal's hand in hers pumped new warmth into her veins.

"Alright, my turn," Cal hummed, his face turned toward the ocean as he led her across the sand. For the moment, the waterline appeared at low tide, and the two traversed dry sands. "What three things in your life could you not imagine doing without?"

"Ooh, that's a hard one. The first one is probably my job because caring for people is my passion in life. Then, I'd say good food because I'm a foodie, and it's my dream to travel and try new cuisines. Last but not least, I'd choose my friends because they're the closest thing I have to family in this world," said Madi.

"I understand that. . . The last one that is. Friendships are everything. I'd consider my friends like family, too." Cal nodded despite his eyes still focused on the waters. He appeared far out to sea mentally, not tied to the beach with her.

Madi tugged on his arm gently until his head swiveled back to hers, already loaded with an apologetic smile. She understood, though. The question game started during their stroll from the Sage & Salt, but the initial questions danced along the line of flirtation. These ones were. . . deeper.

"How about we take a break from the questions for a moment. Let's just enjoy the night?" she offered, and Cal accepted without a protest.

He set down her tote bag, which he still carried for her, into the sand and set his shoes next to it. "Let's leave our stuff here. No one's around, so they should be good over here."

"Alright, I trust you." Madi didn't think Cal would let them stray too far from their belongings. She dropped her shoes and the bouquet onto the pile as Cal tugged her ahead.

They veered from their dry path and onto the thin stretch of sand before the damp part. Water rushed in its cyclical rhythm, quietly roaring into the night without the cries of birds or beachgoers interrupting its melody. Madi stayed on the inner edge while Cal leaned over.

When the waves rolled in, his fingertips ran along the damp sand. He traced the seafoam for a fleeting moment before the waves backed away. He chuckled as he said, "The water is colder than I expected. I'd almost want to jump in it."

"You're insane." Madi scrunched her nose at the thought of diving into the frigid February ocean. Although Cal could probably convince her with enough of his troublesome smile and those pretty eyes. It should be a crime for how long his lashes were natural. "You'd have to walk back to the hotel soaking wet."

Cal laughed, "Oh, I've done so much worse. Remind me to recount my drunken escapades during my first year on the Foxhounds. Now, those days were insane." He dipped toward the water when it rushed in. That time, however, he cupped a little and let it run through his fingers.

Cal popped back up, flicking his fingers toward Madi. Although most of the water slipped from his hold, a few stray droplets pelted against Madi's cheeks and chest. She hadn't thrown up her arms fast enough. She shrank back, squealing loud enough to echo down the beach.

"Evil!" Madi gasped. She broke out of their linked hands and strode a few inches ahead. The next thing she knew, she had scooped up a handful of fresh water and flung it at Cal with no remorse.

The water splattered against his dress shirt, and the fabric stuck to his glorious chest like a fancy wet t-shirt contest. Cal blinked twice, his jaw wide open for any flies to dive in.

Smarter than the average bear, Madi didn't stick around before bolting down the stretch of beach. She giggled, losing the sound in the wind as her legs pumped as fast as possible in her dress. Cal's "You're in for it now!" rumbled from behind her, preceding the thudding of footsteps in the sand.

Madi sped up, but she wasn't a match for the former athlete in Cal, who quickly caught up in a few long strides. His labored breathing pressed against her ear while he caught her with arms around her waist. Madi wiggled around and looked for an escape, finding none.

But on the shifting sands, the two lost their footing and crashed to the ground in a tangle of limbs. Cal's hands snapped into motion, tucking behind Madi's head to shield her from knocking into the sand. Yes, the sand was soft, but the thought counted.

Cal landed on top, offering a wolfish grin. "Was this your plan all along, Miss Caldwell? Trapping me into a beachside rendezvous."

"No, but now that you mention it—" Madi hummed, slotting one of her legs between his. She pushed and angled it, flipping her and Cal over. Cal landed on the bottom, sprawled across the sand with a startled look. "—that sounds like a great idea."

Madi sank into a comfortable straddle of his hips, pinning her man to the sand. Her head dipped down to bring her lips closer, and Cal, catching the memo, met her halfway. Their mouths collided, a twisting tangle of emotions vying for attention. However, desperately aroused appeared the winner by a long shot.

Cal's hands grabbed Madi's hips, pushing the hem of her dress higher as he fisted the fabric in his fingers. Madi's hips swiveled to the motion of the ocean, searching for the friction she craved. Knowing Cal, she could find it fast.

But neither expected the sudden blast of cold to slam into them, courtesy of the tides rising from their low reach. Salty ocean water doused Madi and Cal from the waist down, interrupting their moonlight make-out.

Cal's head fell back, laughter pouring off him like the sweet wine from dinner. "I think Mother Nature is telling us to take it elsewhere. Is there any chance I could convince you to come to my room with me?"

"I won't need convincing," Madi whispered while she got off him. Cal sat up, and the two helped each other off the newly damp sand. "Let's go warm up."

Chapter 12

Cal

IF CAL HAD A choice, he would never step into a hospital for the rest of his life. After months spent either in the hospital for recovery or bogged down by check-up visits, he endured his fill of the sterile smell and sickly florescent lights. He always found his way back there in his nightmares.

But today, when an emergency call hit his phone, Cal abandoned all his plans to rush to the hospital. He had sprinted out during an interview, shouting promises to reschedule to the poor journalist.

He didn't spare a glance at any of the people he passed when racing toward the pediatrics wing, not stopping to ask for directions or guidance to the pediatric wing. There was no time.

On paper, Cal appeared carefree and devoid of responsibilities. He was a twenty-seven-year-old bachelor with a literal fuck-ton of money, fame, and no dependents. Not even a dog. But that wasn't necessarily true—at least not to his best friend, Claire. She and Alex thought it was best to name Cal the godfather of their son, Louis.

So, when a call from Louis' school interrupted his interview with a message that Louis "got hurt on a field trip," that he would be "escorted to the hospital," and "no one could reach either of his parents," Cal made a beeline for the hospital.

Cal paced the small, enclosed space inside the elevator, burning holes into the floor from the sheer weight of his steps. He couldn't manage flights of stairs like he used to—no more bounding up them quickly—so the elevator carried him up the several stories. *Why did the hospital put pediatrics on the top floor?*

His hands fidgeted with everything in reach: his long-sleeved shirt and baggy jeans, the backward baseball cap tucked over his hair, and the lanyard with his keys wrapped so tight around his palm that he might lose circulation to his fingers. Nothing seemed to settle him when the nerves took control, reigning over scattered thoughts and a million different worries.

When the elevator doors swept open, Cal barged through them. He ambled down the hall to the labeled pediatrics area, stumbling into the waiting room. The sight of it stood out like a mismatched place between two different times. The ancient television and faded toys for kids melted against the backdrop of the more technically advanced check-in station and brand-new chairs. But, more importantly, the room had little to no occupants beyond two women seated in chairs. No one manned the check-in station at the front.

Cal paused his frantic pace to a complete standstill, frozen in the middle of the waiting room. *If he stared hard enough at the check-in station, would a nurse materialize to help him find Louis?*

As he waited at the check-in station, a gentle tap on his shoulder snatched his attention away from Louis somewhere behind those muted walls. Beside him, one of the women that had been seated peered up at him.

She cocked her head, knocking a few strands of cinnamon-brown hair from a ballerina-style bun loose around her face. "Sorry to bother you, sir. Are you here for Louis Bridges?" she lowered her voice so the other woman didn't overhear them.

"Yeah, how'd you know?" Cal stammered before his reluctant throat closed on him. He stared at the woman, eyes narrowing while he studied her. Suspicion came out on top in the war waged between the rush of emotions in his head. He had close encounters with paparazzi surrogates before but never this close, never this intrusive into his life. *Not since the accident.*

However, the woman smiled. "Oh good! You must be his dad. I tried to reach you and your wife about Louis being a little clumsy. Thank goodness the school was able to reach you."

"Oh, um," Cal shook his head, "I'm actually the other emergency contact, his godfather. I'm Cal. . . Did we speak on the phone?"

"We did. Apologies for the misunderstanding, Cal. My name's Sierra. I'm one of the new teachers at the elementary school. I volunteered to help chaperone the trip to the observatory when Louis fell. I stayed with him in the ambulance. . . Didn't want to leave without a parent or guardian being here."

Sierra stuck out her hand to Cal, who took it. He remembered all the stress Claire and Alex faced when enrolling Louis in school. They couldn't have picked a better place. Teachers like Sierra must be commonplace there.

"Thanks for being there. As much as we all love Louis, I know he can be a little reckless. That's how his mom was at his age." Cal couldn't stop the snicker from weaseling out of his mouth. He knew all about Claire's death-defying escapades from her parents, who used to regale him with tales over dinner whenever he crashed at their place.

Claire might kill him later for sharing her dark secrets with a stranger.

Sierra snorted, "Honestly, that's not surprising. Louis has this sense of adventure in everything he does; you can see it in his eyes. I figured he picked it up from someone at home. But he does often cite you as his favorite bad influence."

Cal should've seen that coming from a mile away, but he laughed anyway. That was him: *Cal, the fun uncle who came with gifts and no rules.* He liked being the fun guy who occasionally occupied the Bridges household.

He shoved his hands into the pockets of his jeans, content to shrug and feign innocence. Sierra beside him tsked and shook her head. "I can see it. You two smile the same, so he obviously admires you. Kids need that in their lives, even for a little trouble."

Cal nodded. He stepped back from the check-in station with Sierra, and the two took separate seats in the waiting room. He waited for a while—how long precisely, he couldn't say—but footsteps nudged his attention toward the front. A dark-haired receptionist adjusted her glasses while she set down her purse.

"Any new check-ins?" she called to the rest of the room, causing Cal to stumble onto his feet. Sierra did the same, only more gracefully than he had.

"That'll be for you. Tell Louis to get well soon for me, okay?" Sierra picked up her oversized purse from the foot of her chair. Her warm eyes softened when staring past Cal at the hovering receptionist.

"Thanks for staying with him. I'm sure he'll recover faster than we think." Cal watched her leave and checked himself in for Louis. He didn't need to wait much longer this time before a nurse in pink scrubs led him into the pediatric wing. Someone painted animals, nature, and other objects all over the sterile white walls to inject some life into the place, unlike the hollow emptiness Cal remembered about the hospitals he stayed in.

The ambient chatter in softer, high-pitched voices floated in his wake while Cal lumbered behind the nurse whose name he never got. She scurried fast across the linoleum floors, stirring ripples in the distorted reflections like murky waters. He followed her to one of the glass rooms with a curtain pulled over the entryway.

"Here you are," she said before speeding away, likely to attend to another important task besides guiding him around. Cal stuffed the quiet thanks into his back pocket for if he ever saw her again and threw the curtain open.

In the upright bed, Louis grinned with dimples digging into the curves of his round cheeks. His non-injured arm swept away the shaggy fringe of dark hair falling into his eyes in desperate need of a haircut. But in him, Cal saw the inklings of a younger Claire blazing through, bright and undeniable.

A nurse stood beside the bed with her back facing him, adorned in the same pink scrubs as the others on the floor. *Must be a pediatric-specific thing.* The sight of her fiery hair under the lights almost reminded him of Madi's, tucked out behind a dainty hair clip in a matching shade of pink.

"Hey, bud—" Cal began, not expecting the nurse to whirl around at the sound of his voice. He hadn't been expecting the familiar, beautiful face of one Madi Caldwell. Her eyes blew wide when she ran them over him once. . . twice. . . three times. Madi never told him the name of the hospital she worked at; granted, he hadn't asked before.

Of all the hospitals in Los Angeles, he walked into the one where his secret girlfriend worked. *It'll be fine. Play it cool and try not to undress her with your eyes in front of the kid.*

Was it only last week that they had been kissing in the sand while the waves dampened them on a beach in the South Bay? When the world pulled them apart, all those memories felt like they existed another lifetime ago, much less a week.

"Hi there. Are you here for my very brave patient?" Madi asked. If he listened closely, her voice's ever-present yet faint waver lilted in and out. It rode on the tide of her breathing, a little louder and harsher, while she stared him down.

"I am," he promised while stepping into the room and closing the curtain behind him. Cal would never blow their cover without asking her first; he knew better than to think life would be so easy when thrust under the spotlight where the world watched. "My name is Cal. That young gentleman in the sling is Louis, my godson."

He leaned around Madi, catching sight of Louis' newly sheepish grin and avoidant eyes. What had he gotten into while at Griffith Observatory to bang up his shoulder?

"Well, nice to meet you, Mr. Cal. Louis here was perfectly behaved while I took his vitals. I can call the doctor if you want him to debrief you." Madi half-reached for the curtain when Cal's hand snagged her wrist between his fingers.

"No need," he said, voice on the verge of a whisper. Their eyes met in the middle, gazes a little too familiar, but none of Madi's coworkers could see them. "I'd like you to tell me, Miss."

"Of course. From my understanding, Louis had been a little eager to play a game of tag around the observatory with some friends. He ended up slipping and falling on the stairs, resulting in a mild shoulder strain in his right shoulder. Thankfully, he sustained no other injuries. The doctor can offer a better estimate of healing when the parents arrive."

Cal listened to Madi. She put on a different tone when talking to patients, somehow softer and daintier than her usual resonance. He wanted her to keep talking to him, but the thought of her other patients in neighboring rooms stopped that thought.

"Thank you. You're quite the nurse, Miss," he murmured, just then realizing he still held her wrist. He let her go. His hand slithered into his back pocket, finding a frayed thread in his jeans to pull at instead of the temptation to drag Madi into his personal space. *Even the scrubs looked ridiculously good on her.*

"It's my pleasure." Madi lingered on the last word while sidestepping Cal. She tossed open the curtain, all smiles for him and Louis. "I'll give you two some alone time but do ring my button if you need anything. I'll check in on you shortly."

Madi bowed out from the room, but Cal darted to the archway. "Wait, one more question before you go?" he asked, waiting for Madi to turn around. He ran his eyes over her gorgeous face one last time before she left for more afternoon rotations. "Any chance the gift shop downstairs has some games for the next few hours?"

"Do you have any threes?" Louis questioned while his eyes lazily lifted from the stack of cards in his non-injured hand. He examined Cal, who sprawled across the foot of the tiny, cramped hospital bed; Cal preferred that to the chair, which turned his leg into a restless aching lump.

"Go fish, bud," Cal remarked. It earned him a sigh from his godson when he plucked a card fresh off the shuffled pile. "You're terrible at this game."

"You're only better because you played it a lot back in your day. . . because you're old." Louis stuck his tongue out, which was very seven-year-old behavior.

Cal chuckled while he set his cards face down. "Just for that little comment, give me the queen of spades I know you have." His remark elicited an eye roll from Louis, who proceeded to hand over the exact card Cal asked for.

He adored his godson, but he telegraphed *everything* on his cute little face.

Cal would've asked for another card to match the one in his dwindling hand, but the faint exclamation of "Louis?" from across the curtain stopped him. He and Louis perked up at Claire's voice, painted frantic like only a mother's could be.

The curtain swished open, revealing Alexander and Claire on the other side. Claire almost collapsed into her husband's arms at the sight of Louis unharmed. . . Well, mostly. Her sharp blue eyes landed on Cal, who lounged across the bed.

"Thank god." Claire surged forward as Cal slid off the bed, managing to catch her in his arms. She, a petite woman, buried her face into his chest and squeezed him tight. She trembled a little in Cal's embrace when the anxiety cut out, no longer driving her forward. "Thank you for making it."

"Of course. I assumed that one of your mediations went over time," Cal murmured. He clasped Alex's hand for a brief moment over Claire's shoulders and met relief flooding the man's icy eyes. Claire and Alex worked in the legal field but with Alex and Claire as mediators. The two ran a solo practice, often hired by different parties as a neutral third voice in conflicts.

"We normally wouldn't work a double, but the clients insisted." Alex eased his wife from Cal's arms, and Claire molded into his touch. Cal stepped to the side to watch Claire and Alex embrace Louis to the best of their abilities, maneuvering around the cast to hold their son.

Louis buried his face into his mom's auburn hair. "I'm sorry, Mom," he mumbled, less of a rebel when faced with his panicked mom's face. While he looked like the spitting image of his father, his mother's eyes and personality won the genetics fight.

"Shhh, it's okay. You've got to be a little more careful out there, rockstar." Claire eased him with a forehead kiss. However, the red lipstick transferring to Louis' forehead caused Alex to laugh, and Cal's resolve crumbled.

Louis' nose crinkled while looking around the room. "Do we need to call in the nurse? Miss Madison was really nice."

"We can." Cal glanced through the open archway, searching for Madi among the sea of pink scrubs. But his eyes picked her out of the crowd when her laugh rang out. She leaned against the nurse's station on folded arms, her body perfectly arched from her back to those voluptuous hips. Her hair fell loose around her face. A giant duffle bag rested at her feet, propped against one of her pristine white sneakers. "You can press the nurse's button to call her over."

His eyes stayed on Madi, trailing the curve of her back whenever she shifted in her position. The slight bite of her lower lip tested his resolve, forcing him to stay put while the rest of the pediatric wing moved along. *Worlds apart, they stood.*

Cal hadn't noticed, at least not at first, how Claire materialized by his side, peering up at him. When he noticed her in his peripheral gaze, he spotted her arched brow. Her expression, not unlike Daisy's, knew how to slide under his skin and pluck out the secrets he buried under a casual smile.

In her silence, she posed a question left unspoken. *What had his attention grasped by the collar?*

Cal should've turned away and brushed off her stare in nonchalance. Instead, the involuntary heat wave over his cheeks and the rest of his face probably outed him. That lifted brow from Claire transformed into a devilish smirk while her eyes followed his line of vision. Yeah, she knew he had his eyes somewhere they shouldn't be.

Only when the loud buzzing from the bed behind them did the two turn away from staring at Madi. However, Cal would answer for that later unless Claire forgot all about it in the shuffle of getting Louis home.

Louis held the little remote, pushing the "call nurse" button with a wide grin. Alex wrenched the remote from his son's hand with the gentlest hand Cal had ever seen. The two exchanged silent gestures, ending with Louis sticking his tongue out.

Footsteps approached, and another nurse—not Madi—appeared in the doorway. She clasped her hands together. "Hi there. You must be the Bridges family? I'm Nathalie, and I'll be taking over for Madison. Is there anything you need?"

"Could we have the doctor come in and tell us our next steps? We don't know if our son needs to stay overnight or if he can come home with us," said Claire.

"Of course. I'm sure Louis will be discharged tonight, but let me grab him for you!" Nathalie nodded. She gave Cal a lingering once-over before she strode back into the hallway, leaving the curtain open.

Cal peered out, not finding Madi by the nurse's station anymore. He patted his pockets to check for his keys, wallet, and everything else he needed to make a quick break for the elevators. Madi couldn't have gotten far in the hospital yet, not when he took his eyes off her for no more than a minute.

He snatched up his baseball cap, sliding it back on to obscure his face from recognition. He gave Louis a fist bump, winking. "I've got to head out. Try not to break any more bones, kid."

"No promises." Louis snickered despite the disapproving looks from his parents. What a little wild child. "Bye, Uncle Cal!"

"Little hellion. . ." Cal shook his head while hugging Alex and Claire goodbye. His and Alex's bro hug didn't compare to the warm, familial squeeze of Claire's small arms around his waist. They were family; blood didn't mean shit to him.

"Drive safe. And no skipping our monthly dinner next weekend," Claire warned with a stern finger prodding his chest. Cal wasn't in the habit of skipping homecooked meals made by Claire or the chance to hang out with people he actually cared about.

"Of course. Okay, got to go—" Cal headed for the elevators, knowing the way he came after a few trips between the room and the lobby during his stay with Louis. He passed nurses who either smiled, waved, or tried to catch a glimpse underneath his baseball cap when he walked by them. But Cal didn't stop until he saw the elevators in his sights.

As the doors appeared to close, he lunged for the down button. Luckily, he snagged it on time, and the doors opened.

Inside the elevator, Madi stood all alone, shouldering her duffle bag. Her once exhausted expression perked up from the elevator doors opening.

But when her eyes landed on him, life flooded back into her ashen cheeks. The polite smile broke for something startling. Something *real*. Her fingers twitched at her sides, and she beckoned him into the elevator.

Cal darted inside. He leaned against the wall beside Madi, towering over her rather effortlessly. He chuckled when she repeatedly pushed the 'closed door' button, reminding him of Louis.

"So, I don't know what the protocol is for when your beautiful nurse girlfriend pretends to be a stranger while she's taking care of your reckless godson. Is sushi and drinks back at my place a good start at a 'thank you'?" Cal whistled while watching the doors.

Madi fluffed out her hair, laughing. "Oh? Well, I feel like that's a good start. . . but an even better one will throw in the promise of dessert. . ."

Her innuendo hung heavily while she ran her hand down the length of his shirt. Her fingers curled around the hem of his shirt, easing it from his jeans. Cal shivered while Madi pinned him to the wall with her gaze.

"Whatever she wants, my Firefly gets," Cal murmured. As the elevator doors closed, he surged forward, needing a taste of Madi. Spending the last few hours staring out at her where he couldn't pull her close or whisper teasing jokes into her ear to make her blush tortured him beyond compare.

Chapter 13

Madi

MADI'S DUFFLE BAG BOUNCED against her thigh as she climbed onto Cal's porch, brushing loose curls from her face. Those curlers she snatched up on a sale from the local drug store worked like magic, turning her hair into princess-style ringlets framing her bare face. That evening promised a night at Cal's pool, and she finished her last tube of waterproof mascara last week.

President's Day weekend descended on Los Angeles with sunny, temperate weather and plenty of opportunity. Madi, seemingly the luckiest woman in the world, managed to snag some time off. She and Cal had been discussing a long weekend shut-in at his place, planning an overnight stay with plenty of things to do. The time finally came around, and Madi intended to enjoy every moment.

Rocking on her heels, Madi knocked on the door twice before Cal's grinning visage appeared on the other side, warped through the glass. She listened to the locks click before the door swung open, and Cal yanked her inside.

Madi giggled when crossing the threshold, content to crash into Cal's broad, well-defined chest. His arms slithered down and around her waist, resting comfortably over her ass. One of his hands squeezed but stayed over the dress she wore as a makeshift cover-up.

"Hi," Madi murmured, staring at Cal while dropping her bag. She heard the door close and leaned with Cal while he fiddled with the locks. "I see you've decided to skip the shirt. I like the view."

"Oh, you know. . . I figured I'd save us all some time and give you a little snack to enjoy before dinner." Cal's mouth grazed against hers, stealing the ghost of a kiss straight off the edge of her lips before tipping his face back. "Welcome to your humble abode for the next two days."

"Humble is an interesting descriptive choice. More like massive, million-dollar, and made for a celebrity athlete." Sarcasm spun off her tongue, pinging around as a stray bullet would.

Cal, for all her teasing, took her commentary with a shit-eating grin and a playful squeeze of her ass, using both of his hands. "So, there's plenty of room to play."

"Oh, I can't wait to see how we can spend twenty-four hours without responsibilities or contact with the outside world," Madi mouthed. Her voice petered out when Cal's firm grip squeezed her ass again. It threw her off just enough for him to snag her lower lips between his teeth and drag her into a bruising, hungry kiss. His mouth touching hers went from nothing to one hundred as he traced her mouth with a quick, skilled tongue; she knew exactly what kind of damage his tongue could do to her.

He'd turned her into a mess before, an utter puddle of mush.

Between the fervent kisses, like he wanted to devour her on the spot, Cal whispered, "I'm getting ahead of myself. Dinner's sitting in the little oven warmer—which I didn't know existed until Claire told me about them—and I spent some hours preparing outside for us."

The admission almost made Cal bashful. Once darkened by lust, his eyes softened to their resting shade of green while his cheeks flushed in a delicate touch of pink. Both sides of Cal existed in beautiful harmony, but something about his sweetness left Madi craving more. She always preferred the sweet things in life.

"Lead the way, honey." Madi kicked her bag aside as she followed Cal through the living room. He gave her the grand tour last time, leaving no room untouched. Granted, the last time she was here, Madi added *get eaten out on a pool table* to her running list of unique sexual experiences Cal gave her. That man seemed *determined* to either cross off her secret, sexy bucket list or inspire new fantasies for when she spent some much-needed decompression time with her vibrator.

The two headed to the backyard, stepping out into the night. Madi's eyes flew to the new string lights hung over the outdoor dining patio. Cal adorned the table with candles and a flower centerpiece, illuminating the space in an amber glow. Rose petals surrounded the hardwood of the deck in the spirit of true romance.

Cal's mouth grazed against Madi's ear, his hands holding her by her waist, "Because I'm still not the greatest chef—barring a few staple meals—I ordered in food. It'll stay nice and warm inside while we enjoy the pool for a little while."

"The pool sounds amazing right now. The hot tub will probably be so good for me after the last couple of shifts." Madi hip-checked Cal as he stepped toward the table. He revealed several towels stacked on one of the chairs, smiling wide. Clearly, he thought everything through ahead of time. "So glad I packed my best bathing suit."

Madi's hands grabbed the skirt of her dress. In a smooth pull, she worked the dress over her head to reveal her choice in swimming attire—a teeny tiny, string bikini matching the color of a candy apple.

She tossed her dress toward Cal, thinking he'd catch it and set it aside. But the dress harmlessly smacked into his chest and fell to the wooden deck. Cal stared at Madi, jaw slack and eyes fixated on her body. He didn't move or speak while he admired her.

A loaded silence ran free through the backyard as Madi tucked her hands behind her back, further accentuating her hips and chest. The bikini didn't cover much of her body, but that was the intent.

He's speechless. Madi swallowed the laugh begging to come out. If she wasn't already a medical professional, a small part of her might've worried that she had induced cardiac arrest in her poor boyfriend. "Earth to Cal?"

"Huh?" was Cal's response. He blinked hard, even shaking his head until he uncrossed the wires in his brain. "God, Firefly. . . Are you trying to break my patience?"

"Maybe, or maybe not. Depends on if it's working." Madi cheesed when Cal strode toward her. He grabbed her by her hips and lifted her off her feet. She gasped, quick to coil her legs around his waist and bury her face into the crook of his neck.

Cal breathed hard. "You're so damn tempting. I think we need to cool down before things get too hot." His words didn't set off bells in Madi's head until she realized he stepped closer to the pool's edge.

"Cal!" Madi gasped, shrieking with laughter as Cal jumped into the pool with her still wound around his waist. Their bodies crashed into the freezing pool, sinking beneath the waves while tangled together in an unseemly mesh of limbs. Madi slid free from Cal's arms and spiraled through the waters, lighter than a feather. She resurfaced first, gulping the freezing night air as it brushed against her damp face.

After a few seconds, Cal emerged from the water too. He shook out his hair like a dog fresh out of the bath, half-panting and half-laughing. He paddled to Madi, content to nuzzle his face against her damp skin.

It was his hot breath, not the chill of the night pressed against her wet skin, that sent a shiver down her body. Cal hummed.

"The hot tub feels even better after a dip in the pool. C'mon." He swam to the edge, pushing himself out of the pool, allowing Madi to enjoy the view of his muscles flexing while rivulets of water slid down the hardened, sinewy ridges.

Madi swam to the closest staircase and hauled herself to the hot tub, where Cal waited. The two stepped into the frothing, steaming waters together. A whimper slipped off Madi's lips when her legs submerged into the hot waters, scalding compared to the pool below them.

Cal's head tipped back, and he sighed in pure bliss while he sat in the hot tub. The bubbling reached his mid-chest, but hovered around Madi's neck until Cal eased her to sit on his lap. He stared at her through heavy-lidded eyes and his naturally thick lashes, pouting his lips while his thumb traced circles around the small of her back.

"You're so pretty," Cal groaned. "Have I told you that tonight?"

"Oh, I don't know. . . maybe once or twice," Madi played along. She shifted her position from perching on one of Cal's thighs to straddling her legs wide across his lap. She didn't mind the marks of her knees digging into the stone bench if it meant she got to admire Cal like this. *Compliments never came so easy to her until Cal started saying them.*

Cal adjusted her on his lap to where their hips aligned, leaving no space between their bodies. He chuckled when hovering his mouth over the column of her neck. The sound stoked shockwaves to reverberate over her skin. "Well, you're so damn pretty. I almost want to hang a photo of you tonight on my wall like a centerfold."

Heat throbbed between her legs. Those words sent a shot of arousal straight to her clit, which cried out for Cal's hand to push aside the fabric of her bikini bottom and touch. And, almost as if he sensed the dirty fantasy racing through her thoughts, Cal's hand wandered further up her back.

The next thing she knew, Madi felt the thin string of her top undone when Cal yanked it apart. Her bikini top loosened and, with a secondary pull from Cal, fell off. Her nipples hardened fast once exposed to the cold night air, stiff and perky without a single touch from Cal.

But she didn't need to wait for long before his thumb circled around one of her nipples, grinning at the hitched, breathy gasps she let out at every rotation. "Lean back a little for me."

"Okay—" Madi stammered, doing as he requested. She moved, and he followed, running his tongue down the winding path from her pulse point to her breasts. He swirled one of her nipples into his mouth, sucking hard enough to make her hips buck. His other hand palmed at her other breast; no part of her was left neglected by Cal.

Her head lolled back, focusing on the sensation of Cal's hands and mouth having their way with her. Cal's roughness poured accelerant on the heat festering between her thighs. The rush crept up the slopes of her hips and painted her stomach and chest in its burning presence.

Madi began to roll her hips, emboldened by Cal's kisses and bites growing fiercer. He seemed on a mission to mark her body as his. No one could touch her without a reminder of the man in front of her. Water sloshed around them, dousing the ends of her drying ringlets, but Madi couldn't be bothered. Their grinding hips could knock water onto the stone outside the pool and run the hot tub dry, but she might not be able to stop.

Madi ran her fingers through the hair gathered at the nape of Cal's neck, threading her grip to pull his head back. She heard Cal's frustrated, borderline feral grunt. His eyes dipped back into darker shades, drenched from the arousal pooling between their flushed hips.

"If I didn't know any better, I'd think you were trying to eat me. What happened to the romantic dinner plans?" asked Madi. She watched as Cal's tongue roamed along his lower lip, slowly swiping over the puffy skin. He kissed his lips raw from his relentless pursuit of her body.

"Forget that," Cal's voice rumbled, a whole octave deeper, huskier than Madi had ever heard from him before. His hands grasped at the waistband of her bikini bottoms, curling his fingers underneath it. "We're starting with dessert first."

Madi stared at him, rendered speechless, when his hands lifted her straight out of the water. Holding her underneath her ass, Cal rose from the waters long enough to rest her along the rim of smoothed stone lining the hot tub.

His hands guided hers to grip around the far edge, the one that didn't hover above the open pool, smirking down at her. Cal loomed over her, dripping water from the hot tub onto her bare torso by the sheer angle of his body leaning over hers. *She needed him to be on top of her, not hovering over her.*

"Don't worry. . . I won't let you fall." Cal cupped her face for a second. His hand tilted her chin so she could watch the rivulets of water speed down his toned abs and slide underneath the waistband of his swim trunks.

Madi grasped the ledge in anticipation. Her eyes followed Cal when he sank back into the water, lips parted to ask where he was going. But she shut up when his hands dragged her hips to the inner edge and spread her legs wide open, so her pussy was at his mouth level.

Cal expertly peeled the wet bikini bottoms off her body, tossing them into the pool somewhere behind him. The loud 'splash' might've caused her to spasm on the spot, taken over by the downright horny energy swimming laps in her brain. Cal loaded her legs onto his shoulder as wide as he could, leaving Madi's pussy unobstructed.

Eagerly, Cal's mouth attached to her inner thighs. He peppered up and down the length of her thighs, never venturing further than the juncture of her hip with his mouth. Hot, wet kisses adorned her while he teased, always coming close but not close enough for his tongue to graze her throbbing clit. Wherever he bit, he soothed the spot with a lingering kiss and a cheeky stare thrown her way.

Madi could've pouted or demanded he go faster. However, the sight of the soaking wet Cal, with a grin like the devil of her dreams and dark hair framing his face in the shadows of the February night, left her without words. She stared, a willing participant in his game, spellbound.

Cal's eyes held hers when he finally reached the top of her clit. He laid a few rough kisses and firm swipes of his tongue, turning her legs into jelly. So entranced by his mouth, Madi failed to realize one of his hands slipped away from holding her thighs until the sensation of a finger pushed into her pussy.

Madi moaned, unashamed by how loud her panting filled the backyard. Cal's solo finger pumped in and out of her, testing the pace. He didn't stop with his mouth either, wrapping his lips around her clit with a fervor to taste her.

No matter how much she squirmed, Madi refused to let go of the wall. She imagined the stone pressed into her hand was Cal's hair, pretending to thread her fingers through and tug harder, goading him to eat her out without a shred of elegance. She wanted it reckless, sloppy, and unburdened by any restraint.

Cal's mouth made a mess of her while a second finger slipped into her. He crooked his fingers, stretching her pussy out like perfect preparation for his cock. He fucked her stupid on his fingers, slick with her arousal.

Madi couldn't string together a single thought while Cal feasted between her legs, growing more reckless as the seconds passed. His eyes dropped away from hers, focused on her needy pussy. Soft grunts and panting from Cal echoed in the air, twining around Madi's pleasured cries.

Her back arched hard. Arousal coiled low in her stomach, tightening into the world's largest knot. Her orgasm dawned on her without warning, tearing through her when Cal hit a perfect one-two of his fingers curling and his tongue flicking the sensitive nub of her clit simultaneously.

"Fuck!" Madi howled, head rolled back and legs shaking from the aftershocks of her climax. "Cal— Cal— Cal—"

"Mmm, I like the sound of that. My name sounds best when you moan and scream it for all my neighbors to hear." Cal chuckled once he removed his mouth from her. But his finger didn't stop its slow, shallow thrusts while Madi rode out her orgasm. Her hips rocked, shallower and slower than Cal's current thrust. "Do you think you have more in you, sweetness?"

"Maybe. How many more?" Madi gasped. What about the lovely dinner he planned for them? Her eyes fluttered as the aftershocks subsided. Heat fanned at the sensitive skin between her thighs, stoked by Cal's fingers.

"As many as you'll give me. I'm going to fuck you until the only word you remember is my name. It'll be the only thing my neighbors will hear for the next few hours."

Nothing felt better to Madi than running her smoothed legs through soft sheets after a shower. The silken sensation and smell of her favorite body wash set her at ease in a strange bed. Tonight marked the first sleepover of her relationship with Cal, which should inspire a million different butterflies throughout her body.

Instead, her pulse raced like a skittish cat, never settling for longer than a few minutes. Several feet away, Cal finished up in the ensuite bathroom of his personal bedroom. Although he hadn't said anything contrary, Madi waited for the other shoe to drop.

What if Cal changed his mind? What if he told her he didn't want them to sleep in the same bed? What if this is getting too serious, and he pulls out?

The worst of her cumulative dating experiences—a lackluster, demoralizing bout of wasted potential—told her not to expect much. Everyone initially seemed great, but the fairytale image eventually fell apart. Most of the guys who came before fizzled out around the point where things got real. She couldn't let herself be blinded by how great Cal was.

The audible flip of a light switch from the other room shoved Madi out of her mental spiral, reminding her that she was in her boyfriend's bed, wearing her favorite cotton pajama set and smelling sweeter than ever. She propped onto her elbow as the door swung open.

Hot steam escaped from Cal's bathroom while he lingered in the doorway, illuminated by the wash of blue light from the nearby television. The television's glow made his toned body look divine, showing off every part of him except for a pair of dark boxer briefs.

Cal didn't hesitate before climbing into his side of the bed. At first, he propped onto his elbow and smiled at her. Half-expecting him to say their goodnights, Madi prepared to roll away and spend the night on her side of the bed, imagining an invisible pillow wall between them. However, Cal's hand curled around her waist before she smushed against his chest and threw all her worries straight into the nearest wastebasket.

"Where are you going?" Cal teased. He flashed her a smile softer than the usual wolfish grin he reserved for her. "I thought we were going to put on a movie."

"Yeah, let's put something on. You pick." Madi swallowed all the nerves that sprung to life in Cal's absence. *Looked like the shoe wasn't dropping tonight, or maybe not at all.* She cozied up to Cal, tucking her face to his chest.

"Mmm, terrible mistake. I'm going to find the cheesiest action flick from the 80s and crash from the nostalgia," replied Cal. He jumped through the library of potential movies, skimming over several films that Madi recognized.

She dropped her gaze to his hand splayed over her stomach, opting to trace her fingers over his. Madi tipped her head, searching for Cal's face. "Hey, how's Louis doing? I've been thinking about him while doing my rotations. Nathalie told me that she thought his parents were so adorable."

Cal sat up a little more, keeping her close to his chest while he hovered over a potential movie selection. "He's doing better. Claire, his mom, gives me updates about him."

"I assume you've known her for a long time?"

"Since high school. We've been close for years. When Claire met Alex, he and I became close, seeing I was one of his groomsmen." Cal nodded, dropping the remote on the bed. His hand roamed up to her face, cupping her cheek.

"That's sweet." Madi's face softened. "Nathalie couldn't stop gushing about how cute they were when I relieved her in the morning. But, knowing you, they're probably amazing people too."

Cal chuckled. Yet the sound didn't carry the same weight of amusement or warmth she attributed to his laughter. No, it lacked both, hollowed out. "They are. They, and my friends Jensen and Daisy, are the two marriages I think can last a lifetime. Everyone else? I wouldn't bet my money on it."

Madi cocked a brow. "That's quite a strong opinion. Is marriage not something you want in your life? No judgment—"

"Not particularly. My parents are a perfect example of why. Actually, *they're* the reason why I'd never want to get married. Those two spent years in a miserable marriage, constantly doing everything but filing for divorce," Cal remarked. He spoke so casually that Madi nearly took a double take.

His parents? She could count on a single hand the number of times she'd heard anyone speak about their family with such detachment. Sometimes, people loved their families. At other times, they detested them, cursed to share the same blood in their veins. But she rarely met someone who treated family as something amorphous, so far out of reach that she didn't know how to define it.

Cal realized she had retreated into her thoughts, silent. Or maybe her face gave everything away. He sat up, brows furrowed. "Madi? Hey, what's going on in that head of yours, Firefly?"

"Nothing bad. I just realized I have no true metric of what makes a good marriage versus a bad one. I never had an example to compare to while growing up." Madi shrugged. "Growing up in a group home didn't show me a conventional family dynamic."

Cal froze. "I didn't know you were in foster care."

"Yeah, I don't talk about it with most people. No one in my life really knows. It's not something I publicize since I aged out of the system without a long-term foster home. It's not something I'm ashamed of. . ." Madi rambled. She trailed off, nervous when confronted by Cal's quiet expression. *Had she said too much?*

But any questions about where Cal stood fell into the background when Cal's arms looped around her. He pulled her to his chest, and Madi settled into him. His aftershave and the leftover remnants of his woodsy body wash tickled her senses, lulling her into the comfort of Cal's body. His hands kept her close, but she had no plans to move or leave. The conversation dropped without a fight, forgotten in the blue light of the television cast over Cal's bedroom.

Note to self. Madi nuzzled her face into Cal's neck. *Leave the marriage conversation alone.*

Chapter 14

Cal

GOLDEN SKIES STRETCHED OVER the horizon, streaked by strokes of red, orange, and pink. In the last moments of daylight left, Cal basked in the sunset. The quiet settling over the Long Beach neighborhood where Claire, Alex, and Louis lived followed behind the changes in the sky. Cal could see why Claire liked it out there.

Sometimes, Los Angeles felt a little too chaotic with its beating heart in the constant movement of the 405 and the dazzling lights from downtown.

"I've got you!" Alex's triumphant shout and Louis's shrieks dragged Cal's attention away from where he admired the skies. His thoughts returned from miles away, dropping him off at the front porch of the Bridges' house. A few feet away, Alex lifted his son high above his head, careful with his still recovering shoulder when spinning them around.

Louis's laughter filled the air. He kicked his legs through the air, laughter turning into hiccups. "Dad! Put me down!"

"Five more seconds of air jail." Alex smirked, still holding Louis up. He shot a cheesy grin to Cal, who shook his head, content to watch the father-son duo play in the yard. It healed something in him to see a good father. A present father, more specifically.

The door creaked beside him, announcing Claire's return. In her hands, the glasses of some fresh, iced mocktail rattled and sloshed around. Claire picked up mocktail making in college, always the sober one of their friend group. She used to pick him up from the bars or whatever frat party he attended, tending to him like a mother hen.

The practice came in handy eventually, didn't it?

"Here's yours. Are you sure you don't want any fruit pops? Louis worked very hard on them considering he's down one arm—" Claire hovered when passing Cal his drink. She never sat until everyone else was taken care of.

"I'm good. Dinner filled me up after my second helping." Cal took a tentative sip of the mocktail. He sampled lemon, blackberries, and something vague yet earthy he couldn't quite place. Whenever he came to the Bridges', he never left with an empty stomach or hands because Claire sent him home with half the leftovers. "He seems to be in high spirits."

"Nothing gets that kid down for too long. He pouted for the first night because we told him he'd miss out on baseball for a few weeks until he healed up, per the doctor's orders. But he accepted the consequences of being reckless decently well after we reassured him he'd return to the field soon. Sounds like someone else I know," Claire replied.

She shot him a friendly glance, lips curling up at the corners like she battled the urge to smile. Her eyes glinted in the late February sunset, which was a sight Cal knew all too well. Claire cemented herself as a staple in his life back in high school, refusing to go anywhere; he had been on the baseball team since freshman year, whereas she worked on the student newspaper between mock trial practices. She had run a piece on the baseball team's award-winning season. Still, they ironically met by chance in their biology class.

And the rest? Well, that was *much-loved* history.

Claire knew him like the back of her hand and was able to read him better than anyone, including Jensen and Daisy. From a glance, she could tell when something weighed on his mind, or someone had done him wrong. It was the primary skill Claire learned from all the times Cal would crash at her place during high school, tired of the screaming matches at home. She existed like a safe harbor, as bright as the lighthouse beckoning him into welcome waters.

Cal chuckled, leaning back in his chair to the rattle of his iced mocktail. "So, how is Little League? I assume my godson absorbed my pro baseball skills through karmic redistribution since I'm forever out of commission."

"First of all, what did we say about the self-deprecating talk? Don't talk about my friend like that, or I'll punch you," Claire scoffed. She nursed her mocktail close to her cable-knit sweater. "Second of all, he's doing pretty good on his team. They've settled him as first base, but he's developing quite a pitching arm. When he moves up leagues, he might try out for pitching."

"Hey, that's great!" Cal said. He set down his drink to grasp Claire's hand, squeezing for a second before letting her go. "The kid's got some natural talent to pick up those skills already."

"He tells all his teammates that it's in his blood because his godfather is *the* Callum Lambert. I don't have the heart to tell him we're not blood-related. You're his hero, Cal. I don't think there's a single person on this planet who will ever change that."

Those words smacked hard into Cal's chest, strong enough to bruise and yet heart-achingly sweet. His gaze wandered past Claire to find Louis sitting in the grass with Alex, smiling wide. *That kid would grow up to do amazing things. Maybe he'd pick up where Cal left off in the league, escaping the curse of what could've been.*

Louis's eyes spotted him on the porch and waved, sporting a grin bigger than the sunset-speckled sky. Cal waved back, shooting him a matching grin. He held his laughter close when Louis scrambled to his feet, taking off toward the mini baseball diamond Alex and Claire set up in their front yard for his practices. Poor Alex lumbered after him, trying to rein his son in before he undid all his healing in sheer excitement for the game.

"So, we have *something* else to talk about," Claire remarked, voice dipping in a sing-song tone until Cal faced her. He watched her sip her drink, shifting into a coyer version of her 'all-knowing' interrogation. That marked her *hot gossip* look. "Did you end up catching up with the nurse?"

"Huh?" *Real eloquent, Cal.* But the question caught him off-guard, coming so fast out of left field. He averted his gaze from Claire and her raised brow—that damn brow—but he couldn't get far.

"The nurse at the hospital. Louis kept repeating the name Madison. Apparently, you and she spoke when you first arrived at the hospital, and you. . . couldn't stop staring at her when we got there. Oh, and so you don't try to pretend I'm imagining things, she had strawberry ginger hair, medium height, and glowing in her scrubs like a plus-sized model."

Claire recited every detail of Madi she saw in the short glimpse between her arrival and Madi's departure, only because Cal couldn't keep his eyes off her for more than a few seconds. *Fuck.*

"Okay, you got me," Cal admitted. He grabbed his mocktail and downed the entire drink in one go, pretending to get his courage up with a shot of liquor. "I was staring at Madison."

"I knew it! So, did you get her number?" Claire asked, leaning forward on the edge of her seat. Her wide eyes peered at him, eager for an answer. *One thing to know about Claire: she, like Jensen, secretly loved gossip.*

"I did," Cal started, "but there's one small thing you don't know."

"Oh, and what's that?" Claire sipped at her mocktail, and Cal waited for her to finish her mouthful. Somehow, he assumed neither Claire nor Alex wanted sticky stains from Claire's spit on their porch.

Cal sighed, "Madison and I have been together since New Year's. And by together, I don't mean hooking up casually without commitment. I'm dating her."

Within several seconds, Claire gasped, smacked her hand over her mouth, and coughed so hard she might hack up one of her lungs. Shock tinged her cheeks bright red while Claire struggled to catch her breath.

Like a good friend, Cal leaned over and patted her back to stop the coughing. Claire swatted at him, tapping his chest to back off. Cal did as she requested.

"What?" Claire croaked until she regained control of her throat, but her voice remained a tad husky from all the coughs. "You and her? Dating?"

"Yeah. We are." Cal waited for more reaction from Claire. To people who 'knew' him and those who thought they did, everyone assumed him incapable of doing the 'dating' thing. . . ever since his last long-term relationship. He had his part to blame in that image, knowing how much mess he needed to undo for anyone to take him seriously as 'boyfriend material.'

But Cal didn't expect Claire to grab him by his shoulders and shake him. "Callum Devin Lambert, you better not be playing with me right now! Do you know how long I've been waiting for the fuck boy façade to be over?"

"The fuck boy façade?" Cal quirked his brow. Claire's vocabulary never ceased to amaze and amuse him in equal measure.

But Claire shushed him with her hand clamped over his mouth. "Shhh. You need to tell me more because I am so damn happy for you. You are dating someone for real, not the avoidance song and dance you've stuck to like a bad religion."

So, when she eased her hand off his mouth, Cal confessed. He didn't spare her the details except for the spicy ones. Thus, Cal and Madi's secret relationship became a little less hidden.

Claire listened, not interrupting him with commentary or the millions of questions erupting in her brain while the story unfolded. Even Louis's playful shrieks couldn't tear her eyes off him.

Eventually, Claire whistled, "Oh my god. And you waited this long to tell me that you've gotten a woman who puts up with your corny cool guy act, doesn't leech off your notoriety, and works as a pediatric nurse? I want to give this woman a medal."

"If it makes you feel better, you're now the third person to know. . . Jensen and Daisy figured me out right away." Cal dodged around a downright evil glare from Claire. *Okay, maybe telling her she was the third in line wasn't the best idea.* "Anyway, I think you'd like her."

"I can't wait to meet her and tell her all your embarrassing stories. But I wonder," Claire softened as all trace of teasing abandoned her, "what's stopping you from embracing her openly? Is it the media's cruelty toward bodies? The paparazzi and fans' invasiveness? Fear that it'll fall apart like you and she who shall not be named because I still hold a massive grudge?"

Cal found himself at a loss for words, stuck behind the new lump swelling in his throat. All those scenarios flashed before his mind, played out at least a hundred times before when he couldn't sleep.

He shook his head. "It's too much to explain."

"Cal, don't run from me," Claire interjected, not letting him squirm away. She grasped his face between her hands, holding him still. On her left hand, the curve of her wedding band pressed hot against his skin. "What are you so afraid of?"

"Everything. I'm afraid of everything, and you know exactly why—"

"Then, I'm about to tell you something you need to hear. So, stop running and listen," Claire held Cal firm, pinning him down with her stare, "No matter what you think about yourself because of what's *in your blood*, you are not your parents. I don't care what anyone put in your ridiculously thick skull. You are not Sloane and Eric, okay? You never will be."

Cal tried to summon a retort, begging for some reason that she was wrong. However, no words rescued him from his predicament. He hung in silence while Claire stared at him. He wasn't his parents, the serial cheaters who turned his childhood into constant arguments and wishes for a divorce.

He would never be Sloane and Eric Lambert.

Warmth dripped down his cheeks as Cal realized the weight knocked off his shoulders. He almost felt bare without it nagging him, whispering into his ear about how bad any attachment could sour with a guy like him.

Claire swiped away some dampness from his cheeks. Her frown pulled him back into the moment. "Did I finally get through to you? I've been banging on the doors for years, Cal. You've always been free of their mistakes."

"I don't think I was ready to hear it." Twenty-seven years of turmoil abruptly silenced in his head, ushering clarity in with a gentle hand. "Thanks for always trying."

"The day I give up on you is the day the sea swallows California whole. I love you, idiot. You're my best friend." Claire wrapped him in one of her signature bear hugs. Tonight, Cal wouldn't protest or feign annoyance; he sank into the hug, clinging to the sturdiest anchor to the world he'd ever known.

He murmured, "I might need some time to take those steps, but I want you to know her. Madi is good people."

"Good thing I'd love to meet her. You and Louis have nothing but good things to say about her, so I trust your judgment. She's always welcome in our house as long as you want her around in your life. My alliance is to you," Claire promised.

Underneath the darkened skies, Cal grasped the first inklings of something he thought he had lost years ago. Hope fit into his hands, enough to hold onto. For now, that would be enough. What he had with Madi was more than enough. But now the door opened to wonder: what might a future look like?

Their future.

Since his enlightenment on Claire's porch days ago, Cal held onto his new realizations in his back pocket, keeping them close. He decided to keep the comfortable pace with Madi that they set at the start of the relationship.

He owed her a conversation about all the deep stuff, but he intended to enjoy the moment. She hadn't run away when the mention of his parents crashed their romantic staycation. So, he'd like to keep her from running for the hills.

Cal marched down the familiar hallway of Madi's apartment complex, speeding along to her door. He wanted to see her and didn't need to be recognized by someone in the hallway because he took his sweet time getting to her place. He lowered the brim of his trusty baseball cap—repping the Foxhounds for the night—while speed walking down the faded carpet.

When he reached her door, he knocked on it. Cal didn't need to wait long before the door swung open, revealing Madi. Cal's eyes greedily flitted over her body—clad in a cozy, long-sleeved bodysuit and hip-hugging gray sweats.

Sue him, okay? She looked delicious.

"Hi, stranger," Madi cooed. She held the door with her foot, moving enough for Cal to slip inside. As he did, his eyes picked up on the wine coolers gripped in one of her hands, promising a tipsy evening of fun. "I've missed you."

"Missed you more," Cal murmured once the door closed. His hands shot forward, coaxing Madi into his arms with a soft tap against her hips. She leaned in, making it all too easy for Cal to steal a kiss off her glossy pink lips. "Thanks for having me over."

"Don't thank me yet. I'm about to put all those muscles to good work." Madi chewed on her lip when she squeezed his bicep, complete with a giggled "honk."

The further Cal moved into the apartment, the harder the mouth-watering aroma of greasy pizza invaded his senses. After a full day of strength training and rehabilitative exercises at the home gym, several slices of pizza screamed his name.

His eyes traced over the space until he spotted the upright box in the middle of Madi's living room. That must be the replacement couch he bought her. It took longer to arrive than he expected, but he didn't buy her something cheap as a replacement. He was looking out for his future investments of couch sex.

"Do you want to eat first, or should we finish the couch?" Cal asked. His hands shed the bomber jacket he pulled on for the cold February evening. He turned his baseball cap backward, seeing no reason to get rid of it.

"We should assemble the couch. . . and drink first. The pizza is a reward for a job well done." Madi dipped into the kitchen for a split second, only to return with the newly opened wine coolers. She thrust one into Cal's hand.

"Cheers, beautiful." Cal clinked the neck of his bottle against hers before taking his first sip. He, not expecting something sweet, earned a mouthful of cherry alcohol. "Oh shit. That's good."

"Glad I bought a twelve pack then," Madi giggled. When Cal sat by the giant box, seeing all the tools laid out for him, he heard the familiar crackle of static. Then, the sultry, smooth opening notes sang out from the turntable Madi had out for the evening. *She loved R&B and soulful jazz.*

Madi chose the spot right next to Cal, half draped over his lap. She giggled. "Do you want the instructions?"

"Please." Cal grinned. He accepted the neat pamphlet from her hands, opening it to all the different instructions written across several languages. He scoured for English but became down one hand when Madi snagged his wrist to hold.

Cal built things before, sure. However, the gorgeous woman draped over his lap, who probably tasted like cherries from the wine cooler she drank, had his complete focus. *He should've bought the couch pre-built so they could skip to the fun part.*

His furrowed brows must've caught Madi's attention. Her hand lowered the instruction manual away from his face, peering up at him with her pretty eyes. "Cal? Everything okay?"

"Yeah, it's all good. I'm looking for the starting instructions in English." Cal's nose crinkled, thumbing through the pages slower than usual. He finally uncovered the English version between Danish and French.

Madi lounged across his lap while he read over the instructions, pausing after the first few. *Wait a moment. . . it said the couch had already been built.*

"Okay, these instructions say the couch was pre-assembled already. These are for how to use the couch with the pull-out function." Cal showed Madi, who sat up with her wine cooler. She read over what he had, eyes widening.

"Oh shit! Let me clear these tools out of the way and we can move it together!" Madi and Cal rushed to clean up their mess, abandoning the tools and practically useless instructions at the foot of the kitchen.

Together, they lowered the box onto its side, breaking through the cardboard to open one end. Cal took the heavier side, and Madi stood on the other, ready to haul her brand-new couch into the world.

After a few coordinated tugs, Madi and Cal admired a sizeable blue couch in the middle of her living room. The color added something darker to the otherwise light-toned palette, earning a bright twinkle in Madi's eyes.

She turned to Cal. "You said it has a pull-out bed, right?" Her hands dove between the cushions to toss them to the side. As promised, a small metal contraption revealed itself without the cushions to cover it.

"Allow me." Cal leaned down and hauled the pull-out portion from inside the hollowed couch. The bed stretched across the available space and turned into a king-sized mattress with matching blue sheets. "Would you look at that?"

"It's perfect! I can have guests over to stay the night if we have too much to drink, or I can crash on it after a rough shift. I love it!" Madi squealed, throwing her arms around Cal.

He held her close, laughing. "Sounds like a plan. But there's one last thing for us to do." He waited for Madi's curiosity to get the better of her delicate features. No sooner than she arched a brow, he said, "We should test how sturdy this thing is."

"Cal!" Madi shrieked in delight when Cal's hands tucked underneath her thighs, scooping her up long enough to harmlessly toss her onto the pull-out bed. He kicked off his sneakers before crawling onto the mattress.

Madi laid still for him, letting him pin her to the mattress. She gazed up at him, savoring the staring contest before their lips melted in the middle. Cal swept them away on a teasing, cherry-flavored kiss.

Cal held himself up, propped by his hands, while Madi's fingers roamed down the expanse of his back. She scraped down the bomber jacket, telling Cal to take it off before she stole his cap from his forehead.

Cal cracked an eye open to see Madi fumble with his hat, slipping it onto her head. Something about her, wearing his backward baseball cap, did something to his mind. . . because the next thing he knew, Cal's hand dipped under the waistband of Madi's pants.

She gasped, silenced by Cal's palm pressed flushed against her clit. He hummed, "Keep the hat on. I want to see how it looks on you with nothing else to distract me."

Chapter 15

Madi

THE SPRINGTIME BREEZE GREETED Madi as she stepped onto the dusty parking lot outside a baseball diamond in Long Beach. All her spontaneous trips to the South Bay from downtown might've doubled her monthly gas bill, but Cal always sent her extra money after each outing, covering at least two months' worth of gas.

That's why she drove from the city on one of her days off to enjoy the coastal March weather and some Little League.

According to Cal, little Louis had the sling taken off a few days before and insisted on returning to the game. The kid took after Cal in strides, loving the same sport. Since the injury was minor, neither his parents nor the doctors protested his return. However, she became involved because Louis and Claire invited Madi to the game through Cal.

Part of her wondered if Cal told Claire—his closest confidant in the world—about them. She tried her best to be professional while at work, continuing the lie that she and Cal had never met. No one on her side suspected a thing!

But somehow, either Cal spilled the beans or Claire sniffed them out. If they kept the secret between the three, all would be fine.

The dusty, dirt ground crunched underneath the soles of Madi's sneakers when she shut her car door, lost among the echoes of other doors slamming up and down the parking lot. Loud chatter shifted as families headed to the field where two junior teams warmed up.

Madi shouldered her favorite mini backpack—a dark leather thing covered in a pink strawberry pattern—and she tucked behind one of the gaggles of families. People talked amongst themselves, seemingly knowing one another. As the odd one out, she kept to herself and avoided unwanted attention.

She crossed onto a softer mound of dirt interspersed by thick, unruly patches of grass when she met a woman's eyes. Glossy, auburn hair hung in waves around her mid-back, framing her heart-shaped face and the classic, baseball-style shirt in bright green. Somehow, she made the otherwise blinding neon lime look stellar.

The woman cocked her head for a split second, beckoning her over. Madi didn't delay in breaking off from the group of spectators and met the woman halfway. That must be Claire.

"It's nice to finally meet you, Madi," she beamed. Before Madi could say anything else, Claire threw her arms around her in a bone-crushing, soul-snatching bear hug. Madi swore that her feet lifted off the ground from the sheer strength of this woman who barely touched five-foot-three. "Cal had nothing but glowing words."

"Same!" Madi squeaked, lost for words and breath. She patted Claire's shoulders twice before Claire relinquished her from the embrace. "He didn't warn me that you're secretly Hercules. Ever consider getting into sports yourself?"

"My husband and I work out at an MMA gym. We've tried to convince Cal to come with us, but he's afraid I'll knock him out." Claire winked.

Madi giggled at the thought of Claire tackling Cal to a soft, blue mat. Somehow, she imagined the two fought like siblings—without remorse or mercy. "If he ever caves in, I'd pay for a video of that."

"I like you already. Deal," Claire barked with laughter. She reached into her oversized tote bag, which had a bookstore's logo imprinted on the side, *Beehive Books*. She pulled out another bright green baseball shirt from the bag. "This is for you. We had plenty of plus sizes leftover, so I aimed for a 1x."

"That either will be perfect or a size too big, which is always a bonus." Madi gingerly accepted the shirt into her arms, unfurling it. The back of the shirt had the team name—THE RAPTORS—printed in a firm black cursive font. "Oh, this will be my new favorite cozy shirt."

"I'm glad! You'll rock the green with the rest of the team. Everyone wears their shirts on game day as a supportive cohort for the kids. It's also great for camouflage if you catch my drift." Claire dropped her voice when a few more families in the opposing team's color—a burnt orange with a cartoon tiger embroidered on the breast pocket—wandered past them.

"Totally understood," Madi assured her. *Cal needed camouflage to blend into the crowd, hiding in plain sight from any paparazzi lurking around.*

"Great! We have a reserved spot for you next to my husband and me, with the best view and perfect access to the snack shack. The slushies and loaded nachos are to die for, literally."

Madi trailed behind Claire to the bleachers on one side of the field. They passed a guy with the lime shirt, who winked at Claire. *That must be her husband.* Madi tucked that information away for later, taking the empty space in the middle of the bench.

Claire sat next to her husband, accepting a blue slushie from his hands. She gestured to Madi's back before pointing at the seat. It took Madi a moment to catch the suggestion until the strap of her backpack slid down the curve of her shoulder. *Oh, right.*

Madi dropped her purse onto the open seat to her right. The large stretch of metal bleachers to her left remained untouched, but Cal probably wanted to sit close to Claire and her husband. She was their guest.

With free hands, Madi donned the lime green baseball shirt, becoming one with the sea of lime green perched on the bleachers. Being in the second row provided a great ground-level view of the action. By "action," she meant the two teams of kids no older than seven years old stretching on the grassy outer field.

Her gaze leaped across the helmets and baseball caps on the hunt for Louis' face. Despite being fresh off an injury, she suspected he would be off the bench. Cal's personality probably rubbed off on him.

Movement in her peripheral vision startled her away from the field, and she turned to another bright lime shirt on an otherwise familiar body. Cal's muscles bulged against the medium-length sleeves, nearly flexing through the fabric when he sat beside Madi. She quickly moved the backpack, spotting a small mountain of snacks and drinks in his arms.

"Morning," he greeted. Cal went full incognito mode, sunglasses covering his eyes and a non-descript baseball hat tipped low over his face. From a distance, anyone would only see the lime shirt and little else about his face. "I see you've met Claire."

"By met, you mean she almost broke my ribs from hugging so hard?" joked Madi. Death by hug wasn't the worst way to go out, if not a tiny bit embarrassing.

"Sounds like Claire. She nearly flew into orbit when I told her about us, annoyed that I didn't tell her first but thrilled about you," Cal murmured. Although, he sounded on the cusp of cackling with laughter more than an apologetic whisper.

Their knuckles brushed together when Cal handed her a loaded hot dog, drowning in mustard, onions, and relish while smelling of grease from whatever else was cooked in the snack shack. A simple touch generated a million bursts of electricity exchanged between the mere ghosting of skin against skin, innocent compared to the other ways Cal turned Madi into a twisted tangle of desire.

Madi snuck glances at him, following his lead when he bit into the hot dog and when he paid attention to the field. The cheers from others in the bleachers helped, too. She couldn't remember the last time she attended a baseball game—if ever—and didn't want to stick out like a sore thumb.

Cheers and shouts of various kids' names from the crowd announced the start of the game with the Raptors up to bat. Madi squinted, trying to look for Louis among the crowd, when Cal scooted closer to her. Their thighs bumped together before Cal leaned in.

"Louis's on deck. See the chalk circle by the dugout over there? That's where batters wait for their turn and practice their swings. . ." said Cal.

Madi followed his finger to a lone figure, swinging his bat repeatedly in a chalk circle on the dirt. She softened, observing how Louis ran through the motions off to the side. She didn't even focus on the kid on base, listening to the shouts and groans of probable strikes.

"Thanks. I don't know much about baseball, so I'll need an expert commentator to walk me through it all," she whispered before popping one of the gummy bears Cal bought through her lips. Madi felt his eyes on her through the exchange.

"Of course," Cal scooted even closer until their hips molded together like their thighs, "consider me your expert commentator." The heat of his breath caressed the column of Madi's neck, bringing the temperature up at least ten degrees. *This man.*

"Perfect." Their conversation fell apart when the kid up to bat finally hit the ball. The ball rolled toward the third base side of the field, but he took off toward first base, goaded on by the shouting from the audience.

Madi clapped when the kid crossed the base just as the third baseman threw the ball across the field.

Cal whistled, his claps louder than most of the audience around them. "The kids always perform well with their family and loved ones here. But they do even better when their lucky teacher comes, according to Louis."

"Oh? Is that so?" Madi grasped Cal's hand when Louis trudged to the plate, tentatively gripping his bat in his smaller, gloved hands.

"Apparently, the boys always invite one of their teachers, Miss Sienna, to watch their games. She was the one who rode with Louis to the hospital after his little accident at Griffith and stayed until I showed up."

"That's so sweet!" Madi cooed.

"She's sitting behind us in the specially designed Raptors shirt. She's known around the school for attending as many student events as possible to support the kids, especially those without family support." Cal nodded backward to indicate where Sienna perched among the crowded bleachers.

Madi would look for her after, too preoccupied with Louis stepping up to the home plate. She cupped her hands around her mouth. "Let's go, Louis!" she shouted, mingling with the other cheers from the team parents and Cal beside her.

Louis adjusted his grip on the bat when staring down the pitcher from the other team. He braced and rattled the bat as the opposing team wound up their first pitch. The ball shot forward, and Louis swung to a loud 'crack.'

The ball soared above a few heads, landing squarely in the outfield. But before the ball hit the ground, Louis sprinted for first base. His teammate ran, aiming for one of the further bases.

Madi didn't realize that she had shot out of her seat, but the sheer force of her upward propulsion almost caused her to drop her hot dog. She cupped her hands around her mouth, screaming, "Run, Louis! Run!"

"You've got this, bud! Go! Go!" Cal bellowed beside her. His voice didn't need the extra amplification, carrying easily over the rest. Second to him, Claire jumped onto the bleacher where she once sat, clapping and shouting Louis' name.

The sibling resemblance between Cal and Claire—not even blood-related—continues in full stride, Madi thought. *So cute.*

Louis easily could've stopped at second base while the other team scrambled to run after a rolling ball. But he waved to his teammate, who hit third, to keep running. *They were going for a home run.*

Cal and Claire seemed to notice this, growing louder and more fervent in their encouragement. At that point, other families on the Raptors' side got out of their chairs to cheer the two boys to run the rest of the wall.

Madi held her breath when the first boy crossed the home plate with Louis speeding behind him. Louis jumped onto the home plate right before the second baseman tossed the ball to the catcher, doubling the score within the first inning.

Louis spun to face the crowd, flashing a double thumbs up and a wide smile. The audience applauded, chanting his name loud enough to fill a stadium. But his eyes focused on his family in the second row.

Cal flashed Louis a thumbs-up back, not sitting until Louis waddled over to the dugout. He turned to Madi, smiling breathlessly. His eyes sparkled, injected with a rush of adrenaline, or maybe the happiness in his eyes during his pro career. *Take the man out of baseball, but the baseball couldn't be taken out of the man.*

"That was amazing, yeah?" Cal asked her, chest heaving and voice breathless. "That kid has so much potential. It's torture to wait for him to start climbing leagues."

"He did amazing." Madi grasped Cal's hands until he turned away from the next batter up. She ran her thumb over his knuckles as the jittery breathing slowed. "He takes after his godfather. What a lucky kid to have someone like you."

Cal's throat bobbed in response, defaulting to a quiet scan of her face with his loaded eyes. His gaze lingered on her lips for a split second too long before a thankful nod spoke its piece. Madi wished she could do more than hold his hand.

But the audience would be watching. Neither of them needed that; today wasn't about them.

After the Raptors' 4-2 win, Madi anticipated driving home for lunch and some vinyl time on her new pull-out sofa. But Claire and Louis had other plans, and they convinced her to come over for a meal at the Bridges' family home.

Who could say no to not one but two successful negotiators? If Louis didn't want to pursue baseball as a professional career, he could easily follow in his parent's footsteps with negotiation. *The kid knew how to get what he wanted, spinning the world around with a bat of his eyelashes and a cute half-smile.*

"—and so, Miss Sienna rearranged the seating chart. Now Olivia and I are seat partners all day!" Louis gasped, bouncing in his spot on the couch. He clapped his hands over his mouth as if trying to fight away the grin.

For the last hour, Madi listened to the whirlwind saga of Louis and his massive crush on a cute girl named Olivia in his class. Apparently, at least three other boys liked her, but Miss Sienna was his ally in the battle for Olivia's heart. The whole thing would've kept her entertained for hours if she heard the story from one of her peds patients.

Madi propped herself up on the arm of her couch with her elbow. "So, how does Olivia feel about the seating arrangement?" she asked, happy to be a new fan of his budding crush.

"She told me that she likes sitting next to me. She also promised that we could share her markers during arts and crafts because she has super fancy markers!" Louis recounted to her, kicking his feet when mentioning art time and markers. *Ah, to be young again, hyper-focused on the small things that seemed more important.*

"Sounds like art time is about to be your new favorite class." Madi smiled while Louis continued to bounce in his spot. He hadn't settled down since the end of the game, running off the field with a dozen things he wanted to tell Cal and his parents. "Make sure to thank Miss Sienna for the new seats."

"I did. But Miss Sienna won't be back at the school next year. She said that she was moving back to Santa Monica in the summer. Is Santa Monica far away?" Louis pouted.

Before Madi answered, Cal re-entered the room with Claire on his heels. Claire sported a dish towel over her shoulder, devoid of the casual jewelry she wore while cooking.

Cal raced over, scooping Louis off the couch like he weighed less than a feather, resulting in a frenzy of shrieking laughter from Louis. Louis kicked his feet to Cal's evil cackles, running out of the room.

The shrieks rang down the hall, fading with distance and time. But that left Madi and Claire alone in the house since Alex stationed himself outside at the grill. The two insisted on a home-cooked meal instead of take-out; who was Madi to suggest otherwise?

"Mind if I sit with you? The macaroni and cheese tray is baking in the oven, and the veggies are staying warm." Claire hovered above the spot where her son once sat. Madi nodded, scooting over to give Claire enough room to lounge comfortably.

Claire perched up on the couch, legs tucked close to her chest. She long abandoned the Raptors shirt for a soft blue blouse and comfortable jeans, still managing to look expensive with minimal effort. Madi wished she looked half as put together; on her good days, she had the extra time to be dolled up instead of her scrubs, minimal make-up, and comfortable hairstyle of choice.

But as Claire waited, the light flashed on in Madi's head. *Claire wanted to talk about Cal, didn't she?* Madi sat up taller, crossing her legs and offering a smile. Claire studied her without a word, trading a passive expression for steeled eyes.

"Do you know how special you are?" Claire asked, immediately throwing Madi off. She swallowed the knee-jerk "huh?" ready to jump out.

Madi stammered, pushed onto the defensive, "I don't think I'm all that special—"

"But you are," Claire interrupted. She crossed her arms over her chest. "I don't know how much you know about Cal's family life, so I won't get into the details. Before fame and baseball changed Cal's world, his home life was a nightmare. I'm the person he came to for safety. I've seen every side of Cal."

Madi stared at Claire, somewhat confused. Was Claire against her, or did she like her? Somehow, Madi couldn't figure out what angle Claire came from, so she was lost. She nodded as she said, "Yes, of course."

"I say that to illustrate that I can see what he hides no matter how hard he tries. Cal has a habit of burying his true emotions, bottling them up instead of dealing with them. He seeks to avoid the pain, self-medicating in other ways," Claire hummed. "When he started playing pro, he changed. Happiness unlike anything from our younger years became his default."

"Baseball was his life."

"It still is. So, when Cal lost it, I watched him revert to the sad boy I knew in high school, aimless and withered without baseball to make life better. I didn't know when I'd ever see that happier version of him again, who saw life as worth living. But you've brought him back to us. He has that spark in his eye for the first time in months. So, you're clearly exceptional."

Heat welled up in Madi's eyes. The sensation pricked along her sensitive waterline, but she didn't want to cry in front of Claire. At least not yet.

She cared for Cal so deeply that it ached. They shared maybe two months but made a million memories within that time. She never stopped to second-guess that they ran past the milestones too fast or wondered if they were the right fit. She knew how good he made her feel, and now she knew she did the same for him.

"I want to try to make him that happy. He's always treated me like I'm priceless, giving me anything I want or need without me having to ask twice. I care about him deeply, with or without fame." Madi clasped her hands together, squeezing hard while carefully choosing her words. She needed to speak delicately in front of Cal's family.

Yes, Claire, Alex, and Louis were his family—blood-related or not—and he loved them. She never had a family, not one like the Bridges. *Maybe one day, there would be a space for her to be part of the family too.*

Her and Claire's conversation ended abruptly when Cal returned to the room with Louis on his back. He appeared mid-piggyback ride when Louis wiggled out of his embrace. Landing on his feet like a cat, he sprinted toward his mom.

"Dad wanted me to get you. He says that a work call came through!" Louis announced, all smiles when his mom pinched his cheeks. She scooped him into her arms as she headed to the backyard.

Then, Cal and Madi stood alone. His eyes caught hers, and he stepped closer, saying, "Hey, Firefly? What were you and Claire talking about?"

"Oh, nothing important." Madi looped her arms around him, greeted by his mimicking the motion. She laid her head against his chest, closing her eyes. His cologne and the lingering notes of the fresh-cut grass smell from the baseball diamond painted Cal so vividly in her mind. She recalled how bright his face became when watching Louis play. Did he seriously look like that when she came around? "Just how annoying you are."

Chapter 16

Cal

SNIPPETS OF CONVERSATIONS GREETED Cal as he entered the packed restaurant, followed by the aroma of seafood, herbs, and unrelenting heat. Jensen promised a full-bodied ambiance if he booked a night at Lumina. His recommendation hadn't disappointed.

Cal had been looking forward to some alone time with Madi since the baseball game with Claire, Alex, and Louis last weekend. Sharing her with the people closest to him would be better later on. Yet, a small part of him didn't want to give his secret away, to have to share her with everyone else who fell for her sweetness and perfect smile. *She was his secret to keep, his love to hide from the world that would impart unnecessary opinions.*

He shooed his thoughts away for the night as he searched the tables for his firefly. Cal sifted through the strangers until he spotted Madi seated at the opposite end of the room. She chose a table underneath a painted mural of the ocean and the cliffs, popping off the walls with the vibrant colors and the glossy finishing coat.

From a distance, he ran his eyes over her slicked-back ponytail and the tiny golden hoops. As he came closer, however, his eyes admired how the soft, gray fabric of her knit sweater dress clung to every inch of her body. It accentuated the fullness of her hips and thighs while not shying away from her stomach. Putting Madi on full display was the best thing the dress did.

What a beautiful sight.

Cal maneuvered around the tables of dinner patrons until he reached Madi. He shrugged off the leather jacket he grabbed for the March evening. "Always shining bright, aren't you, Firefly?"

Madi's head swiveled away from her phone, perking up with shining eyes at the sound of his voice. She grinned hard, wiggling out of her chair to throw her arms around him. In return, Cal hugged her tightly, molding their bodies together.

"Hi," she giggled, voice soft as a whisper when it curled around the shell of his ear. Anticipation jostled in his head with all the ways the evening could go. Her fingers raked through the hair at the nape of his neck, scraping her nails upward. Cal swore his tongue nearly rolled out like a dog, eyes squeezing shut while his hands gripped her closer. "You look nice tonight."

"Me? You look good enough to eat." Cal's hand snuck a firm squeeze of her ass. The tiny squeak muffled against his chest earned a grin from him. "I'm glad you like the dress."

"Thank you for buying it for me. . . along with every other item in my shopping cart. That was nearly $500 in clothes, and I have so few places to wear them all." Madi propped her chin on Cal's chest, staring at him sweetly.

During his visit to assemble the brand-new couch, Cal might've taken her tablet and done some snooping through the half-dozen tabs she left running. Three had been new clothes, many of which were basic necessities. So, Cal bought every item he saw before Madi returned to the room to catch him with her tablet. His sheepish confession earned him a half-hearted lecture and nearly an hour of her mouth on his.

That $500 appeared to be a purchase well-spent if all the outfits fit Madi perfectly.

Cal nuzzled his face into her hair, being careful with the gel slicking her hair back when pressing a kiss to the crown of her head. "Maybe. You'll have to take me home and give me a private fashion show. I seem to recall some lingerie finding its way into your cart between all the skirts, dresses, and new shoes for work."

Pink flushed along Madi's cheeks when Cal's gaze landed on her again. Busted. She offered a timid lip bite. "Oh, that was a given."

They let go of one another, remembering they were in public. Granted, Lumina promised exclusivity for its dinner guests, which meant they had a strict guest list policy. Still, Cal refused to be reckless with Madi, to let her get too close to the tabloids with their never-ending hunger for people to exploit. Once they got their teeth into someone, they never let go until that person offered no value to their pockets.

Cal pulled out Madi's chair for her, playing the role of the gentleman. He settled across from her and grasped her hands when a waitress approached them. She carried a tray of drinks, setting down the waters and a tall, dark glass with fruit floating through a reddish liquid. He cocked a brow at Madi, who grabbed the cocktail.

"It's sangria! Want some?" she asked, taking a coy sip of sangria through the straw. She fluttered her lashes until Cal gestured for the drink. *He didn't need much convincing to enjoy alcohol.*

Madi passed the drink, trading it for the menu beside his silverware. Cal tipped his head in a silent toast before wrapping his lips around the straw, covering the exact spot where Madi's pink lipstick print resided. Instantly, his tongue twisted around the sangria's light-bodied, fruity flavors. The medley of different fruits and what he assumed was wine hit him all at once, overwhelming yet refreshing.

"Woah." Cal studied the giant glass. "That is really good."

"It's a good thing it's big enough for us to share." Madi winked. "Unless you brought Tommy tonight to drive you, then we can get a second one."

Cal laughed, "Fuck, I like the way you think. Tommy drove me tonight, so I'll order all the sangrias your heart desires. We have a full meal ahead of us, though."

"Oh, I saw the menu for tonight. How'd you know I was craving surf and turf?" Madi scooted her chair closer. Their hands slid together, drawn in like magnets, interlacing their fingers nice and tight.

"What can I say? It's a gift—" Cal's stomach rumbled at the mention of food, but it at least had the decency to not announce it to the nearby tables. He spent the last few hours in a physical therapy consult with a private trainer, pushing himself to the brink. Exhaustion and hunger chewed at him, devouring more of his thoughts than he'd like. He *deserved* an evening with Madi to enjoy, not wrapped up in the things that dragged him down. "—Did you see any appetizers you wanted?"

"They'll bring a complimentary breadbasket when the waitress swings back our way. I watched all the other tables get theirs when they ordered food," Madi hummed. She gestured with her head, ponytail swishing over her shoulder.

Cal spotted a nearby table—the one Madi pointed to—getting the baskets of pita bread while the same waitress from before whipped out her notepad. He swapped the sangria for the menu, burying his face into its offerings. He might order half of the menu after the day he had.

With his face buried in the menu, Cal failed to notice someone approaching their table. He felt the presence first, hovering over him almost impatiently. The sensation came in waves, forceful and demanding for his attention. But until Madi tapped the back of his hands, Cal hadn't taken his eyes off the menu.

Was it wrong that he half-expected it to be a fan or someone he tangentially knew?

Instead, his eyes swept over designer clothes to a face he knew too well. Sunken cheeks and greying blond hair cut into a sleek bob stared at him, patronizing alongside the disgruntled purse of coral-colored lips. He didn't know Sloane slithered back into town.

"Callum," she greeted him, ignoring Madi seated across from him. *That* brought a scowl out of him, one almost as ugly as her blackened heart. "Funny seeing you here."

"Mom. I didn't know you were in Los Angeles or on this side of the world. Been a while since we've run into one another," Cal replied. His hand, no longer preoccupied with the menu, grabbed Madi's fingers. He turned her hand into his lifeline, pinning him down to the table rather than indulging the urge to rise from his chair. His mom stopped being able to loom over him the day he moved out, the night of his eighteenth birthday.

"Well, you would've known if you answered any of my calls or texts," she huffed, managing to look at him with her nose turned upward. "Ruben and I bought a summer home in Napa, but he suggested we return to town for a few weeks."

Ah, Ruben. . . His mother's new husband. Apparently, Ruben did something lucrative for his work. He also came from wealth, culminating in being the perfect candidate for his mother's expensive lifestyle. He abstained from attending their wedding, even with the afterthought invite a week before the ceremony.

Some part of him—as morbid as it might sound—always wondered whether the "lucky" guy Sloane Bellingham settled down with after his father knew of her penchant for other men. Ruben could either be the most oblivious man in the world. . . or he might've been one of the suitors of his mother's past infidelity.

Regardless, he wanted her anywhere but at his and Madi's table. His mother hadn't addressed her yet. Cal knew better than to let his mother have the chance to say anything unkind about Madi; he lived with the harpy for eighteen years.

He plastered on a smile as painful as carving into his skin with a knife, swallowing the foul words flooding his mouth like gasoline. "Sounds nice. You have a good evening, Mom." Cal went to sit back down, ready for her to leave.

But his mother stayed put, crossing her arms over her chest to jostling of her leather handbag. "Excuse me? I'm not done talking. You've become an ungrateful bastard since you and Sadie split. She's doing magazine covers, you know. And you're—"

"Done with this conversation," Cal snarled. He kept his voice low, not interested in offering a free show to the rest of the restaurant patrons. "You can return to your table with Ruben, and I'll enjoy my dinner in peace."

"Maybe you'd be happier if you had a partner who matches you. Downgrading isn't beneficial to anyone with standards." Sloane clicked her tongue, having the gall to parade around with disapproval. Where did she find the entitlement to judge him?

Her eyes dropped to the table where Madi sat, squeezing Cal's hands tighter than before. Cal couldn't look back, knowing any tears in Madi's eyes might break the last shred of patience he clung to.

He leaned closer to his mother, bringing their faces level. "Don't even look at her. Don't address her. The woman sitting at the table behind me is better than you could ever dream of. Never in an infinite number of lifetimes would you measure up to the grace, kindness, and beauty she exudes. Speak to her at all, much less without the proper respect she deserves, and I won't hesitate to turn this dining room into an expose about the real Sloane Bellingham."

His words landed heavy. Their gravity slapped across Sloane's face, blending in with the ashen cast overtaking her. She didn't speak as she stumbled backward, almost crashed into a waitress, and scampered to whatever hole she crawled out of.

Still strung tight from all the adrenaline rattling around his head, Cal knew he should sit down and apologize to Madi. *Assure her he didn't believe a word from his mother, especially not about the "downgrading" comment.*

When he faced Madi again, he observed the concerned tilt of her head and frown. Thankfully, her eyes appeared untouched by tears, cheeks dryer than his throat. He reached for the water or sangria, something to dampen the strain.

"Firefly, I'm so sorry—" he started, silenced by her spare hand cupping his cheek.

"Cal, you're shaking," she whispered. Her thumb stroked over his cheek. She never dropped the worry etched so hard into her features. Gone was the soft, rosy glow adorning her cheeks, promising an evening of laughter and endless flirting over gourmet food. "Are you okay?"

"Me? Are *you* okay? My mother, ever the saint, couldn't help herself from being a massive b—" Once again, Madi shushed Cal before he got too ahead of himself. Sure, calling his mother a bitch would've felt good at the moment, but it opened the door for guilt later. That's why he left the chewing out to Claire, who wouldn't hold herself back and apologize afterward.

Madi shook her head, lacing their fingers. "I've been mistreated by plenty of people. My weight is not something I'm ashamed of, and it's not something people can hurt me with. Some families of patients and ex-boyfriends have said much worse."

"That's not okay."

"It's not, but it's in the past. You defended me, and that's what matters." Madi reached for her purse. "We should go back to mine. We'll get the bill, pick up some takeout, and forget all about that woman. She's not worth the mental energy."

"I'll cover the bill and have Tommy come get us. . . or whatever the car situation will be. Doesn't matter to me if we get to your apartment within the hour," Cal agreed, flagging down their waitress.

"Can I turn around now?" asked Cal from his spot in the tiny hallway between Madi's front door and the open kitchen of her apartment. Clutched in his hand, the brown bag with Mexican takeout from this neon-colored truck Madi spotted parked on Melrose Ave crinkled in its agreement.

When Cal and Madi entered her apartment, Madi ordered him to stand and face the door. He did as told, listening to the scattering noise and Madi's mumbling to herself while she. . . He had no idea what she was doing over there.

"Almost! Be patient!" Madi exclaimed. Her words came before a few harmless clatters of what sounded like plastic and wood. *Nothing dangerous.* So, as promised, Cal stayed at his post, facing the wall. He occupied the time by counting the grooves in the paint, searching for spots where the color appeared thinned out compared to the rest of the wall.

He stumbled free from boredom when Madi's hand slid into his, curling around the takeout bag. Even the slightest shift sent the mouth-watering scent of birria tacos, churro chips, two orange drinks that Madi insisted they get, and a massive chili verde and chicken burrito to spread over the apartment.

Madi giggled. "Okay, it's ready!"

"Finally. I almost considered demolishing the tacos and seeing how mad you'd be," teased Cal. He followed behind Madi, who dragged him into the kitchen with a barely concealed smile. Then, his eyes landed on the kitchen table.

Madi had covered the surface with a bright white plastic cover. Two easels, canvas, and small palettes of paint sat on the table in front of a respective chair. Spare brushes and a giant bowl of water like that for a fish made up the centerpiece of the makeshift art station.

Gesturing with a grin, Madi spoke with pride, "The girls and I were supposed to have a sip and paint night the other day, but everyone had to cancel. So, I repurposed the paint for us to use. Now, we get Mexican food and messy painting. I hope this is an okay replacement for dinner."

"Okay? Madi, this is awesome." Cal set the food down on the table, taking up the remaining space not monopolized by the painting kits. "Sit, and I'll pass out the food."

"I'm glad you love it!" Madi flounced to the seat across from him. She took her plate with her burrito and two tacos, complete with the frothy orange drink. *Orange Bang*, he remembered.

Cal piled the rest of the food onto his plate before crashing into his chair. He and Madi divided their attention between their dinner and the canvases. Cal hadn't even realized he began to speak, mouth full of handmade tortilla, "What're you painting tonight?"

"Don't know yet? Maybe a beach landscape. I'm not good with people or animals, but semi-decent with landscape stuff. How about you, honey?"

"Probably something natural too. I haven't tried to paint since middle school art when my counselors forced me into ceramics. My glaze layers were always uneven and patchy, but I had good shaping on the potter's wheel." Cal's chest puffed a little. He swore Claire kept one of the mugs he made in her kitchen cabinets to this day, so his skills seemingly held up over time.

"Is there anything you can't do? You're artistic, athletic, funny, handsome. . ." Madi sighed, pretending to swoon in her chair.

She tossed her head back to the jingle of her earrings and threw her hand across her chest.

Cal chuckled, shaking his head at his girlfriend's antics. *Oh, if only she knew how much he wished that were true.* However, the lighthearted comment sank when sailing onto darkened waters, grazing against the rush of thoughts contradicting Madi's assessment.

There were so many things he couldn't do anymore: baseball, handling his parents, accepting when life changed around him, painting him in new shades of surprise.

His silence caused her to sit up straight, her face morphing into that sweet concern. "Cal? Did I say something wrong?"

"We haven't talked much about my family situation. For as long as I can remember, my mom and dad existed in an unhappy marriage. Unlike the parents of kids my age, neither could stand to be around the other. Either they ignored one another or argued, nothing in between. And they cheated on each other a lot. It wasn't some secret, not when they would devolve into screaming matches about their affair partners. They poisoned any interest in marriage I might've had," said Cal.

He paused, soaking in the kaleidoscope of emotions fractured across Madi's eyes. He searched for pity or disgust, which he expected whenever he approached his childhood in otherwise pleasant conversation. But unlike the one therapist he tried in his late teen years, he couldn't find any of it in Madi.

Instead, she softened with sadness. "I'm sorry. You didn't deserve that."

"Yeah, it left a lot of bad taste in my mouth," he replied. "I shouldn't be complaining that I had two parents and grew up in an otherwise ideal home. It's wrong of me to dump all of this on you."

"Good thing you're not. I guess we both know a thing or two about unstable home lives. . . Is that why you spent your time with Claire in high school?"

Cal nodded. He could pull countless examples of him knocking on Claire's door late at night, teary-eyed and carrying a duffel bag. Her parents, bless their hearts, never complained when he arrived. They made up a couch for him and saved an extra breakfast plate in the morning.

He swallowed. "I was there more often than my own house. It was safe there."

"I get that. I do. But do you know what I also see? I sit across from an accomplished man, better than any of the circumstances of his childhood. Your parents have nothing on the man you've become. Besides, marriage isn't for everyone... so you don't have to chase someone else's dream." Madi winked.

Her words pulled Cal straight out of his chair. He rounded the table and tugged Madi into his embrace, forgetting the meal and painting. Madi melted into his touch, curled up against his chest with her head tucked into his neck. Her touch beckoned him closer, closing the door on that conversation in a simple promise. *It'll be okay.*

But it was his honesty that set him free. He let the secrets go into the night without a fuss or a fight. Madi deserved an honest man, and he would try his best to be that man for her.

Chapter 17

Madi

THE SUN'S GENTLE RAYS skimmed the apples of Madi's cheeks while she basked in the balmy morning. March should've brought more showers, providing the perfect weather to crash in her bed after an overnight shift. Instead, the sunny, cloudless day brought her, Janet, Sonia, and Alaina out for brunch.

The waiter swung by their table at a dainty little café several blocks from New Horizons, the name written in a different language. Madi swore up and down it sounded Spanish, but Sonia, the resident Spanish speaker, didn't recognize it. It became a forgotten thought when the first round of fruity margaritas hit the table.

"—Oh, please. Having a client throw up on you is light work. Madi's had several kiddos hurl all over her and did it with a smile." Sonia cackled, which knocked Madi out of her aimless daydreaming. All she could remember was Cal's arms and the smell of his cologne, lost when three pairs of eyes blinked at her expectantly.

Madi offered a shrug to the table, and a tiny "occupational hazard" slipped along the rim of her margarita glass, which was pressed into the curve of her lip. "Kids are sometimes prone to being a little gross, especially sick ones. I don't take it personally.

Now, if a grown adult hurled all over me, I might be less nice about it."

"Valid!" the table chorused as their waitress swung by, dropping off another helping of freshly pressed tortillas at the table. She came and went with the flutter of her patchwork skirt, dancing around the tables to the melody of the live mariachi playing nearby.

The conversation fizzled out with more carbs dropped onto the table as everyone's hands dove into the middle. Madi cast herself back out to the lazy flow of thoughts—somehow all of which involved something about Cal.

She had an undeniable obsession with that man. . . Namely his hands and those breathtaking eyes.

Ever since she confessed that she had someone in her life, her friends became "interested" in the details. And by interested, she meant they took every chance to pry, trying to tease a confession out of her. Alaina and Sonia had their respective approaches, always willing to back off after a certain number of denials in a given conversation.

Janet, however? She seemed to make it her mission to figure out who Madi kept her *dirty little secret* whenever she got the chance. Madi swore she caught her friend checking through her social media following for someone new, biting back the amusement at the fruitless endeavor.

She wouldn't be finding Cal on the following lists. Madi did all her snooping without following his social media profiles, likely run by the publicity firm his agent chose for him. The occasional shirtless photo thirst traps someone posted on that account gave her butterflies in her stomach. Yes, she'd seen the real-life version up close and personal. . . but she'd still kick her feet and blush over a perfect angle of his abs.

Madi slumped back into her chair, head rolled back to embrace the sunshine pouring down upon her. She closed her eyes, surrendering to the faint breeze sweeping over the open-air deck with its stained promise carried along the undercurrent. Her mind took her back to the beaches of Del Mesa, at peace with the cold margarita glass in her hands and the ambient chatter singing all around her.

Madi could've stayed there for hours, content to sprawl out in the vibrance of the morning. But, like all things, it came to a swift end when the table rattled. A loud whine from Janet coaxed Madi to crack open an eye.

"See? I would kill for a brand deal like this! The minute I get something even half as big, I'd never need to work another shift again," Janet said, thrusting her phone into Alaina's hand and slumping into her chair. Her pout drew Madi upright, and curiosity beckoned her back into the conversation.

Alaina stared at Janet's phone, wide-eyed and jaw slack. "Forget that! I would kill to look like her! She's got a literal six-pack, sculpted by the hands of God. This is a sports magazine cover model in the making."

She rattled Janet's phone in front of her face, urging her to see the image again. On their side of the table, Sonia and Madi's eyes caught one another, swapping looks with their raised brows. No words were needed to understand the universal undertone of *kindly what the fuck is that about?* all over their faces.

Sonia cleared her throat, "Care to share what's got you two twisted into knots over there? You're scaring the margaritas." Teasing danced on delicate turns, dousing Sonia's question in a helpful dose of reminding Alaina and Janet that the rest of the world still existed around them. And Madi thought she was the worst, considering how often she let herself wander away from daily life with Cal on the brain.

"This social media influencer I follow, Sadie, just got a luxury brand deal with one of my favorite fashion designers. She's been my inspiration since I started because she gets the best brand deals," Janet remarked, passing the phone to Sonia, who gave the image a cursory glance and a nod.

"Alaina is right. She's an attractive woman," Sonia conceded while Alaina threw her hands into the air, pointing to Janet in a silent but oh-so-obvious 'I told you so.' Vindication stretched over her face.

Madi reached for the phone next, or rather last, steeped in her curiosity. She didn't have an expectation when first greeted by the photo, but she probably should have. This Sadie woman—leggy, platinum blonde, and built like a lithe dancer—would match the image of a supermodel. She stood tall and radiant, wearing next to nothing and dripping from the water pouring over her.

"She's gorgeous, yeah. But so are you, Alaina," Madi murmured, scrolling through the photos in the news article. She skimmed over blurbs about Sadie's personal life and her latest modeling campaigns.

"Aww, Madi. You're such a sweetheart." Alaina feigned tears and dabbed at her eyes, teasing in good fun. "I might be beautiful, but she's like a total goddess. She needs to drop the fitness routine or the meal plan. At least give us normal girls a chance with the skin care suggestions."

"One word: money. Sadie has access to fitness trainers, personal chefs, cosmetic alteration, and more because she has a lot of money," Sonia jumped back in, always the voice of reason. *Money couldn't "buy" happiness but could buy comforts to make someone much happier.*

"Which is why I *need* those brand deals," Janet interjected. She snatched up her third margarita and sipped it, still pouting. "My following would explode if I got anywhere near a hint of designer—"

Madi assumed one of the other girls swung back with some sage pearl of wisdom or something to lift their friend from one of her usual spirals. Janet lamenting over what she wanted versus what she had wasn't rare. But the noise around her cut out, plunging her into silence louder than the nearby traffic through the busy downtown streets on a weekend morning. Ringing thrummed in her ears—low and heavy-footed—while she stared at the article.

She hadn't intended to fall so deep into the rabbit hole about Sadie Marks. Yet, she arrived at the small section devoted to Sadie's past love life and stopped by the familiar face of her secret: *Callum Lambert.*

Although younger in the photographs, his eyes were unmistakable. The two posed on a red carpet for some event, with Sadie's back arching off Cal's chest and his hands gripping her waist. But the way the two looked at one another, twinkles of unspoken admiration caught by the camera on full display. He looked so *in love* with her.

A lone pang of something ugly jostled into her stomach, disturbing the balance of greasy brunch and cheap margarita. Madi wanted to throw up her guts and confess her fears to the table of friends. However, she *needed* to get out of there before she devolved into a mess.

Madi handed the phone back to Janet, trying hard to keep her cool instead of tossing the offending screen away like a hot coal in her hands. She mumbled some hazy excuse about needing the bathroom and her stomach hurting. Madi shrugged off their chorus of concern, turning around before heat pricked at the back of her eyes.

She stepped forward, one wobbly stride after the next, searching for a quiet place to decompress. To think.

Madi liked Cal. She liked Cal a lot. Some might even say she'd be approaching dangerous territory with how fast she fell for him. In the back of her mind, she always knew that a guy like Cal went out with women who belonged by his side: athletic, lean, and beautiful. His past girlfriends or flings were models, actresses, athletes of their own high caliber. . . not ordinary people like her.

After her last few relationships, Madi promised herself several things: First, she would never date a guy whose whole life revolved around the gym. Second, if a guy tried to neg her in their pick-up lines, she'd hit them with an instant block. Third and most importantly, she would never allow herself to be a placeholder for someone else.

With that tiny morsel of information about Miss Sadie Marks, Madi wondered if Cal had fitted her into the spot made for another woman.

The dimmed lights of her vanity mirror cast strained shadows across Madi's bare face, and makeup scattered over the bathroom sink. Her skin gleamed after a fresh scrub, her cheeks a little raw from her rougher hands. She spent the last hour fiddling with everything—her hair, makeup, and clothes—stricken by the indecision.

Cal would be there any moment, ready to sweep her away from her apartment for a romantic night out at the movies.

Going in public had some risks, sure. But Cal and Madi spent so much of their time shut off from the world, constantly perched along the thin tightrope of 'too exposed' and 'cowering away from living.' If she and Cal settled in for the long haul together—whatever that looked like for them—then the world would eventually know the truth.

The thought didn't comfort her. The sheer burst of nerves spun her into a fresh wave of Sunday scaries, unsure of how to process the war ongoing in her head before the week began. She couldn't spend her free days hiding from everyone she knew, curled up in bed, and feeling sorry for herself.

"Get a grip," Madi murmured to her reflection, staring at the slight puffiness around her eyes and the cracks in her lips from where she chewed too hard. Thank goodness that the movie theater would be dark. "If Cal notices you look like a wreck, you'll start crying again. It's embarrassing enough."

Her thoughts derailed the second she heard a knock from the other room. *Cal was there, don't leave him waiting!* Madi's body jolted out of the room, ungraceful and disjointed, tripping over her feet in her stumble for the door. She made it in one piece, barely checking through the peephole before opening it for Cal.

He stood there, hiding in his favorite incognito outfit behind a pile of things in his arms. A dark, hooded jacket and a baseball cap to hide his face from cameras shouldn't look so good, but Cal elevated the classics. His head lifted at the creak, catching sight of Madi as she flung the door open.

"Hey," he grinned. His arms rustled while he ducked into Madi's apartment. "Special delivery for Madi."

"Are you serious? Cal, that's— you didn't have to splurge on me more than you already did. Movie tickets are a luxury nowadays, and you never let me pay for my meals when we go out," Madi spluttered. Her eyes probably blew wide when surveying the sheer amount of stuff piled into his arms. He seemed to like spoiling her, even while her blood pressure skyrocketed when she thought too long about the total.

"Please, I have more money than I know what to do with. Not to brag, but the MLB paid me pretty well for the last few years," Cal's chuckle swept up her spine, raising a rush of shivers in its wake. "I got you a mixed bouquet of daisies and white tulips. Also, I stopped by Buttery Bites and picked up a pastry tray, so you have food for the next week. Finally, you're always borrowing my hoodies, so I picked out one for you to keep. It's from my college days and very nostalgic."

Cal shifted the items in his arms to pass her the bouquet and drape the hoodie over her shoulder. His eyes raked over her, pinning Madi to her spot while she gasped. Before she lost herself to her wayward thoughts, Cal moved into the kitchen to drop off the pastries.

He flashed her a cheeky smile when swiping one of the honey-drizzled beignets from their cluster. Cal inhaled the pastry before Madi could say another word. He winked, "Oh, and don't worry about snacks for the movies. I picked up your favorites, and we'll stuff them in our clothes to smuggle them in."

"You've thought of everything, huh?" Madi asked as she approached the counter. Her eyes focused on Cal cleaning off his fingers, popping them into his mouth. His hums, though? Those might be the death of her. Unrestrained desire could drive her straight into his arms, planting her mouth against his neck before self-consciousness could slow her down.

Madi held herself back, however. She leaned against the counter, leaving some space between them. Setting those barriers kept her thoughts in check, away from the sensitive spots where open wounds lay festering.

"I do try. I'm working on my romancing skills."

"Well, Mr. Romantic. . . when are you going to let me pay you back for all these grand gestures of your affection?" Madi watched Cal scoot closer to her, not stopping him or moving. His eyes sparkled in the light, spinning into a breathtaking shade of green. The bright jade stole any follow-up from her throat, rendering her speechless.

Cal's hand cupped her face, coaxing her eyes to close on pure instinct. He tipped her face until her eyes opened again, finding his staring into hers. She waited, half-expecting him to call out the last remnants of her tears.

Instead, he smiled. "No payback necessary, Firefly. Although, if you're inclined to provide a generous tip, I'll accept payment in the form of a kiss. . . Maybe with some interest on that too." His cheesy remark nearly knocked her knees out.

"You're so ridiculous," Madi breathed out before her lips found their proper place, crushing against Cal's. He sank into the embrace, taking the lead from how his warm mouth pressed hard into her. He gave them a chance to start slowly, savoring the taste of honey and powdered sugar that slipped down her tongue.

Madi could've lingered forever in the moment, preferring Cal without all the doubts rattling around her head, critiquing every move and wondering where reality might kick in. But when Cal's hands traced down her spine and crossed the threshold of her waist, Madi's body pulled her out of the haze.

She tensed. Tight shoulders and an even tighter grip broke the immersion for her. . . and for Cal from how fast he pulled back. His head cocked to the side, revealing more of his face to the light overhead. "Hey, are you okay? I didn't hurt you, did I?"

"No, I'm fine," Madi lied, almost too fast. Her response elicited a quiet, probing stare from Cal, who didn't seem entirely convinced by her comments. "Don't stop."

That did the trick, bringing Cal back into her orbit. His mouth gave chase before colliding with hers again, slotting right into that perfect angle. She marveled at how he read her body like an open book, knowing exactly what she liked and committing it to memory. If he traced her lip with his tongue a specific way, she only needed to vocalize it before he made it part of his repertoire.

Madi tried to stay on top of how Cal kissed her, steeped in heat and want so evident to even her. The sensations radiated off his body in palpable waves, luring her in deeper. So, she tried to let go of the thoughts, ready to enjoy the moment.

Yet his hands dipping a little too low again jerked her headfirst into the worst of her thoughts. *Maybe Cal liked her for the sexual gratification. . . Ever consider that?* That kicked off the flood of insecurities, rushing forward without a linchpin of composure to hold her back.

Madi hadn't realized she tensed again until Cal's body leaned away from hers. His hands grasped her face to hold her still, and his brows furrowed. "Okay, you're not fine. What's going on?" he whispered.

Damp warmth sliding against her cheeks told her about her tears before she even registered them. Madi averted her eyes, her breath shaky when she inhaled to find the words. She might sound deranged if she brought up his ex or the insecurities inspired by the realization that Sadie Marks had been "his" Sadie.

But she needed to start somewhere, so Madi let all the words fly out of her, catching up to them afterward.

"—So, when I saw this woman, who looks like a literal goddess per my friends' commentary, used to be your girlfriend, my brain started running with the worst possible scenarios. It's not uncommon for guys to use a girl like me as a placeholder, as a convenient substitute for sexual desire when the lights are off until they find someone they actually want to date."

"Madi—" Cal started, face torn between the apparent concern splashed across his face and the vague hint of amusement peeking out from behind it.

Madi rambled on, unable to keep herself from spewing all the thoughts and secrets rolling around her head, "And I didn't look for her intentionally! I didn't even know she was *your* Sadie! After all the trouble you've had with the tabloids making shit up, I promised myself I wouldn't dig into your public persona. You deserve someone you can trust—"

"I appreciate the thought, but she's not my Sa—"

"I just want to know why you like and want me. And I want you to be honest with me because I can't continue this relationship without knowing." Madi gasped when Cal's hands squished her cheeks, cutting off another bout of word vomit.

Cal's gaze held hers hostage, boring into her soul. "You want me to be honest?" he asked her, waiting for her tiny nod before he resumed. "Okay. I want you because you make me feel grounded. I've spent the last decade of my life in the public eye, always sought after for what I provide, whether my athleticism or fame. But you? You make me feel like I could be the most average person on the face of the earth, and you'd still look at me like I hung the stars in the sky. My fame isn't the selling point or even a consideration. You like me *for me*. That's merely the start of why I like you. You're gorgeous, funny, full of laughter, smart, kind, and a woman of undeniable taste in music and food. You're a never-ending source of comfort and a good time all wrapped together."

Madi's breath trembled when she sucked in a breath. "Really?"

"Really," Cal humored her disbelief, stroking his thumb along her rounded cheeks. "You will never be a placeholder to me. I want you, not Sadie or anyone else the world could offer me. I had my time with Sadie, which ended because she wanted to use our relationship to invite more fame into our lives. . . and I hoped to keep the press out of our home. Our views on fame were incompatible."

Madi took all that in, anchoring herself into the real world. She spent the last day so trapped in her head, detached from rationality. Cal's hand holding her steady seemed the only thing keeping her from collapsing into him.

But, as if he could read her mind, Cal's hands dropped to coil around her waist, tugging her to his chest. "C'mere. You look like you need a hug."

"I do." Madi sniffled, burying her face into his chest. "That and the movie to take my mind off me being ridiculous for the last twenty-four hours."

Cal's hum rumbled deep in his chest. "Your feelings aren't ridiculous. Do you know why I call you Firefly?" he asked, prompting Madi to lift her head off his chest. "The night I met you, you wore that golden dress. It reminded me of when I spent nights with Claire and her family during summer camping trips, chasing all the fireflies that gleamed brighter than the stars. You glowed brighter than any of the strobe lights or neon in that bar, so I couldn't take my eyes off you."

Heat prickled around Madi's ears. *Oh, that's sweet.* The innocence of it all turned her stomach into knots; it was gentle and kind. Her hands laced with his, keeping him close while they shuffled around the kitchen. Sometimes, a gesture said everything when words failed to reach.

And as the conversation closed on a quiet, unremarkable note, Madi swore her light roared to life again, twinkling brightly for the man who used to chase fireflies.

Chapter 18

Cal

SLINGING A DUFFLE BAG over his shoulder as he slid from his car, Cal stepped into the sun of the late March afternoon, greeted by the thundering of metal bats colliding with baseballs. The bag in his hand carried all his training equipment from his time before the Foxhounds, which he hadn't touched in years.

Although the thought crossed his mind once or twice, Cal refrained from throwing away or junking any baseball gear. Some online collectors or charity auctions would foam at the mouth to get their hands on these, but there would come a day when Louis could use it instead. It would be better to repurpose the gear as a gift for his godson, fostering his shining talent.

Who knows? Maybe Louis might take that borrowed gear to a stadium, standing underneath the lights while a major league crowd roared his name. That sounded like a legacy to transcend Cal's abruptly ended career.

Cal locked up his car before hustling over to the batting cages. Behind his sunglasses, he searched the different sections for the familiar faces of his old teammates. According to the numerous texts spammed in the old group chat, Mason, Gage, Diego, and Jordan should be there.

The chat remained so quiet for the last month that Cal wondered if his friends had forgotten his existence. But with baseball season starting soon, he likely fell lower on the priority list between all the training sessions and press. His friends had their lives, and Cal had his.

But when his eyes skipped over a few heads, he spotted Mason's favorite, camo-patterned bucket hat, sticking out of the crowd like a sore thumb. Cal fought a smile. *They hadn't forgotten about him yet.*

He whistled, approaching their reserved cage in several bounding strides, "Got room for one more in there, or did I drive to Torrance through mid-day traffic for no damn reason?" he asked, mostly teasing. A dull ache flared up in his left leg that morning, finicky after too much movement or moving too fast.

His body hadn't recovered enough to allow extended periods of physical activity, not like the old him. His physical therapist, Jesse, told him recovery came with diligent practice and an understanding of non-linear results, whatever that meant.

At his voice, the guys turned, clamoring for his attention simultaneously. Their voices overlapped, drowning out each other's greeting into one loud, knotted noise. A little noise occasionally lit the right amount of fire under Cal, taking him back to the years before it all came crashing down. Sometimes, he sought peace, yet others found him waiting for the rush of the fast-line life to kick in.

"It's good to see you, man. You're all smiley and stuff." Mason gestured to all of him before giving the first hug in the round of embraces, coming with their own personal greetings. "Are you ready to get back into the *swing* of things?"

"That was terrible. Don't quit your job to pursue comedy," Cal snorted, shifting between Gage and Diego. At that moment, he caught a glimpse of a fifth person sitting on the bench—someone he *didn't recognize*. "Thanks for inviting me out today."

"Of course, man!"

"We wouldn't dream of coming to town and not visiting our favorite retired player."

"Especially since you're buddies with Joe Avery now! You're a superstar compared to the rest of us."

That last comment from the gallery earned a ripple of laughter from the group, except from the stranger on the bench. He appeared preoccupied with his phone in his hand until he slid it away into a nearby duffle bag. The second he looked up, a strong dose of nostalgia sucker punched Cal in the stomach.

It was like looking in a mirror, warping the ravages of time and tragedy, undoing them between nimble, wizened fingers.

Fuck, the kid couldn't be older than him when the league first drafted him, somewhere around his early twenties. He sported one of the Foxhounds caps given to all team members, a blond buzz cut, and the type of athletic attire all the professional-level guys wore. His eyes zeroed in on Cal, studying him without a drop of emotion to give away the thoughts churning behind his cold blue eyes. *Odd, but hey–*

"Are you going to introduce us?" the new guy asked. Despite the firm stare, the shackles of youth still clung to his voice. He pushed off the bench, tucking his hands into the pockets of his shorts.

"Right. Cal, this is Luka Hartman. He's the new guy on the team. We called him up from the Minors," Gage cleared his throat. Although quick to define him, Cal's brain filled in the necessary context that Gage left out. *Luka was his replacement.* "Luka, this is the Callum Lambert. He's about to be sports network's newest star."

"Gage, please. It's a pleasure to meet you, Luka—" Cal extended his hand to the new guy, quick to plaster on a smile. The name 'Luka Hartman' buzzed around his head with the same annoyance as a persistent fly. But it wasn't all bad; he recalled the name mentioned once or twice in a text conversation with Joe and his future co-hosts for *Beyond the*

Bases. Athletes could go from a no-one to one to watch within a single game. Stars came and went, either burning up in the atmosphere when they failed to stick the landing of longevity.

What kind of star would Luka be? Probably not as short-lived as Cal.

Despite his hand outstretched to him, Luka gave it a mere glance, never taking his hands out of his pockets. "Same." Through it all, his face remained stony; features darkened in opposition to the flat words leaving his lips.

Sensing the awkwardness in the air, the others ran full steam ahead with side conversations. Someone lifted Cal's bag from his grip to toss onto the bench with the others. Others ushered him to his seat, conveniently on the opposite end of the bench from Luka.

Deigo's hand clapped his shoulder as he leaned in, speaking quieter than the others could hear, "Hey, thanks for coming. None of us would've blamed you if you turned us down or met us later. But the fact that you're still willing to give this a shot inspires all of us."

"Of course. I love baseball," Cal murmured. He shrugged out of Diego's grip to take his seat. That plastered smile he put on for Luka's unwilling benefit stayed firm, stretched to the edges of his face and the brink of his patience. "It's been a minute since I've used any of my gear or done drills, so I might be rusty!"

He emphasized the latter for everyone else to hear, tempering their expectations of him. His comments elicited a wave of friendly laughter from his former teammates—well, except from Luka, but he hardly counted. *He and the kid ran in different lanes, that's all.*

"Let's send the new kid up first." Jordan clapped. Luka said nothing when grabbing his gear from the bench.

Cal focused on Luka's approach to the batting cage. The kid took measured steps like each one amounted to some unseen tally and strode around, shoulders squared back. He looked as if he had something to prove. *It was hard to be the new guy.*

A few seconds stood between Luka stepping up to the plate and the first ball shooting out of the machine, speeding toward him faster than a bullet. The ball came and went in a blink to the average, untrained eye. For a star player, however, their reflexes did all the talking, and the difference between the Major and Minor Leagues showed in a million slight variations.

Luka connected with the ball, resulting in a loud *thwack* that inspired a shot of adrenaline through Cal's seated body. All the energy bounced through his skin and bones, spiraling out somewhere around his legs. They couldn't stop shaking to an inaudible beat, full of restless energy.

He watched every swing Luka took, the ones he nailed and the others he missed. Each one earned a smattering of applause and playful taunts from the other Foxhounds on the sidelines. They did that for everyone, not to haze the newbie or anything nefarious.

Yet Cal found himself tangled in his assessment of his replacement. The kid had *potential*, standing on the cusp of greatness, separating the professionals from those who fell short of those standards.

As the machine slowed to a stop, Luka dropped his bat away from his face to the hoots and applause from the others. He joined them, not inhibited by whatever stick someone rammed up Luka's ass.

"Nice job, Hartman," Mason whistled. "If you bring that energy to the next practice, Coach might run laps around the field faster than when the social media interns bring his morning coffee."

"Yeah. Well, I have plenty of years left to improve," Luka remarked. For a split second, his eyes snapped between the others and Cal. The statement had an intended recipient, and *fuck*, it tasted bitter.

Cal's gaze narrowed. His hands flexed hard at his side, squeezing warm, sweaty palms into tight fists. *Don't punch the rude punk. He's not worth the fight.* Cal might've been cocky in his rookie year in the majors—he definitely had been in college—but he never stooped low enough to shit-talk the greats who came before him.

When none of his friends reacted to the jab, neither chiding nor uncomfortable, Cal swallowed the ire flooding his mouth until all that remained would be its rancid aftertaste. His fists loosened enough for the circulation to return to his fingers, and the roaring in his ears was silenced. The one thing he had plenty of throughout the shitty hand the universe forced him to play—*anger.*

Luka sauntered over to the bench, ditching his gear. While one of the other guys hustled to prepare the machine, a hand clapped Cal on the shoulder. It was Mason's hand, "Your turn, Lambert."

"Are you sure we shouldn't save the best for last?" he joked. Everyone laughed, but the joke soured on his tongue. He'd never let the other know that; he spent time with Jesse on drills to brush up for the batting cages.

He rose from his seat, quickly grabbing his gear from his duffle bag, "Alright, I'll go. I don't leave the house often, so I should make the most of it."

Cal hadn't lied there. Beyond mandatory engagements Desmond signed him up for, visiting the Bridges and the Ramseys, or whenever Madi enticed him onto a date, Cal stuck to the four familiar walls of his new home. It promised safety from the prying eyes of the world. Compared to the man he used to be, his turnaround painted him as a newly minted recluse, shunning the limelight he once chased after like a dog let loose on speeding cars.

Cal stepped up to the plate with his bat gripped in his hand. Feelings rushed him all at once, ranging from the relieving familiarity of the bat in his hands to the sudden urge to throw up his entire breakfast on the side of the batting cage. None of them asserted their dominance until he stepped up to the plate. Everything went quiet beyond the tunnel vision, narrowing in on the machine.

Cal curled his grip around the bat, moving on sheer muscle memory. His entire life existed in the context of baseball, and he, a devout practitioner, studied his craft as if his life depended on it. All those years ago, it had. . . Even if it didn't anymore.

His eyes narrowed, waiting for the ball to shoot toward him and scream its arrival through the narrow tube of the machine. However, in a single inhale, the world around him fell perfectly silent where it had once teemed with noise. The applause of his friends on the sidelines muted as if someone had clicked the wrong button on the television remote. Their stand-in for the adoring crowds who used to chant his name, jeer, and holler in the name of the sport vanished, replaced by a loud, agonizing screech of metal.

Cal's body froze. Every muscle pulled taut underneath his skin, tensing and bracing for the impact that never came. But Cal heard it: the sickening crunch of metal and his body colliding into stone, tumbling onto the asphalt. He might throw up if the smell of gasoline reached his nose and throat.

The "whoosh" of something past his body knocked the world back into focus, resuming all of the noise on top of the recollection of that night and the stretch of highway. Cal blinked, dropping his eyes enough as the first baseball rolled harmlessly next to his feet. He hadn't swung.

He hadn't moved.

Hollowness circled around his head until his thoughts went off-kilter. Gage leaned into the batting cage and slapped the red button over the machine, stopping it before another ball shot out at Cal. His furrowed brows said, "Cal, are you okay?"

"Hey man, we didn't mean to push. We can have someone else go and give you more time—" Diego chimed in from the bench.

Luka, who had kicked up his feet with the extra room on the bench, hummed, "We can slow it down for him. He's still rusty." That comment earned a rough shoulder check from Mason beside him, including a sharp glare screaming for him to *shut it or else.*

Cal snapped, struck by a sudden case of gritted teeth. "I'm fine," he lied. Nothing about him was alright.

He bounced back as much as possible from the accident, barring the metal plate existing in his leg and the fact that professional sports would forever be lost to the cruel whims of time. At least, he thought he had. Yet the second he took a bat into his hands, his progress was knocked back to the start.

No matter how much he gained in the physical, the scars promised he'd never climb out of the dark hole of that night. Fuck, what did he do to deserve being broken?

Cal didn't make a single swing. Not a single one.

Despite any protests or gently worded suggestions, Cal insisted on trying to land a hit. He struggled through his turn on the machine, stubborn as could be, missing every ball shot out at him. And when his turn ended, he ambled over to the bench and never got off it until the session ended.

Two hours of pure shame. Cal must have a fucking fetish for public humiliation.

The entire while, he fielded dueling reactions from the other guys. Luka—the damn bastard—stayed smug throughout the two hours. He enjoyed the occasional jab, which slipped out as a casual comment or "observation." On the other hand, the rest of the guys danced around the subject like Cal's massive failure was a game of limbo. He didn't know what he hated more—Luka's satisfaction at his fall or the other guy's pity.

Cal spent hours aimless on the road. He pulled over once or twice when the tears blurred his vision too much to manage. The gas tank dwindled to nothing as he pulled into the parking lot outside Madi's apartment.

Cal punched in the code and buzzed himself into the complex. He moved past closed doors, ignoring the ache in his leg, which started its wounded cry when he marched out of the batting cages. *Cal didn't ask if Madi was even home before showing up—the audacity of his selfish, pained brain.*

Still, he knocked on her door, leaning in to listen for noise. Thankfully, he caught hints of something playing on her favorite turntable and ambient noise clattering around the kitchen. Cal envisioned Madi with a messy bun and an oversized shirt or hoodie swamping her figure.

Footsteps echoed closer until the door swung open, bringing Madi into view. She looked exactly as he imagined, down to the borrowed hoodie and something red staining her cheek. *Was that pizza sauce?*

Cal might've laughed and joked any other day, using the excuse to cup her cheek and wipe her face clean. But he, suffering from a face aching from all the crying and his leg screaming for relief, mustered a pitiful, "Hey."

"Cal, come in," Madi yelped. She hauled him inside without a second thought, bringing him stumbling over the threshold. Her gaze fixated on his face, and her hands grasped him by his shoulders to hold him still. "Are you okay? Do I need to get you medical attention or ahold of someone?"

"No. Please."

"Okay. Let's sit down. Then we can talk about it," Madi said, guiding him to the soft couch. She didn't make him kick off his shoes or explain much of anything. Instead, she wrapped her arms around him while the two sunk into the couch cushions.

She sat on the right side of him and propped his left leg onto the couch, elevating it from the pain. "Do you need something to eat first? Water? I made pizza."

Cal nodded. To what? He wasn't sure.

Madi brought him a glass of ice water and a slice of cheese pizza on a paper plate. Cal scarfed these items down, chasing an excuse not to speak. Madi, bless her, didn't push him for answers either.

She merely rubbed his back. "You'll stay here tonight, okay? We can talk about it or run the shower and go to bed. Sometimes, that makes me feel better after a day that's *too much*."

"I went out to see some of my old teammates today. They invited me to go to the batting cages with them and the new guy on the team, Luka. He's my replacement—" Cal's words trembled on the back end of shallow breaths, still ready to succumb. Hyperventilation waited for the best moment to pounce, to pull him off guard and send him back down the same damn spiral he spent the last several hours fending off. "I *choked*, Madi. I couldn't move or hit a single ball. I couldn't think because all I felt was the accident—"

"Oh, Cal." Madi's face dropped. But she didn't devolve into pity, which Cal would take a dozen times over than people's well-meaning, off-putting pity. He endured his fill of that shit whenever he made the mistake of wearing shorts that showed off his scars or talked to people who knew of him before the whole fiasco.

Cal shook his head, eyes stinging. "It was bad enough that I couldn't hit a single ball. It was bad enough looking at the faces of the guys I used to run with and seeing pity in their eyes. No, my replacement making snarky comments about how he'll never end up like me really sold the whole shitstorm."

Madi's face warped, twisted up in anger that time. "What a pathetic piece of—" and described Luka Hartman in a slew of colorful, downright degrading curses that Cal never imagined she knew. She cussed like a sailor, unburdened by remorse. "If I weren't so nice, I'd probably do something that makes Tonya Harding look tame by comparison."

Cal's mouth hung open, awestruck. "Could you do that again? That was ridiculously hot." He stammered, stricken by how heat enraptured his face and neck. Even his ache muted underneath the touch of admiration for Madi.

She shook her head. "Thank you. . . but we should get back on track." She cupped his face where Cal couldn't look away from her. "What happened at the batting cages? The panic attack? Those are common symptoms of post-traumatic stress disorder. I'm sure your doctors explained all that to you during the first parts of your recovery. A therapist would be better suited to explain this, but trauma impacts us in strange ways. I see this in some of my peds patients, especially the ones with chronic illnesses or who survived freak accidents. It can change how we perceive our bodies and engage with the world."

"I. . . The body thing. I felt that a lot with my scars and how certain clothing showed them off. You are one of the few people who don't treat my scars like some freak show." Cal's throat bobbed hard. Even saying that out loud felt akin to someone carving into his chest with a kitchen knife, digging around for his wounded heart.

"I've seen many scars in my line of work. Yours tell me that you've been through a great ordeal. Scars will never scare me away from you."

"A great ordeal is a nice way of putting it. It was an accident, kind of. I used to drive a motorcycle, which wasn't an unknown fact about me. I had been visiting Los Angeles to see Claire and the family again when someone started following me. We were on the freeway when I spotted them in the window. They were fans, trying to take photos." Cal waited for his throat to close up on him as he spoke or for the tears to spring in his eyes. He expected them this time, giving himself distance from the story.

Madi stayed quiet, her hands holding his face. She didn't interrupt or prompt him to move along with the conversation; the space did all that on its own.

"These were dumb college kids, tailgating me to snap a few photos to brag to their buddies or post online. I didn't want them to photograph me, so I merged lanes to escape them. But a car on the lane to the left decided to merge, not paying attention to their blind spot. Their front bumper collided with the back of the motorcycle, causing me to spin out and crash into the freeway divider," Cal choked out, almost gagging when the impact replayed in his head like spotty B-roll film. "I fell off the bike, and it fell on me, pinning me there. I couldn't feel my legs. . . which was later revealed to be two broken legs and a dislocated pelvis. My left leg still has a plate in it. *That's* what happened to me."

Cal glanced at Madi, whose face walked the line between anger and horror. Claire had the same look when she rushed to his bedside. Her jaw clenched before she said, "I hope those stupid kids feel guilty for a long time. They could've killed you."

"During the accident and for a while after, I almost wished they had," Cal confessed. He didn't know what prompted the impromptu admission, but Madi became his sacred sounding board. At that point, he needed her to understand the extent of the damage she worked with. "My career died instead."

"And I can't imagine how heartbreaking that was. But, Cal. . . you're more than that jersey, more than that career. Even though you deserve that dream career, your life is still worth living. I know people see you like I do—still an amazing, accomplished man on and off the field," Madi whispered.

Staring at her, Cal listened. Not that he hadn't before when the rest of his closest friends promised him that his potential didn't die on that freeway. But from Madi, he believed it.

So, he collapsed into her with a hug, burying his face in her hair to smell her favorite shampoo and body wash. Chia milk and cherry set him right at home, mellowing the jagged and raw edges. No thank-yous needed to be said, conveyed through the weight of his embrace in Madi's arms.

And when she hugged back, Cal sank further in. The old him might've sought out the comfort of the flesh, chasing away the feelings and shoving them down while he busied himself against the bare skin of a woman whose name he might forget the following day. He didn't need to do that with Madi.

She wouldn't let him. Madi forced him to confront what he tried to avoid, embracing it for what it was. Unlike the collision on the highway, however, Cal stepped into the open without a secret and with a woman who embraced the darkest side in open arms.

He wasn't alone.

Chapter 19

Madi

WALKING OUT INTO THE springtime evening, freezing air hit Madi with a nice pick-me-up after another long day at the hospital. Although she usually waited to get comfortable, the day encouraged a fast shower in the hospital's facilities instead of at home. She washed off every moment of stress or sadness, letting anything that no longer served her circle the drain.

Her bag thumped against her side with every step she took. The strap slid along her shoulder, slipping against the plush fabric of her hoodie. Her friends said the sunshine yellow paired nicely with her hair.

Speaking of the girls, they walked beside her with their bags. They'd spent lunch together that afternoon, but someone suggested regrouping for the evening. Somehow, Madi sensed an unspoken promise of chaos on a night out with the girls.

"So, what are we thinking tonight? Club, bar, or dinner? What's the vibe?" Janet shook her phone. A toying smile overtook her glossy pink lips, shimmering after a full day without any smears. She gatekept her makeup products close to her chest from her followers. . . and *sometimes* her friends too.

"Bar. Val asked to join us tonight, and I figured that everyone might consider inviting their partners out tonight for one big quadruple date," said Sonia.

Coincidentally, Alaina interjected at the same time, "Dinner! I've been dying to try out that Italian place you mentioned seeing on Daisy Ramsey's social media stories. I would die for some tiramisu with you all." Her suggestion ran head-first into Sonia's, blending together in an unseemly word soup.

"Huh," Janet sighed. "I'd been chatting up a club promoter at this new rave-themed club in Hollywood. It's ladies' night there, and they're offering $5 drinks to every group of three or more who show up at the door."

Sonia shrugged. "Well, that means only one thing." She glanced around the entire group, which stopped outside the hospital doors. Patients, their families, and New Horizon staff could walk around them while they hashed it all out. "It looks like Madi is our tiebreaker for the night, as usual."

More than once, the three had tapped Madi to decide what to do on their girls' nights out. She didn't mind the club per se. Yet, after a long, laborious day around sick or injured children, she couldn't muster the energy for nightlife. But she tried to alternate whose side she chose, never wanting to indicate favoritism.

When all three of her friends turned to her, eyes expectant, silence jumped into Madi's throat instead of the answer. Her lips parted, preparing to make a snap judgment and seal her fate for at least the next two hours.

However, the loud buzz of her phone from inside her pocket diffused the tension as everyone focused on the buzzing sound. Madi snatched her phone, opening it away from the prying eyes.

CAL: what's my Firefly up to tonight?

> **CAL:** any chance you'd be free to see me?

> **MADI:** Well, any excuse to get out of playing referee for my girlfriends sounds ideal. Did you have something in mind?

> **CAL:** Oh, I do. Tommy will be pulling up to the hospital in less than a minute. As for what we're doing, it's a surprise.

Madi's brows must have shot up into her hairline as Sonia cleared her throat. "Madi, are you okay?"

"Huh— Oh, I'm great!" Madi assured them as she liked Cal's latest message. Her gaze darted past the girls toward the parking lot entrance. Sure enough, as Cal promised, the familiar dark sedan rolled into the lot and circled to the sidewalk where they stood. "I won't be able to decide for you guys tonight. My ride's here."

"Oh, do you have plans with your beau tonight?" Alaina gasped when the front door to the car opened, revealing Tommy. They likely thought he was her Cal. Tommy was objectively attractive, so Madi didn't hate the implication. "Is that him?"

"I do. But that's his chauffeur," Madi explained. She hoisted her bag higher onto her shoulder before jogging across the short distance between her and the backseat of Cal's car, hoping to find him in there. "See you guys soon!"

"Have fun!" Sonia waved while Alaina whistled, smiling and sending her on her way. Janet watched the scene unfold, frozen in her shock.

Tommy opened the door to the backseat, quick to shield the space with his body. "Good evening, Miss Caldwell."

"Madi's fine, Tommy. Thank you." She grinned while sliding into the backseat, right into Cal's waiting arms. Smirking Cal, who rocked a classic black suit. Madi dropped her bag on the spacious floor and leaned into her boyfriend's chest. "Hi there."

"Hi, gorgeous." Cal winked. He waited for Tommy to shut the door before his strong hands hoisted her halfway onto his lap. Madi's legs fumbled outward, stretching into a half-straddle over one of his legs with how wide he spread them. "How was work today?"

"Oh, you know, the usual. Any chance I get to know what plans you've got for us tonight?" Madi asked, all coy from how her words adopted a sultry edge.

"With a little convincing, maybe—" Cal tipped his head, feigning innocence until Madi's lips grazed against his, tempting the answers out of him with a bit of loving leverage. Cal never said no when she involved kisses in the equation. When his hands flexed around the curve of her ass, ghosting over the pair of comfy pants she wore, Madi knew she had won. "We're going to a jazz club. Claire and Alex worked on negotiations that helped the place navigate some legal battles before their grand opening, scoring tickets. There will be dinner, dancing, and a live jazz band, except Claire and Louis caught the flu, and Alex will take care of them. So, they gave me the tickets to use."

"Oh, let me text Claire. I know a few home remedies for the flu." Madi probably should've first reacted to the "exclusive jazz club" thing. But she hadn't shut the nurse mode off in her brain after a long shift. Flu season left a unique imprint on her, with plenty of hands-on experience helping sick kiddos.

Cal handed his phone over without a fuss. "Actually, I'm sure that'll be great. You can text Alex since Claire will probably be sleeping. It's like she remembers what sleep is only when she's sick."

"Night owl, huh?" Madi giggled while sending a quick text to Alex from Cal, signing off on behalf of both.

"More like a major insomniac since college," Cal snorted. He pushed the phone lower from her face. "Thoughts on the jazz club?"

"It sounds amazing. . . Although I don't know if I'm properly dressed. Any chance we can stop by my place? I'll see if I have anything better." Madi eyed her bag. She swapped out her scrubs for cozy clothes after her shower.

She caught Cal's lips twitching at the corners. Oh, she knew that look. He reached for something dark tucked against his side, which she hadn't noticed before. He shook out the folded garment bag. "I called in a favor. Claire and Daisy gave it the stamp of approval. . . Something about green looking nice with red hair?"

Madi's hands fumbled the garment bag open. She ran her hands over the vintage swing dress in a breathtaking emerald shade, spellbound by the softness of its touch. "It's my size?"

"Yes. I double-checked with the nice ladies who worked the shop. It's from a plus-sized specific store." Cal nodded. "I got some masks since tonight's theme is masquerade. Do you like it?"

"I love it!"

"And for my final surprise, before you worry, I grabbed some of the makeup I've seen in your bathroom in case you wanted any." Cal nudged a small bundle with his foot. *That* would happen to be a makeup bag. Cal played her Prince Charming and her Fairy Godmother all in one go.

Madi shook her head. "You're actually insane for this. Thank you." She reached for the dress again, unable to help herself. "I wonder if you get the perk of seeing me undress out of this."

"Is that what you think?" Cal whispered, yet his breathy, husky rasp confirmed everything she thought. "If I wanted to see you naked, I could just ask."

Madi's tongue trailed over her lower lip, taking its sweet time until Cal's eyes dropped to follow its movements. *Predictable.* "Yeah, but where's the fun in that?"

Her hands peeled off her hoodie, and the tank top she wore underneath it came off, too. Cal's hips shifted to accommodate her position when Madi slid further onto his lap, giving him a perfect show since the window between them and the front seat remained rolled up.

Cal's hands roved over bare skin. They gravitated around the waistband of her pants, not shy when dipping right underneath the hem. Calloused fingertips branded her skin in their warmth. Fuck, Madi might tell him to forget about date night and take her home. Cal could manhandle her just fine.

Cal's eyes flickered between hers and her mouth, which hovered mere inches from his. He swallowed to the bob of his throat. "I want you. Can I have you?"

"You always have me." Consent barely passed Madi's lips before three things happened. First, Cal kissed the *living daylights* out of her, causing the world to slam in technicolor. She swore she could suddenly taste the desire twining around his tongue, commanding her to let go. Second, nimble fingers curled into the waistband of her pants, shrugging them down the expanse of her thick thighs. Air from the A/C caressed newly exposed skin, chasing the heat of Cal's touch. Third, the fingers didn't stop at the pants. No, they slipped between Madi's thighs, walking along the fabric of her boy shorts. A faint stroke over her clothed clit awakened the shivers, but two fingers pressed flat knocked Madi's head back. "Cal—"

"Have I ever told you how pretty you make my name sound?" Cal grinned, taking his time to attach his mouth to the side of her neck. He adorned her skin with licks and hot, open-mouthed kisses, all laid against the column of her neck. But it was the sharp, sudden love bite right along her pulse point that caused Madi's hips to jerk.

Oh, the neckline of her surprise dress wouldn't hide a thing.

"You're— trouble," she breathed out, in short supply of a reply when her brain barely remembered anything beyond Cal's name. She stilled when his fingers pulled her underwear to the side, just enough for them to push his index finger into her.

A gasp escaped her when a filling sensation stretched her out, greeted by wetness gathered faster than she even realized. Cal sank his finger into her, knuckle deep, while his mouth traveled down the expanse of her skin.

Cal's teeth nicking her breasts startled her once again. That time, however, her hips shuddered on Cal's fingers, fucking herself open to the obscene sounds of his digit coated in her arousal. Cal could probably slip another finger in there, or maybe two, stretching out her pussy and making her come from his fingers alone. She acted *deprived* like no man had ever touched her before.

But none had, not the way he did.

Cal's hushed groans lilted against her ears, muffled against her skin while he continued to mark her breasts. For every little bite, he offered two more kisses—pleasure intertwined with the pain so tight, she couldn't tell where one began or the other ended. So, Madi's head lolled back and offered him whatever he wanted.

When Cal slid his second finger into her pussy, he curled them hard. The motion brushed against the sweetest spot, causing fuzziness across her vision. Jostling down the road in the backseat of a darkened car added a new dimension to the sensation of Cal's affection, amping the friction between them.

Madi gripped Cal's biceps like her anchor, unable to stop her eyes from fluttering shut. Instead, she dove head-first into the raw sensations. Cal's fingers stretched and scissored, loosening her up. Her pussy throbbed around his digits, staining them in her slick while their quick thrusts teased the tight coil of arousal sitting in her stomach. But despite the warning signs of her body racing toward the euphoric end, Cal's mouth continued its ministrations to her neck and breasts.

He moved with insistence and determination to leave his mark on her as if he hadn't already irrevocably changed the trajectory of her life. He wanted to be *seen*; she *saw* him.

"I'm— Cal, I'm close—" Madi panted into the air, closer to a whimper than a steady response. When the car around them drove over a rough patch in the road, the sensation of Cal's fingers pushing deeper into her was nearly unbearable, with the sensitivity spreading across the apex of her thighs. "Shit. *Shit.*"

"It's okay, gorgeous. I've got you." Cal broke his lips away from her skin long enough to utter those words, raspy when promising. His ragged breathing echoed in her ears alongside the frantic cry of her pulse, teetering so close to the edge that she could taste the incoming crash. "Come for me, Madi."

Her name. Her name was what did her in, coupled with a perfectly timed curl of Cal's fingers. She came hard enough for her vision to go white, blinded for a split second before slumping into Cal's chest. She laid still, relishing the fullness of his fingers while the orgasm rocked her body.

She swallowed through her dry throat. "What about you?" she questioned, remembering Cal hadn't even touched himself or put his pleasure into focus. Guilt reared its head; she'd never not helped her partner get off before. *How selfish of her.*

Cal shook his head. "No, I'm good. Tonight is about you." He silenced those thoughts, swift to act without a word from her. He read her thoughts, much to her surprise.

"Okay. . . Thank you." Madi's eyes fluttered closed while she lay against Cal again. His warmth beckoned her, and a small part of her screamed to never leave. *A few moments of rest couldn't hurt.*

The rest of the car ride to the venue remained uneventful.

Since he made the mess, Cal did help clean her up. Thank goodness Madi always kept spare wipes in her work bag, stocked to the brim for emergencies. Sonia joked that her bag secretly held a black hole to hold the sheer amount of shit in there.

He even held up the compact mirror so she could put on some lip gloss. Since their masks covered the upper half of their faces, Madi opted to stay light on makeup. When the car rolled to a firm stop, she brushed out her hair with the travel brush she kept in her work bag.

The window rolled down, showing a sliver of Tommy in the driver's seat, "We're here. I'll be parked nearby, enjoying my break."

"Thanks, Tommy." Cal tossed something through the crack made by the window, but if Tommy's pleased grunt was anything to go by, he appreciated it. "Ready?"

"Born ready!" Madi and Cal left the car together. They slotted themselves into line until reaching the front. Cal handed over the printed invitations to the security, smirking proudly. They were waved in soon after, stepping into the smokey den of conversations and people dressed in a mix of black tie or vintage.

Her eyes leaped across the walls—screaming art deco with the two-toned color palette and geometric patterns splayed across the space—and the dark dancefloor shy of the clusters of tables and corner booths in black leather. A live band stood on a raised stage in the northwestern corner of the room, their brassy instruments gleaming underneath the overhead spotlights.

The place looked fantastic. . . Radiating the energy Madi imagined of an old-timey jazz bar. History had never been her strong suit in school; she always considered herself more of a science and math girl if her attempts to establish a Science Olympiad team at her school indicated anything.

She followed Cal's lead while his hand curled around her waist and guided her through the crowd, taken by the alcohol flowing and all the hubbub around them. He leaned in, close enough for his mouth to nick the shell of her ear. "Dance floor or dinner first?"

"Dancing," Madi whispered back. She had seconds to prepare before Cal swept her into the corner of the dance floor, which was less populated than other sections.

Their arms coiled around one another into a poor man's imitation of one of those fancy ballroom holds while the band struck up their first song. A raucous, vibrant melody erupted from the band at a pace entirely too fast for Cal and Madi to catch. Their bodies mimicked an amalgamation of the other dancers in the crowd, some much better than the others.

Cal stilled to spin Madi underneath his arm. His movements were alright, albeit a tad clunky—no need to book one of those televised celebrity dance shows anytime soon. Although, she had no excuse for being such an off-beat dancer.

She laughed. "We're so bad at this," she told Cal, chewing down on her lower lip to avoid a full-on laughing fit. "Everyone probably thinks we've got the collective rhythm of a drunk elephant."

"Maybe, but who cares what they think? I'm enjoying the sight of a beautiful woman who asked me to dance," Cal replied, smothering his face into her hair while he tugged her against his chest. While the rest of the world could pass them by on the count of a fast-paced jazz, Madi would follow Cal's slow and steady lead.

Why? Because, for the first time in a long time, she swore she knew what her future looked like, and no version of it existed without a pair of green eyes and an effortless smile. Not a version she wanted to live in.

Chapter 20

Cal

PUSHING THE DOOR OPEN to Buttery Bites, Cal didn't expect the hot, full-bodied aroma of brown sugar and baked bread to rush past him into the early Santa Monica morning. The sun hadn't risen over the horizon quite yet. But, on their laughter-filled drive down the side streets by the Pier, Madi spotted the bakery lights on and the open sign welcoming all.

Madi insisted on grabbing some of Buttery's finest treats before they spent the sunrise in the cramped backseat of her car. Since today was her idea, Cal agreed, hopping into the metaphorical passenger's side. He'd let her drive, trusting her judgment.

Madi's hand slipped into his. The feel of her fingers clasping him close and tight, snug as a fitted glove, quickened Cal's pulse, skipping the occasional beat with sheer ease. He'd become accustomed to the weight of her hand in his, but the warmth from her palm to her fingertips never ceased to pierce through his skin.

"We should get some of his 'Santa Monica Sunrises.' He combines strawberries, cream cheese, and honey and stuffs it all into a flaky pastry crust." Madi giggled into the crook of his neck while they entered the empty front of the bakery. "They sell out so fast since strawberry harvest begins in March."

"Whatever you want, it's yours," Cal promised. His eyes jumped around the room. He spotted several big doors throughout the space. One pair, wooden and painted over in a rustic shade of brown, led out to a deck facing the busy intersection. Through the frosted glass of the window panels in the doors, pops of orange and unfamiliar flowers decorated the space. Inside the room where he and Madi stood, a small cash register and a giant dessert rack behind glass took up the rest of the space. Behind those, stainless steel doors like those of a fancy kitchen led to somewhere else, obscured from view besides the small port-shaped windows on the doors.

The few times Cal ordered from Buttery Bites, someone else picked up the goods. He'd never been able to admire the space and see what captivated Madi's endless praises.

Distracted, he missed Madi leaning over and ringing the bell on the counter. Its shrill ring summoned a faint clatter of noise on the other side of the steel doors to the kitchen. Echoes of footsteps approach before the doors swing wide open, revealing a man with flour smeared on his cheeks and a stained apron stretched across his broad chest.

"Well, look who decided to stop by." The man's face brightened when his gaze landed on Madi. When people were described as a "teddy bear," Cal might picture the baker behind the counter. A stocky frame and rounded cheeks, tinged rosy, gave way to a broad, toothy smile. "It's been a minute since I've seen you, stranger."

"It's been a draw with all my shifts, Evan. You usually handle the baking while one of your employees rings me up." Madi waved him off, not rushing forward or spurning Cal's arm holding her close.

Ah, so *this* was Evan, the baking genius Madi gushed about. Madi sent him a few promotional videos from the bakery for social media advertising. Everything the man touched looked mouth-wateringly good. He must have the Midas Touch of Baking.

Evan nearly carded his hands through his sandy hair but stopped short by an inch. He shrugged his near miss off with a snort, "Which is a damn shame. You're one of my favorite customers. You always give me your honest opinion about my random strokes of madness."

"I think you mean genius," Madi corrected, using the same tone Cal heard from Claire when gentle parenting Louis about why he couldn't have dessert after nine. She stepped toward the counter but rocked a little when the feel of Cal tugged behind her. She turned, blinking and chewing her lip. "Evan, I'd like you to meet Cal. Cal, this is Evan. He's been a generous supplier of delicious pastries to Santa Monica for the last three years."

"I've heard nothing but good things. It's nice to meet you, man—" Cal nodded first, catching himself before he offered his hand.

Evan's smile didn't falter when he swept his eyes over Cal. "Hey, any friend of Madi is a friend of mine. Besides, thank you for all the free beers you earned with my buddies. I learned to bet on Lambert a long time ago."

Cal couldn't help his laughter, especially when Madi's brows shot up into her hairline. She hadn't expected such a warm reception or for him to be recognized. *It was okay, though.* Evan approached him more carefully and casually than most encounters with fans; he could handle a few moments of chatter.

"I appreciate that. My little Firefly here put me onto your bakery a while back, so we thought we'd stop by and get some breakfast," said Cal.

"Of course. Feel free to take a few minutes to review the menu. I've added some new seasonal dishes based on what television show my sister's been binge-watching on my couch for the last two weeks." Evan gestured to the laminated menus mounted onto the wall behind them.

"I just might." Cal flashed Evan a thumbs-up. He nuzzled Madi's hair, burying his nose into the crown of her head. "Order whatever you want, and I'll put it on my card," he instructed, giving her a gentle pat along her hip.

"You don't know what power you've given me." Madi borderline *cackled* when she scampered forward to the glass with all the pastries. Evan quirked a brow and said something lost on Cal when he turned away from the two.

He wandered to the back of the room where the menus took up wall space, cluttered by a dozen local and national culinary awards or achievements. He couldn't miss the newspaper clippings framed either. Evan did his job well, clearly. Cal knew the type of dedication and pride that went into such a painstaking, thorough reputation of excellence.

He used to be on the field, and now, he planned to use his skills in front of the cameras. March would end in a matter of days, rolling into April and the robust start of the baseball season.

Studying the menu, Cal tuned out Madi and Evan's conversation, keen to give his girl her space. She didn't need him hanging all over while catching up with Evan, who seemed nice.

His eyes glossed over the menu a few times, reading the words but never fully processing them enough to know what he wanted. Cal kept re-reading until the door next to him swung open, welcoming a customer into the bakery.

Cal intended to focus, ignoring how the excited rush of a morning draft sped past him. He did. But he switched his focus onto the new arrival when he heard Evan call out, "Can I help you, sir?"

"I'm here to pay the remaining balance for a wedding cake. Should be under my fiancée's name, Jillian Sharp," the man said.

The statement seemed casual enough, except for how deep the dagger of nostalgia cut through Cal's chest.

His head snapped to his left, where the greying but all-too-familiar visage of his father, Eric Lambert, stood shy of the doorway. With Cal's eyes on him, he turned his face and froze, looking as shocked as Cal felt inside.

The two eyed one another, even when Evan replied from behind the counter, "Give me a moment, sir, and I'd be happy to grab your invoice. Thank you for coming in."

"Sure thing." Eric nodded, but his eyes never strayed from Cal's face. He and Eric's relationship suffered the same strains and scars he held against Sloane. The main difference? Sloane tried to erase the pain through denial and manipulation. Eric gave him the space to feel, relishing in the absenteeism. "Hello, Cal."

"Dad." Cal swallowed back any illusion of fondness for the older man. The two looked similar; Cal took his mother's coloring in his eyes and hair but his father's facial features and tall, broad stature. Eric had been an athlete back in his day, promising a bloodline of strength. *How ironic, now.*

Cal could count on a single hand the number of times Eric texted him before the accident, which seemingly shattered the haze over his eyes. Their texts elevated from occasional texts—reserved for holidays and birthdays—to a little more frequent and a phone call once in a blue moon.

While he lay in the hospital, Eric visited him. A small part of Cal remembered this as clear as day: despite the pain meds in his IV, Eric apologized to him for his failings as a father. Neither addressed the apology since then, treating it as an unspoken acceptance. They walked the tentative ground of knowing but never addressing it for fear of the fragility beneath their feet.

"How've you been?" Eric asked.

"Fine." Cal sensed Madi's eyes on him, boring holes into his back. He thought to meet her eyes and silently assure her that things were fine. Instead, he tipped his head toward Eric. "I didn't know you were getting married. That's. . . unexpected."

"For us both. Jillian, my fiancée, is lovely. We met through some mutual friends. She's also a divorcee and a therapist."

Cal managed to keep his face level, ignoring the strong urge for his eyebrows to shoot up. "That's—" *Age-appropriate? Normal-sounding?* "—great. She sounds lovely."

"She is. We know everything about each other—the good and the bad—and strengthen each other. I don't know how I went my whole life without such a steadying presence." Eric murmured. Cal's ears almost burned with how fast Madi's face popped into his head, reminding him of her presence behind him.

Yeah, he understood the feeling.

"Everything, huh? That includes me?" Cal didn't know why he asked. The words blurted out, slipping past all his defenses too nimble for him to catch on its way out. But they had their intended effect on Eric from how several different emotions flashed across his face. Shock stained his mouth while a tiny glimmer of hope lightened his dark eyes.

He, after a moment, nodded. "Jill was the one who told me that it wasn't too late to try. It's what brought me to you while you were in the hospital, especially when you were touch-and-go. She told me, in no uncertain terms, that I needed to stop hiding behind my ego and unstick my head from my ass."

Cal could've laughed. Oh, he *liked* Jill. "Very wise of her. I feel like teenage me would've appreciated that advice." He jammed his hands into his pockets while turning a little more toward his dad, putting him in a perfect angle to see Madi.

She leaned against the counter while Evan flipped through a giant binder. Yet her eyes flitted between Cal and the exciting sight of her sneakers scuffing against the floor in the same circular pattern. At one point, he caught her eyes long enough to still her nervous fidget. Her mouth twisted into the faintest image of a smile when holding his gaze.

But when Eric hummed, that brought his attention back to the unfurling tension. "She knows everything about you since she moved here from Virginia a few years ago. It would be great for the two of you to meet. . . maybe at the wedding. We've reserved a spot for you and a plus-one. If you want, it's yours."

Cal's throat tightened into a vice grip, trapping his voice somewhere amid the rush of thoughts roaring in his ears. Attend his dad's second wedding? Silence spun between Eric and him, perched on the unsteady proposition.

He sighed, "You want me there? Does your wife?"

"We both do. And for the plus one, we figured you'd ask your friend, Claire, to accompany you. I assume you're still in touch with her; you were always close. But we'd also be okay if you bring the special someone in your life. . . say like the pretty redhead watching us from the counter." Eric mused, dropping his volume while his eyes studied someone over Cal's shoulder.

Heat flooded his face, tinging his cheeks with prickling numbness. "Uh—"

"I still can tell when you're lying, Cal. Is that your girl?" Eric questioned, yet Cal knew better than to assume he had doubts about his answer.

"Yeah, she is. That's Madi."

"She's beautiful. I hope you two have found happiness within each other, the same way Jill and I have. You deserve that much, especially after everything you've experienced." said Eric.

Cal's shoulders hunched over a little. *The implication stood tall, unflinching while it stared Cal down.* He inhaled before he said, "I appreciate that. You can send me an invitation, and I'll consider it. I moved, so you can text me for my new address."

"I appreciate that. A lot."

"And, for what it's worth, I hope your and Jill's marriage is happy. At least, happier than you and Mom." Cal meant it. At the end of the day, his parents didn't slog through a happy marriage, and neither did he. It would be best for all of them to go their separate ways, searching for happiness that's too short for the lifetime they'd live.

Eric managed to smile a little. "Thanks, Cal. You turned out to be a good young man." The two stepped apart. Cal let his father go to the counter, swapping places with Madi. Her brows furrowed while she studied his dad, occasionally breaking to trace Cal's face. Recognition flashed in those pretty brown eyes, painting her face in the color of shock.

"Are you okay?" she whispered, grasping his hands. Honestly, he would be just fine.

"Yeah, I'm good. Let's let Evan finish up, and then we'll grab our stuff to go," Cal assured her, pulling her closer to him. He kissed her forehead while her arms slipped around his waist, sinking into his frame. "Things are okay."

The invitation question hadn't been solved on the same night. No, Cal mulled over the idea for days, weighing the pros and cons of attending his dad's second wedding. He discussed it with Madi, Claire, Alex, and Jensen in great detail. Yet, no one managed to give him the perfect answer.

So, while he lay in bed and waited for Desmond to call him back, Cal stared up at his ceiling, aware of the crossroads he stared down. Change peeked over the horizon of his life, promising the start of new things—a *new* job, *new* milestones to reach, and *new* relationship waters to navigate.

At some point during his aimless, empty lounge, Cal switched on the television. Noise shot out at him from the random commercial flashing across the screen, bathing the room in a blue, startling light. His finger nudged the volume to non-existent, loud enough to be heard but not enough to drown out his thoughts.

He should RSVP soon, whether as a yes or no, and Desmond could be his tiebreaker. His agent always managed to become the voice of dominance throughout his career, never swayed by indecision.

Still, Cal couldn't help the itch settling under his skin to call Madi. *She'd be the plus-one invited, after all. Shouldn't she have the final say?*

Cal held himself back, though. Madi was finishing a hectic shift at the hospital, focusing on the people who needed her. He needed her, but he could wait.

So, he waited. And waited. And waited more. Even with the television to distract him, time trickled through his fingers slower than his anticipation could bear. Cal's hands fumbled for his phone charging on the end table, quickly firing off another message to Desmond in delayed succession with his other ones.

> **CAL: Hey. Call me when you get the chance.**

> **CAL: It's urgent. Something came up at the end of April, and I wanted to check my calendar before I commit to anything.**

> **CAL: Is everything alright?**

As soon as the text read *'delivered,'* an incoming call from Desmond buzzed through. Cal didn't wait to answer, perched on the edge of metaphorical pins and needles. He'd lay the issue to rest for good, free to bypass the crossroad choices he needed to finish.

"Hey, what's—" Cal got out before the rattled, echoey sound of Desmond's heavy panting interrupted his thought.

"I need a favor," Desmond spoke over him. The urgency, however, slammed Cal back into his place. A favor could mean anything. Getting bailed out of jail in Vegas flashed across Cal's mind, a fuzzy recollection of his "proudest" moments.

"Anything. At least promise me you're okay, man." Cal sat up from his cozy lounge across his bed. His almost dry hair flopped into his eyes, in dire need of a trim. Some of the guys suggest he grow his hair out, let it brush his shoulder, or reach man-bun status. He elected to let one of them try it out instead; he preferred his hair on the shorter side, or at least long enough for a lady to pull-

Desmond sighed, relief palpable, "I'm fine. Some punk kid nearly ran me over with his skateboard, and I tried to chase after him. I'm old now, so that didn't go well." He barely took a breath before pivoting. "You remember my grand-niece, Shaylee, right? Petite, bright pink hair, wants to be an influencer. . . whatever that means."

Vague recognition hit Cal. A woman with bubblegum pink hair crossed his mind, but he couldn't pick her out of a lineup if he tried. Beyond the hair, not much stuck with him, which would disappoint Desmond. He probably shared videos of her before with Cal, who tended to brush them off with a polite comment.

"Yeah, I think so. Is she okay?" Cal jumped down the line of emergency concerns that could bend Desmond so out of shape. Family issues ranked second on the list, which wasn't a small collection of potentials.

"She's doing great. In fact, her viewership numbers and followers on her social media pages are growing fast after a few viral videos. She seems happy about it. I wouldn't know how those things work—" Desmond snorted. "—but she's who I'm asking the favor for. She says she keeps getting rejected from brand deals that would boost her star power to the next level. I figured I could lend her one of my clients to take her out for a night or two."

And there it was. The implication swung and punched straight through Cal's chest. Oh, Desmond wanted them to *be seen*. Girls who were photographed with him got their names printed in media outlets. Nosy people fed on the attention and dug for information about the girls to publicize further, churning out a week of content for the "beauty of the week" in Cal's orbit.

Some girls in the past used PR to their advantage, and the short relationship springboarded them to new levels of visibility in their careers. He spent his fair share of time with influencer girls or wannabe models, always seeking the star-studded life. Few wanted to keep him like a boon, and others were content to slink off with what he offered.

However, Cal wasn't that man anymore. . . He didn't want to be when he had Madi.

He could've phrased it better, but the denial came swiftly onto his mind, ending up with him blurting out, "No. I can't."

"And why not?" The furrow in Desmond's brow was audible, even behind his heavier breathing.

"First, I'm trying to leave that part of my life behind. Has anyone considered I might want to give up the 'playboy' image? Second, I'm dating someone. . . and it's serious."

A pause ensued on the other line. Tiny blips of noise interspersed through the cracks, conjuring up the visual of his stunned agent standing inside the lobby of his firm, or maybe he walked down the busy Los Angeles streets, propelled where words failed.

"Since when do you actually date people?" Desmond spluttered. Yeah, that cut. Cal found himself wincing when the echo replayed. *Maybe if he wasn't forced into the playboy box still, then perhaps people might respect him more.*

"Since New Year's. I mean it, Des. This girl means the world to me, and the media would run with it."

"Only three months. Is it really a big deal to this girl that you can't do me a favor?"

Hurt melted into something sinister, burning at the edges of Cal's hands from how fast they curled into fists. "It is a big fucking deal. She would be devastated by any implication of me stepping out on her, and I wouldn't dream of hurting her."

Desmond scoffed, "You'd rather put this girl you've barely known for a quarter of a year first over me? Me? Have you forgotten who made your whole career? You owe me."

"Like I didn't do the hard work to get myself to you in the first place?" Cal kicked off the sheets, now angrier than ever. "As for my girl, she doesn't use my fame as a leverage point. She sees me for me."

"How romantic. And how are you planning to keep this relationship alive for over a few months? Every girl you've ever picked has an issue with your fame. You might be in the love haze now, but I'll be the only one there for you when she decides you come with too much baggage and not enough perks. Get your head in the game and show up for dinner later. I don't want to show up at your house and chew you out for your temper tantrum." Desmond ended the call on that note, leaving the air sour.

Cal didn't pause to mope. His fingers dialed Madi's number into his phone and waited on speakerphone. He paced his breathing to the ring, forcing himself to be calm.

However, Madi didn't answer. Instead, another voice picked up, one higher and a little more nasally, "Hello?"

"Uh, is Madi there? I need to speak to her," Cal replied. Noise in the background—giggling and clattering—drew his focus in.

"I'm a friend. I can pass on a message because she's a little occupied." The woman suggested, rushing out each hushed word.

"Alright. Just. . . tell Madi that Cal called and it's urgent." Cal's hand rubbed down the length of his face. Tonight was the worst time to give her a crash course on how his fame sucked, but Desmond's insistence worried him.

"Will do. Bye." The woman on the other line ended the call, abandoning Cal on the ledge of uncertainty. *Come on, Madi. Call him.*

Chapter 21

Madi

MADI HADN'T NOTICED THE phone ringing at first. Alaina and Janet's laughter about some video they watched reverberated off the bathroom wall like bass rattling the floor at a club. Since Madi postponed the girls' night the other day, she promised them a do-over. Of course, they took her up on the offer.

That evening, Madi sided with Sonia and Alaina for a casual night at a local karaoke bar Sonia recommended. The girls needed a night to let loose and be silly without the pounding bass or strangers dancing up on them.

Somewhere between Madi setting down her liquid liner to check her wing and reaching for the purple glitter eyeshadow palette propped on the counter, she finally noticed the phone ringing. "Whose phone is that?"

"I don't know—" Sonia glanced over her shoulder to Janet's bedroom. The girls stashed most of their personal items there for safekeeping. They'd go in one car and return to Janet's place to head home, acting as their collateral to not stay out too late or drink too much with work tomorrow.

Before anyone else could, Janet flounced away from the counter. "I'll see who it is." She exited the room to a chorus of "thank yous" from the others.

Madi angled her body back toward the mirror and pushed onto her tiptoes to reach a sliver of visibility in the crowded reflection. Soon, her dark eyes gleamed with a small puff of purple, shimmery powder. In the right light, those flecks of glitter spun in kaleidoscopic colors, brightening her already vibrantly colored makeup.

"Pass me the wipes, Mads," Alaina's voice hovered somewhere to her left. Madi tossed her the crinkling package of makeup wipes, still focused on the mirror. She acknowledged Alaina's thankful response with a hum, trying to finish the rest of her makeup. "So, are we ready for karaoke?"

"You know I am. Val wanted me to take videos of me embarrassing myself up there, so I'm relying on you guys to back me up when I say I forgot." Sonia laughed off to her right and behind her, her voice jingling and her choice of bangles lining the lengths of her wrists.

Madi joined in with the laughter, hands wavering as she exchanged her eyeshadow for another fresh touch of mascara. The rest of the world filtered out while she finished the rest of her makeup in her tiny section of the mirror. She didn't realize Janet returned to the cramped bathroom.

Not until Janet's shoulder knocking into her back almost smeared lipstick down Madi's chin.

Her eyes jumped in the mirror, watching Janet's scowling face ripple in the crowded glass. Although Janet's eyes faced the nearest wall, the harshness of her gaze cut like daggers. She looked angry, *betrayed* even.

The look kicked Madi's heart into her stomach. *Did she get some bad news? What had her so upset?* She knew Janet better than to ask outright, for Janet might deny any issue and leave it to simmer if she came on too strong.

Madi wiped the bottom of her lip clean, focused on the tiniest smudge of lipstick poking out of her defined lines. She hummed, "Was the call important?"

"No. Nothing important. It was just some stupid telemarketer." Janet's curt, borderline hostile reply punched through the once palpable excitement in the room. All emotions rushed out of the room, eager to be away.

All the girls turned to her, watching her aggressive rustling through her drawers for her makeup bag and a light-up mirror. Janet perched on the closed toilet lid, tucked the mirror between her thighs, and freshened up without another word.

Alaina, Sonia, and Madi's eyes descended into a silent exchange of pointed stares, daring one another to prod a little further for answers. Janet's bad moods were somewhat. . . volatile, and none of the girls liked to intercept her anger. It was a total evening killer.

Eventually, Alaina shrugged, breaking the wordless discussion between the three while Janet stormed through her beauty routine. She sighed, "The first round of shots is on me tonight. We'll need a little something to get our performance vibes flowing."

At this, Janet glanced away from the mirror, inky liquid eyeliner grasped between her fingers. Her face softened a little, bringing a sparkle to her eye. "Sounds good to me. I need something strong." Her gaze swept over Sonia and Alaina, still calm and friendly.

Yet when she landed on Madi, Madi swore something dark crossed over Janet's eyes, passing within a blink. It came so quick that Madi almost assumed she imagined the change. Almost.

She held that thought close to the vest while returning to her scattered cosmetics. Her hands swept everything back into her bright pink bag, trying to push the unease gnawing at her chest out of focus.

There was no need to overthink. Janet's bad mood shouldn't impact her night.

Madi cleaned everything up before all her friends clamored to head out, ready to hit the karaoke bar with full wallets and a taste for fun. She swapped her little bag for her phone and the fanny pack with her cards and other items, tugged out of the bedroom by an excited Alaina.

As her friend pulled her along, a stolen moment to check her phone for any missed calls or texts. Although she had only one person on her mind since the rest of her social circle rushed out of Janet's apartment.

A blank screen greeted her, free of any notifications or missed calls.

Cal must be busy. He mentioned dinner with his agent the other day, and that must be tonight.

Madi debated the merits of texting Cal when Sonia nudged her into the backseat of Janet's car. She never got around to it, not when her friends' upbeat chatter and the blurring of the world around her pulled her attention every which way. Since Janet marched into that bathroom with her sharpened glare, the world felt slightly bent off its axis.

And Madi couldn't figure out how to right it. The unsettled feeling would linger, sitting on her shoulder until someone plied two shots into her hand, and Sonia dragged her onto the stage to scream off-key to Kate Bush and Madonna.

The wheezy purr of her car's engine as Madi rolled into a reserved parking spot could've put her back to sleep. She spent last night trying to chase away the anxiety loitering in the back of her mind, tiring herself out with a few shots and plenty of performing.

The cheerful smile she plastered onto her face worked harder than her vocal cords, still aching from too much singing. But none of the girls suspected the discomfort sloshing around in her gut, numbed and heightened by each shot she had swallowed. The numbness won out until she, sober enough to drive, had driven home to a restless sleep.

Madi picked up the green tea from the center console. Her fingers warmed from holding the sunshine-colored travel mug until they became slippery with a thin layer of sweat. She groaned, stealing her first sip since breakfast. "How lucky am I to be working on April Fools? I must be the luckiest girl in the world," she grumbled, sarcastic for no one but herself.

She drove in early enough to sip her tea and enjoy her breakfast in the quiet of her car, safe from the urge to call in 'sick' and pull the covers over her head. Madi reached into her bag, pulling out the two egg muffins she had meal-prepped and the fruit leather bar. *The Breakfast of Champions, right?*

Madi ate in silence beyond the occasional noise in the distance like sirens, honking horns, or maybe the faint growl of a jetliner flying overhead—the noise of life within the city. Part of her yearned for sleep. The rest of her, however, retained the good sense to find something positive to start her morning.

It was her anchor, keeping her grounded when all else threatened to fall around her.

Lately, Cal had become that anchor for her. Even on the days when their schedules left them at odds, transformed into passing ships in the night, his texts always found a way to bridge the space. She never woke up or went to bed without a message from Cal, a video call soon, or the promise of a date to hold her over. He built himself a space in her life, leaving pieces of himself with her like the indent of his body on her well-worn mattress.

However, she waded into the unknown—Cal hadn't texted or called since last night. Her last message remained lonesome in their text chain. Part of her worried, taken aback by the emptiness left in Cal's absence. How soon did she take his presence for granted?

Madi considered texting again, checking in. The little voice in her mind, sounding suspiciously like her friends, called her '*desperate.*' Double texting landed Madi into her fair share of awkwardness with men she thought liked her as much as she wanted them. But oh, why was playing the "cool girl" so difficult?

At some point, her worries grappled with a callous, cold reality check, once again echoing the voice of her friends. That time, however, Sonia's gentle mothering overpowered Alaina's scandalized gasp or Janet's scoff, promising her he likely got busy with his commentator gig starting so soon.

He told her all about it, spending the last week mentioning his hopes, fears, and everything in between. *Work came first.*

So, Madi assured herself the uncertainty would pass soon. Nothing happened to give her any doubts about their relationship, and she wouldn't overthink things. That sounded great—until a loud knock on her car window caused her tea to spill over the center console.

Madi's gaze jumped to the passenger side window, where Janet hovered. She cocked her head, brow raised at the sight of her outside the car. *Didn't she have today off?*

Madi rolled the window down enough. "Janet, what's up?" she asked, gesturing to her lack of scrubs. "I thought you were off today."

"I am. But I knew you were working, so let me in," Janet replied. She put aside her attitude from last night and seemed in a much better mood. In fact, the color in her cheeks and the glint in her eye flagged Madi's focus. *The look in her eyes glinted like she knew something.*

Madi unlocked the door for Janet, and the two sat in the car, perched along the silence. Despite her shift being due to start soon, Madi waited for her to speak. Something weighed on Janet enough for her to show up at work on her day off.

Maybe she wanted to discuss yesterday?

"So, is there anything you'd like to tell me?" Janet questioned. Her fingers coiled her hair into a sloppy updo, very unlike her. Madi could count on one hand—maybe two if she defined this broadly—the number of times Janet looked anything less than pristine. She liked to describe herself as "perpetually camera-ready."

"Me?" Madi snatched up her tea, pacing herself with drinks. What was with all the theatrics? "Jan, you're acting weird. You've been off since last night, so why don't we square away whatever has you bothered."

"I'm the weird one? I'm not the one hiding such a big secret!" Janet's voice pitched to a near shriek, but her saccharine smile awakened a warning. Those eyes, however, glinted dark compared to the bright, wide smile and flashing pearly white teeth. "I know who he is."

"He?"

"You're sleeping with that baseball guy, Callum whatever— or at least you were! I finally figured out what you've been keeping to yourself," Janet said, speaking so casually while Madi swore a bomb went off in her stomach.

She stared at Janet, mouth fighting the urge to fall open and gawk. *Oh no. No, please.* Madi set her tea down before her fingers dropped the scalding liquid onto her lap and gave herself burns. "How did you—wait, did you say were?"

Her small interjection appeared a non-issue to Janet, who laughed and smacked Madi's shoulder. Pain blossomed from the roughness of her hand, especially from the rings adorning her fingers. "I saw something on your phone last night, and it got me thinking about New Year's. That's when you met your mystery man. . . The same night he was spotted with a mystery woman, only photographed with a sliver of a golden dress. . . like the one you wore. I'm not an idiot, Madi."

She shrugged, kicking her feet up onto Madi's dashboard. "Honestly, I can see why he was so tempting to keep to yourself.

He's hot, rich, famous. The total package. . . if only he wasn't such a player. I did try to warn you that he wouldn't be loyal to you. But sometimes life is a learning lesson—" Janet's eyes narrowed.

Madi's jaw clenched. "Fine, you know. But Cal isn't a player, not how the media portrays him. So, I'd ask you to stop talking about my boyfriend like that."

Janet laughed. She had the audacity to full-on cackle, her head tossed back and her hand waving through the air while she caught her breath. She hauled out her phone. "No? Do you know better? Then, what's this? Looks like he went out with someone else last night."

Flipping her phone around, Janet swiped through a few photos screenshotted from a gossip magazine. Source aside, the photos snapped a story in several heinous parts. Cal, dressed nicely, sat across the table from a pink-haired woman and an older man seated in the middle. While the latter two looked at Cal with stars in their eyes, Cal's posture reminded Madi of a cat with its hackles raised.

Madi pushed the phone away from her face, desperate to ignore the hot swell of emotion rushing into her throat. Heat stung at the back of her eyes, "That's it? No kissing? No physical touch? The media likes to twist things—"

"Oh, get a grip, Madi," Janet scoffed. "You have photographs of your man at dinner with another girl. Your track record with men isn't a stunning list of winners, is it? Every single time, you're either ghosted, used, or the one left behind when they stray. And you know what the common denominator is? You. Maybe pick better next time and listen to those of us who know more about romance. . . You wouldn't be the girl men get bored of, then."

With that final jab, Janet left Madi's car, slamming the door on her way out. She sauntered away in the half-empty parking lot, unafflicted by the mess she threw at Madi's feet. "Mess" put it lightly; no, that revelation unfolded like a trainwreck, leaving Madi in the wreckage of her confidence.

Cal wouldn't. . . *right?* He couldn't. . . *right?*

Her hands shakily fumbled for her phone, blinded by tears. She'd give Cal a call, leave a text or two when he probably ignored her, and then she'd head into the hospital for her shift. As much as the kinder side of her breaking heart might suggest she go home and call out, in no state to help others, the rest of her refused.

The world didn't stop just because hers might've.

Chapter 22
Cal

As Cal looked into the sunrise cresting over the horizon, he listened for the approach of footsteps on the wooden planks behind him, hoping Madi would show. They'd agreed on a neutral meeting location—a quiet segment of the Santa Monica pier—needing to discuss things.

Cal really wished things could be different. Fuck, he'd surrender all the money in his bank account, sell the house and car, and strip himself of everything he owned for a time machine to take it all back.

For the second time in months, a series of paparazzi photos threatened to upend Cal's entire life. But unlike the night he met Madi, these photos threatened to undo months of progress and the first taste of happiness he'd found since the accident.

All because of Desmond. Cal didn't do anything wrong, yet he *should've* known better.

When the photos dropped, his first order of business hadn't been to pick up the phone for all the concerned calls from Jensen or Claire, who were worried about him and full of questions. No, it had been to march straight into Desmond's office and scream at him loud enough for the entire block to hear him. He didn't stop chewing Des out, not even when he wore his vocal cords raw from all the cussing he leveled at Desmond.

The horrified paleness across Desmond's face triumphed over his usual bluster and confidence. He looked on the verge of cardiac arrest, shrinking away from Cal until security entered the room.

So much for an attack dog.

The rest of the day—April Fools *of all fucking days*—he lost to putting out small fires and issuing "no comment" to any news organization or tabloid bold enough to contact him instead of his representatives. Granted, Desmond likely wouldn't handle it anyway, so he took over PR.

And when he had lay in bed, the reminder of Madi hit him with full force. Bypassing all the other messages left for him to see, he had listened to her voicemail. He couldn't move, couldn't breathe when hearing her pained sobs between every word. She choked out an apology—an *"I'm sorry"* when she was the casualty—and her tears wore Cal's walls down. He nearly started to cry himself.

Back on that bench at the Pier, Cal's eyes followed a flock of seagulls coasting over the water, greeted by their shrill squawking ringing out. They soar across the vibrantly painted skies, specks of shadow across the streaks of red bleeding into orange and gold. If his heart still jolted in the disjointed song it sang without Madi's voice in his life, the world around him finding a small semblance of peace rubbed its balm over the ache.

But oh, what a heavy, hateful burden his emotions offered just for the chance to feel something other than numb.

Madi brought a new dimension to his life, a new light to the colors that ran gray after the accident, but in her absence, everything ached. She had upended his entire world in three short months, and he wanted it back.

Footsteps creaking against the dock set every nerve in Cal's body on high alert. His breath stalled in his throat while he waited for the steps to approach or fade into the distance. Each time the footsteps faded when the stranger walked past, Cal could never bring himself to look back. If he caught a glimpse of Madi walking away, that might crush whatever resolve he had left.

However, the steps grew louder this time until she appeared in his peripheral view. He first recognized the pink of her scrubs, fixating on everything but her face when the soft sniffles reached his ears. Hearing her cry *almost* broke him. *Seeing* her cry would carve into his chest, pulling his heart out and tossing it into the sea.

"Cal," Madi greeted when sitting on the bench, posting at the furthest spot away from him. Although he understood her hesitance, a gaping chasm between them stung. It was salt in the wound, stinging harder than alcohol against cut skin. "Are you okay?"

Cal could've screamed. Her asking *him* if he was okay while fending off tears fucked him up. *What had they done to deserve this?*

"No, I'm not. . . but I'm worried about you," he admitted, swallowing hard to hold back the flood of apologies he recited through the night. "We need to talk about what happened, and I'd like you to get everything off your chest. If you hate me—"

"I don't hate you. I wish I were that type of person, but hate doesn't help me. So, no. . . but I'm going to ask that you let me speak, no interruptions or excuses," said Madi.

It was then that Cal spared a glance toward her. Her hair billowed around her face, knocked askew by the breeze while she stared ahead at the water. Her arms coiled around herself, squeezing tight in a hug as the cardigan she wore over her scrubs slipped off her shoulders. But her face echoed exhaustion in the bags under her eyes, casting shadows across her pale skin. The world drained her of her color and light.

Cal's hand traced beside him on the bench, faced by the gap between his body and Madi's. "Okay," he agreed.

"I've never been the lucky in love type. I didn't get the bedtime stories about princesses and handsome knights rescuing them from danger. I didn't watch happy parents be madly in love. All my perceptions of love came from the small observations I collected throughout my life and the hope for something more. The world isn't kind to women like me, the ones who exist in bigger bodies. But for the first time in years, I thought that maybe. . . Maybe I could fall in love with someone who would love me back."

If Cal's heart stopped beating then and there, he wouldn't have noticed. A meteor could plummet out of the sky, killing him on the spot, and he still wouldn't notice. Madi said she was in love? Falling in love? With *him*?

Madi's breath shook, screaming for Cal to pull her in and muffle the sound into his chest. Her tears should stain his shirt and not the apples of her soft cheeks. But he stayed put when she continued, "Those photos *gutted* me, Cal. Seeing you with a girl at least half my size awakened this fear that you'd realize you didn't like me all that much and chase after someone who looks like a star athlete's girlfriend. I couldn't function after seeing them, hiding in the bathroom and supply closets at my work to cry or dry heave in between patient rotations. Help me understand what happened. Why did this happen? Who is she, and am I the last to know this relationship is over?"

"No—" The word shot out of him, hurried and panicked. Madi's shoulders stiffened, but she managed to look at him. Cal's eyes met hers, rimmed with red and puffy from plenty of crying. "—Madi, I can promise you our relationship isn't over. Those pictures aren't what they seem. I'm sorry that I've hurt you and that my fame's caused you pain. Can I explain?"

"You better. But if you lie to me and I find out. . ." Madi trailed off. However, Cal understood better than challenging the threat or cracking a joke. Today wasn't the time for jokes or anything less than sincere.

"I wouldn't."

"Okay. Your turn on the floor."

Cal nodded, pushing his hands down his thighs to stop them from bouncing. "I was ambushed. Desmond, my agent, had called me the other day to ask for a favor. He wanted me to be seen with his grand-niece, the girl with the pink hair because she's a social media personality and I'm star power for those looking to climb the social ladder. I told him no, that I was seeing someone and she was too important to jeopardize for a photo op. We argued about it, said many hurtful things, and screamed. I thought he'd back down—"

"But he didn't," Madi whispered, quickly clapping her hands over her mouth. Guilt spilled into her eyes, lightening them like a watery sheen of tears. "Sorry, I shouldn't have interrupted."

"It's okay. You aren't wrong, either. Des and I met for dinner, and I thought he'd leave the subject for good. His grand-niece joined us at the table, and I spent fifteen minutes there before Tommy arrived to pick me up. But the damage was already done since Desmond called the paps on us, setting the entire thing up." Cal rubbed the back of his neck.

Madi's hands dropped from her mouth. "Are you serious?"

"Serious as a heart attack." Cal handed his phone to Madi, who almost recoiled back. He slipped the phone into her hands, opening his conversation with Desmond—if anyone could call a string of angry texts with the occasional interjection from the other side a "conversation." "—Read it. I have nothing to hide and never want you to lose your trust in me."

With coaxing, Madi accepted his suggestion. They lapsed into silence while she scrolled through Cal's phone. He turned away, knowing better than to hover over her shoulder or give an expecting impression. She needed to feel safe with him again. He loathed Desmond for hurting them, violating his trust, and stealing Madi's by association.

The minutes trickled by while he counted each new strand of color added to the morning skies. Cal almost forgot where he was until a gentle tap on his shoulder brought him back to reality. His face tilted enough to find Madi scooted a little closer to him than before.

"That's a relief, honestly," she said, despite the wobbling of her voice. Madi sucked in a breath, fighting for her composure. "I believe you. I'm so sorry that your agent did that to you. He seems like a jerk."

"He's. . . We can leave it at a jerk. I don't know what to do about him yet, but I need a level head before making big decisions. I haven't been myself since the photos dropped, but I needed to solve all this first," Cal murmured.

Madi nodded. "I wish I had gotten a heads up about this, you know? There's not much we can do now about it. It's not your fault."

"I wish I called too. I tried reaching you before it happened when I had the initial fight with Desmond." Cal's brows furrowed. He remembered that much despite every chaotic moment over the last three days.

Madi paused. She couldn't stop her frown, twisting her features into a portrait of beautiful confusion. Color flushed into her cheeks, softer than the harsh red of fresh tears. "Cal, when? I didn't get a call or a text."

"The same night the incident happened. I called you, and someone else picked up. She said she was your friend. I heard noises, so I assumed you were busy with something. I asked her to tell you I called and to call me back because it was urgent," Cal replied.

Madi stared at him, jaw slack. Cal blinked at her, unsure what else to say until tears sprung into Madi's eyes. Her hands clapped over her mouth, muting the strangled choke escaping her. Recognition bled into her bloodshot eyes, newly horrified, while she shook her head.

"No. . . *Fucking* Janet," Madi hissed. She pushed off the bench, rocketing to her feet for a split second before she crashed back down. Tears slipped over her cheeks, streaming without hesitation. "The girl who answered, Janet, never told me you called. She also showed me the photos and said I should've known better than to get my hopes up with you. I didn't understand how she learned about us, but she probably snooped through my phone after you called. She did that purposefully to point out how dumb and naïve I am."

Madi swiped the sleeves of her cardigan over her face, rough when clearing the tears off her face. But they kept coming, and Cal couldn't bear to watch.

He slid across the bench, closing the gap between him and Madi. One arm snagged her waist while the other reached for her face. Madi froze at his touch, letting his thumb brush the tears away.

Her wide, watery eyes peered up at him, lip quivering. "I'm so sorry. I should've known better than to jump to conclusions. Please don't hate me."

"It would kill me to hate you, firefly," Cal whispered. "What can I do to make you feel okay? To make everything right?"

Madi swallowed. "I don't— We need space to process all of this for at least a week or two. In the last few days, our relationship has spun out of control and into the hands of people who don't respect us. We should probably handle them first, take a breather, and then discuss what comes next."

"As long as you're not breaking up with me, I'll give you anything you ask. You mean the world to me, Madi. . . and I want this more than I can ever say," Cal exhaled. With a break-up off the table, much of the tension abated from his body. He imagined it washed into the sea a few feet from where he and Madi sat, vanishing into the deep blue.

His arms held her still, squeezing her tight. Madi reciprocated, giving another glimmer of hope before the two mutually let go.

Madi rose from her seat on the bench, hoisting her cardigan back over her shoulders. She glanced past Cal briefly, but that didn't stop her from grasping his face.

Cal stared up at her, helplessly attending to her call. "I'll see you soon?"

"Yes. See you soon," Madi promised. Her eyes met his in their sweetest goodbye before she walked away from the bench. Cal's eyes followed her figure retreating down the pier, a shining point among all the noise and attractions settled on the dock. He waited for her to become a blip indistinguishable to his teary eyes before he dropped his gaze.

Cal pulled his phone out to get some counsel when he turned away. He'd hit up the ever-wise Claire if he wanted some clarity and emotional wisdom. Yet, anger tumbled around in his chest, crying for retribution. So, he called someone else.

Jensen answered the call on the second beat, voice cutting through the rush of life behind him. "Cal, you okay?"

"I'm fine. You in town?" Cal asked, leaning back on the bench while he fixed his gaze on the rising sun. A new day began, and his to-do list would be complete within the next hour.

"New York, actually. We flew in this morning—"

"That's fine. I need revenge advice."

"And you called me?" Jensen questioned, sounding half-confused but also amused by the choice. "I'm flattered, but I think you could do better."

"I know. Pass the phone to your wife," Cal snorted. It felt nice to laugh after days of screaming. He listened to the scrambling of the background and Jensen's *"for you"* and a muffled *"give me a moment, Giselle"* before Daisy's voice hit his ears.

"Cal, thank goodness you're okay. We were worried when the news dropped. . . Tell me everything," Daisy commanded in that firm yet honeyed tone reserved for the inner circle. Cal did as he was told, spilling every detail about his side of the dilemma.

"—I'm so pissed, but I don't know how to respond without going full tilt. You're the best person I know to coach me through it," Cal finished. He imagined Daisy—and Jensen, who was he kidding—listened to the entirety of his rant.

"Alright. You'll listen very closely because this could implode your career if you do it wrong. Are you comfortable with that risk?" Daisy broke the silence first, eliciting a heavy exhale from Cal.

"Yes. I know that there are risks to this, but it's what I need to move forward. If Desmond wants to hold me back, then he's a loss I need to cut. If that means my illustrious career as a sports commentator might end in its first season, so be it. I'm not scared of starting from scratch," Cal agreed.

And he meant it. He knew what bridge would burn and crumble if it came down to Madi or Desmond. Some things deserved to be left in the past a long time ago.

Chapter 23

Madi

IF JANET DODGED HER calls and texts for another day, Madi might consider doing something bordering on a felony.

Coasting on the last tiny shred of her patience, Madi tried to reach Janet for a chat. As if she sensed the trap, Janet decided to avoid her instead. Her texts went unanswered, and her calls were sent straight to voicemail. She even dodged the chatter in the JAMS group chat.

Thus began an all-out hunt for the object of Madi's greatest ire. A week had passed since her goodbye to Cal in Santa Monica, and Madi missed him like crazy. However, while saboteurs waited to strike, she wouldn't allow herself to give away the rest of her heart in that relationship.

Luck hadn't been on her side. She and Janet ended up on opposing shifts at the hospital for an entire week. She couldn't recall when that happened since they first began working at New Horizons. Janet knew what awaited her the second she crossed Madi's path.

But today, Madi had had enough of the waiting.

Brushing her hair out of her face, Madi didn't dally when her final rotations for the afternoon. She counted the minutes until her lunch break under her breath, passing each room with a patient of hers with a smile and a wave. Her sneakers thudded against the linoleum floors while she approached the nurse's station.

Kiara, standing behind the counter, brightened. "Ah, Madi! Are you heading out to lunch?"

"Yes, please. I'll be back soon." Madi didn't stay long. No, not when her plan needed every second to work. When her notes crossed the nurse's station, she bolted for the locker rooms to grab her phone.

Madi switched on her phone, greeted by the bright flash while her texts came flooding in. Several from Alaina and Sonia rolled to the top of her unread lists. She smirked, reading them while bounding to the elevator.

> MADI: hey. How's lunch sound today?

> ALAINA: of course! Girl, we were so worried about you!

> MADI: I'm fine, I promise. Just had to work through some stuff.

> ALAINA: glad to have you back. Heartbreak never keeps you from shining bright.

> MADI: you want to get the girls together for lunch today?

> SONIA: yes! Alaina and Janet are working today, too. She texted me her schedule earlier.

Madi hadn't told the others her side of the story yet, keeping Janet's involvement in the "demise" of her relationship close to the vest. All would be revealed, of course. But apparently, Janet shared bits and pieces without Madi's permission, which was evident by the original flurry of "We heard about Cal" and "Are you doing okay?" texts in the days since the photo fallout.

So, Alaina and Sonia knew about Cal being Callum Lambert, a baseball superstar and all-around hottie, and that he callously "broke Madi's naïve heart" via paparazzi photographs. Madi didn't ask the others, but a small part of her would assume Janet handed over the photos in question, quick to rub salt in the wound and feign concern.

She'd pay for that, for all of it.

Madi hitched a ride on the elevator, fortunate enough to catch an elevator without the others. She didn't want Janet to see her coming, unable to run from the ambush Madi laid. It wasn't so nice when it happened to *her*, now was it?

She smiled at the people in the carriage, feeling less fake than the ones she had plastered onto her face for the past week. Today marked a turn in the circumstances, a chance to clear the air and start fresh with Cal.

She was in for the long haul if potentially imploding her friend group indicated anything.

Madi flounced ahead of the lunch hour crowd as the elevator doors swung open, making a beeline for those front doors. Through the influx of entering patients, Madi caught sight of

Alaina, Sonia, and the back of Janet's head waiting shy of the doors.

All was going according to plan.

So, Madi sped up, borderline running for the door. Anticipation nipped at her heels, quick to light a fire under her ass and propel her forward. She ducked around patients, offering them a polite "excuse me" but not backing down until she emerged into the chill of the foggy April afternoon.

She stepped over to the girls, hands tucked behind her back, and a smile loaded onto her lips. "Hey, girls!"

Sonia and Alaina faced her; relief was undeniable in their smiles. On the other hand, Janet tensed so visibly that the girls eyed her, fast to swing back into concern. Madi stood there, waiting for Janet to make her move.

Come on. She pinned Janet underneath her gaze, prepared for when Janet turned around and tried some dumb excuse. *No more running from the mess you made, Janet.*

The thought repeated until Janet spun on her heel, wearing a smile Madi knew to be painfully fake. Sympathy never met Janet's eyes, always falling short but only noticeable to Madi's newly opened eyes.

It was all about Janet to Janet, huh? No room for anyone else in her world.

Madi matched her smile, head cocked. "Janet, it's been a couple of days. Everything okay with you?"

"Me?" Janet stammered out, losing control of herself too fast. She schooled her face back into that polite mask of hers. "No, I'm all good. But what about you? How have you been holding up since the whole Cal thing?"

"I've been better. It can be hard to learn awful things about someone you thought you could trust," said Madi. On its face, she sounded like the brokenhearted girl whose boyfriend stepped out with someone else in public, sure. Yet, Janet's eyes looked anywhere but her as those words settled.

Janet managed a nod. "I get it. It can be hard when a guy goes back to his old ways. Guys like Cal never change. It sucks that he used you for entertainment, though."

Her words inspired quiet reactions from Sonia and Alaina—the poor girls left out of the secondary, subliminal conversation ongoing. But Madi tried not to smirk, knowing how soon everyone would enter the fold.

"Funny you should mention Cal. I decided to speak with him the other day to get closure about us, and he told me the weirdest thing." Madi stepped closer to Janet. She watched the snake she once called a friend rocked backward on her heels, ready to inch away from Madi's approach. *She knew what was coming.* "He explained the timeline of events but said he called me on the night the photos were taken. He said that someone picked up on my behalf and said I was too busy to answer. That same person must've erased the call and messages. . . Any idea how that happened, Janet?"

By then, mere inches separated Madi and Janet from one another. Alaina and Sonia rushed to join the two, flanking them on either side, but their wide eyes had nothing on pale, horrified Janet when confronted by the truth.

Madi's jaw clenched at her silence. She wouldn't be absolved of anything by keeping her mouth shut. "I asked you a question. Only one person left the room long enough to answer a call and stayed gone long enough to do the snooping around. You didn't figure out about Cal and me through the photographs. You *snooped* through my phone and decided to take it upon yourself to ruin the best relationship I've ever had, didn't you?"

"Janet, are you serious? That's fucked up!" Alaina gasped, unable to keep herself from chiming in. Beside her, Sonia said nothing, but her stare spoke volumes from how harshly she glared at Janet.

All paleness in Janet's face vanished, replaced by the bluster of an angry red. "Are you kidding me? I did her a favor! Madi wants to play naïve and thinks someone like Callum Lambert is interested in her long-term. She's setting herself up for failure."

"Is that so?" Madi scoffed. "I don't buy it. You didn't do this out of misguided altruism to protect me from hurting my feelings. That's a whole load of bullshit I'm not accepting. . . Are you jealous, Janet?"

"Me? Jealous?" Janet's eyes bulged when Madi dropped the 'j word.' Hell might've frozen over from how the world around them dropped ten degrees. That, and the ever-cool Janet Coleman fumed hard, evident from the steam billowing out of her ears and the red staining her face. "What on earth would I be jealous of?"

Madi smirked. "Oh, I don't know. What does a tall, skinny, and conventionally attractive blonde woman have to be jealous of? Maybe because I, a fat girl, have something you want? You're used to being the center of everyone's attention and admiration. But now I have Cal, a conventionally attractive man, who is head over heels for me, and that doesn't make sense to you. You think it should've been you, not me."

In all her life, Madi couldn't ever recall speaking so boldly, so unafraid of the potential consequences. She prioritized kindness to others at the expense of kindness toward herself. That would end today.

Janet's redness darkened to a plum shade of purple, turning her perfect, symmetrical beauty into a mess. Madi's words must've hit a sore spot with how Janet got all up in her face. Maybe she intended to shove Madi or spit some nasty retort back into her face, driven to the brink of her anger.

However, Sonia and Alaina's arms looped into Janet's, hauling her away from Madi. They created enough space to step in, inserting themselves between Madi and a fuming Janet.

"Don't even think about it, *bitch*," Sonia scolded. Several nearby gasps and some curious eyes from stragglers entering the hospital perked up at that bomb. Betrayal tainted the pure, unbridled rage on Janet's face. "You've done enough."

"I don't know why you're taking her side—"

"Because she's our friend. . . and you're not anymore. Friends don't destroy each other's relationships or treat them like they aren't deserving of love. Madi is a beautiful, kind, funny, and amazing person. Of course, someone fell in love with her. It's a bonus that the guy has the total package," Alaina interjected. Usually the fun, energetic member of the group, her disappointment radiated in palpable waves.

"You can't be serious. Stop being delusional that a guy like Cal wants anything more with Madi than to string her along until something better comes." Janet acted like the rest of them were insane to even consider the proposition of Cal enjoying Madi's company or seeing her as anything more than a breathing sex object to use and discard when he was done.

"He wants me, and he'll have me as long as he continues to want me. I can't predict what will happen, but I won't stop loving simply because someone's feelings might change. I'm tired of holding myself back, shrinking myself to fit in the boxes people like you construct for me. . . When he never made me bend my shape to be pleasing to his whims," Madi snapped back.

"Madi has spoken. We're all done with you. Good luck finding new friends with that shitty attitude of yours." Sonia's nostrils flared, giving the final word to the conversation. Even if Janet wanted to respond, the silent ire of Sonia's stare slammed the door on any more talk.

They decided. It was final.

Smart enough to see where she couldn't argue, Janet shoved past the others, heading back into the hospital. She didn't look back or issue some half-assed apology to Madi for all the trouble, and maybe that was for the better. Madi didn't need her words to fix things, nor did she want them. Good *riddance*, Janet.

Sonia and Alaina's arms circling around Madi grabbed her focus before crushing her in a hug. Madi sank into the embrace, struck by how sisterly it felt. Was that what it felt like to have siblings, especially ones who cared?

"We're so sorry that she acted like that, babes! If we had known, she would've been exiled ages ago!" Alaina exclaimed, burying her face into Madi's shoulder. Madi believed her; Alaina might seem sweet, but when she set her mind to something, she stuck to her guns with the stubbornness of an angry bull.

"We should've noticed," Sonia added. She fixed a stray hair of Madi's, swiping it away from her forehead. Guilt darkened her features. "I can't believe we didn't notice her issues for so long-"

"Don't beat yourselves up about it. I thought Janet was mostly nice for a long time, but this experience opened my eyes. Her true colors came out, and we don't need to think about her any longer than strictly necessary. We'll be okay without her," Madi cut her off. No one needed to play the blame game; only Janet was responsible for her actions.

The three sank back into the hug, soft squeals and sighs becoming the sole continuation of the conversation. However, the moment lasted an extra minute before Madi's phone cried out from her pocket, muted and buzzing.

"Hold on—" She wiggled out of the embrace and grabbed her phone. Cal's name called to her from the top of the screen. Madi couldn't wait when her heart tried to make a run for it and got stuck in her throat. "—Cal texted me."

"What? Are you guys still together?" Alaina questioned. Her mouth fell open, and she clasped her hands together, utterly breathless.

Madi's brow tightened. "Sort of. We agreed to take a week or two to handle the fallout of everything since the photos dropped. Then, we'd see where we stood as a couple. I asked for it, and he obliged me." She stared at the notification, not opening it to read the message. Could he have made up his mind?

Her finger hovered over the message, shaking slightly until she tapped the screen. She did it twice, clicking on the text when it popped up.

> **CAL: thechangeupchats/interviews3813**

She watched the link's pop-up reveal a video thumbnail with Cal's face. He wore headphones and sat at a microphone... Did he go on a podcast?

Sonia and Alaina stepped out of her space, giving her room to play the video. The buffer stalled the playback for the first few seconds, freezing on the image of a different guy, likely the show's host.

"—and for our next "Ask A Pro" question, this comes from user @foxhoundfiend472. They want to know: Cal Lambert was recently seen with a minor-level social media influencer at dinner and his agent, Desmond Dellbook. Is he returning to his playboy past? What do you say to that, Cal?"

"I'm so glad you pulled this one, Donny. I've got some misconceptions to clear up." Cal appeared on screen after his voice hit over the speakers. Despite sitting indoors, he looked downright sinful in a tight white tank top, showing off his well-built arms and a backward baseball cap. *"If you'd let me use the pod to make a statement."*

"Of course, man! Please enlighten us!"

"Thanks. So, those recent photos with Desmond and Miss Dellbrook were arranged PR by Desmond. If they look like a romantic outing, that was his intention. Because of that little stunt, I'm seeking a new agent. I don't enjoy working with people who violate my consent or ignore me when I say 'no' to PR that ignores my boundaries." Cal adjusted his hat, as calm as possible when the camera flipped to show the show's host gawking at his revelation.

Other reactions were captured by quick cuts of the camera, none as outlandish as the host. Cal stayed emotionless, unaffected by the shock.

"Am I hearing you correctly? Did you fire THE Desmond Dellbrook for meddling?"

"Yep. Actually, I fired him right now." Cal popped the 'p' in his affirmation, gazing at the camera. Pride swept across Madi's lower abdomen while she watched her man fight back his smirk on camera.

"That's one hell of an exclusive." Donny laughed, torn between his shock and the awkwardness of wondering what came next. *"So, are the playboy rumors laid to rest then?"*

"I'll admit that after my relationship with Sadie ended, I went off the deep end for a year. That was a genuine cry for help, and the people in my life intervened. After that point, the media ran with a "playboy narrative," Desmond told me to roll with it. But I hadn't chased after a relationship until after my accident. . . and I'm seeing someone now," said Cal.

"You are? Tell us about her!" Donny perked up in his seat. It seemed he realized precisely how big of a story he landed on by sheer coincidence.

"She's amazing. We met on New Year's. It was funny because she knew nothing about my baseball history or fame. We've spent the last few months getting to know and enjoying each other's company. She has a fulfilling career and is a joy to be around. With her, I don't worry about what I regret or what other people think about me. She brings me peace," Cal remarked, only stopping to breathe. His breathless laugh and red cheeks encouraged ribbing from the hosts, which he swatted away and shrugged off.

He seemed so happy. . . because of her. She made him happy. That was more than enough.

Madi dove into the comments, propelled forward by a newfound bravery striking a match in her chest. Thousands of comments from social media users flooded the comment section, shockingly positive to her bewilderment. Many of them cried the downfall of Desmond Dellbrook while others swooned over Cal's recollection of his and Madi's love story.

They were public now, unchained from restrictions placed upon them by expectations. Whatever came next, Madi couldn't care less. She needed to be at Cal's side, riding the waves past the rough patch.

She closed the video, stalling long enough to see Alaina and Sonia's smiles. They clearly heard enough from how hard they flashed her their approval.

"First of all, he is so crazy about you! Second, we will interrogate all the dirty details about this new relationship from you later," Alaina declared, dabbing at her eyes like she expected tears to come.

Sonia shook her head, still smiling. "That's a problem for tomorrow. Madi needs to get her man tonight and seal the deal on getting back together."

"Oh, I'm already on it." Madi chewed on her bottom lip, embracing happiness instead of succumbing to self-doubt and sadness. "We will be talking this over tomorrow. . . Drinks on me," she said, all while typing out her shot to reel Cal back in. *Come back to her, honey. Please come back.*

MADI: I watched the clip. You looked amazing.

CAL: Does that mean I can come over tonight? I've fucking missed you.

MADI: I've missed you too.

MADI: I'll be waiting after my shift. Say 7:30?

CAL: Flowers and me at your door at 7:29 sharp, got it.

Chapter 24

Cal

As soon as 7:27 flashed up on his sports watch, Cal jolted forward from his spot in the backseat. Tommy snorted when he almost faceplanted into the curb, tripping over his traitorous feet and eagerness to be inside.

"Have a good time, boss." The cheeky fucker smirked from the driver's side, his favorite sunglasses lowered to the bridge of his nose. "The parking says I can wait ten minutes without paying, but I can stretch it to fifteen in case Miss Madison tosses your ass out. That should be enough time to confirm if you'll stay the night successfully."

"One, stop smirking at me like that. Two, you'll come pick me up in the morning around ten because I'm staying the night. But thank you for waiting for the confirmation. You're the best," Cal remarked before shutting the backseat door.

He adjusted the strap of his bag slung over his shoulder and the bouquet of two dozen red roses stashed against the crook of his elbow. He promised flowers, so he couldn't be there without them. In his excitement, he had nearly forgotten his overnight bag. Who could blame him?

A week without Madi drove him nuts. He yearned for the delicate reminder of her scent and the warmth of her body pressed into him. The minute he got the chance, he'd reacquaint himself with the sensation of not knowing where he began and Madi ended, joined in interconnecting lines of skin and soft, synced heartbeats.

Cal jogged up to the stoop of her apartment complex, graced by a good, pain-free day. He buzzed himself into the complex with that month's security code, sent via text by Madi. No longer daunted by being seen in public, Cal sped into the building, straight for the elevator.

The plastic wrap around his flowers crinkled with every step closer to Madi, announcing his presence to the rest of the apartment in a soft-spoken scream. The tiny voice in him dreamed of climbing onto the roof and shouting, "Madison Caldwell has stolen my heart," until the entire city block knew it.

He'd spare Madi the embarrassment of being romantically linked to an idiot like him. . . for the moment.

Cal's pace sped up as soon as the elevator doors spat him out onto Madi's floor, greeted by the familiar hallway he walked dozens of times in the last few months. His heartbeat rattled in his ears alongside the crinkling plastic, drowning out his footsteps carrying him to Madi's door.

He knocked twice—trying to hold himself back from more—and stood listless until the door swung open. Madi entered the frame like a vision, backlit by the light from her kitchen in a soft golden halo.

Her eyes brightened when taking him in, but he soaked in every detail of her. He'd want to remember the reunion forever, immortalized by the hazy air in the apartment and the soft lightning. She tossed her hair into a messy ponytail, but a few strands hung around either side of her face. Dressed in one of his dark shirts he left behind to keep her drawer company and a lightly discolored pair of gray sweats, casual felt just right on her. She could wear a trash bag, yet it would still take his breath away. She shone bright, *his* Firefly.

"Hi. I brought you these," Cal blurted out, thrusting the flower bouquet toward her. Madi accepted them into her arms, tenderly cradling them. She gave them a brief admiration, but soon, her eyes returned to holding his captive. "Can I come in?"

"Of course, you can." Madi stepped to the side. The two retreated from the hallway and into the kitchen of Madi's apartment. No vinyl spun around the turntable, serenading the evening with its chosen melody for the night. The kitchen lacked its distinct aroma of something cooking or still-hot takeout on the counter. But those were small things, not the whole sum of why Madi's apartment elicited the feelings of home.

Madi held the flowers and stared at Cal, in no rush to spark more conversation. Her stare—heavy in its comfort—stirred up the uneven racing of his heartbeat.

It was now or never.

"Can I hug you?" Cal choked on those words when Madi's hand gripped an entire fistful of his shirt, dragging him closer to her. She dropped the bouquet onto the table before their bodies collided, and her mouth found his, insistent and hot.

Forget about a hug. Cal wanted *this* instead.

Following her lead, Cal dropped his overnight bag onto the floor. His hands snared her hips between a firm grip and the wandering caresses of his thumbs sliding along the juncture of her pelvis. The repetitive touch elicited a shiver and a moan, barely audible when it slipped into Cal's mouth.

Cal pushed deeper, grazing his tongue over hers and claiming her as his. She probably ruined every other woman for him for the rest of eternity simply by being everything he needed and desired. *Madison Caldwell was the love of his life.*

What a sobering thought to ease Cal out of the kiss, desperate for air. He angled his head back, pulling his mouth away while Madi gave a tiny chase as she leaned forward. She almost recaught his lips between her teeth, and Cal might've given in despite how his lungs wheezed for oxygen.

"Madi," he rasped, run ragged by the sheer return of her lips in his life. "Firefly. Baby. Please."

"Mmm... what's the emergency? I've been deprived of this for the last week. I'm entitled to compensation for all the lost kisses with interest," Madi hummed against his mouth, falling short of a purr. Cal swore his heart skipped several beats, running laps around his chest faster than his run records.

"Two things. First, I need to tell Tommy if he can leave and pick me up tomorrow morning," Cal mumbled, speaking into her mouth from how close their faces hovered above one another. "More importantly, I don't want to save all the talking for later. We should put things the last few weeks behind us."

"Oh! Yeah, go ahead and text Tommy. I'm keeping you tonight." Madi stepped back, letting him handle business with a quick text.

"Thanks. Okay, now... about us." Cal slid his hands down the slopes of Madi's hips, digging his thumb into the juncture of her hip. "How are you feeling? I fired my agent and announced that I'm a taken man in a very public venue... and I hope the latter still stands."

Madi's eyes twinkled in the dimmed lights of her apartment. "It does. I handled the friend responsible for the miscommunication. I'll be better off without her in my life anyways, so it's no real loss."

"Good. Good. I don't know how things will shake out with Des, but I'm done with him. I know the people in my corner will have my back if things get ugly." Cal and Madi's standstill in the living room turned into a subtle sway, reminiscent of a slow dance with its unhurried pace.

"You were bold. I found it very attractive—" Madi giggled.

"I have Daisy Ramsey to thank for that. That woman does it all—business, astrophysics, being a fashion icon, crushing her enemies underneath her red-bottomed heels. You'll like her when the two of you meet." Cal snorted, which prompted more giggling from Madi.

"Oh, is that so? And when would we meet?" asked Madi.

"Whenever you'd like. I'm in it for the long haul with you, Firefly." The brush of their noses when Cal leaned in sparked all the nerves in his body. Wandering hands resumed their playful descent, hinging on the whispered conversation between the lovers' lips.

"I'm in the market for new friends. You've got some pretty good ones that I can't wait to know better." Madi nodded. Their noses bumped together, drawing them further into one another's orbit.

"Same here. I think there's only one order of business left to address," Cal hummed when Madi's arms curled around his shoulders, scooting their bodies together. "Would you be interested in being my plus-one to my dad's wedding? I accepted the invite to go, but I wouldn't have as much fun without my favorite dance partner."

The way Madi's face was illuminated at his request told Cal he had made the right choice. She nodded as she said, "Yes! I'd love to go!"

Cal beamed, scooping Madi straight into his arms. Her legs wrapped around his waist without a single hesitation. Their lips crashed back together, hungry and in search of something familiar. Madi kissed him like she'd waited for him all her life; he kissed back like he was returning home.

Their bodies melted into a twisted tangle of limbs, keen to grasp one another and explore the expanse of skin and desire. Cal hoisted Madi higher into his arms, stumbling toward her bedroom. . . or the couch if he felt impatient. The venue hardly mattered as long as he had her.

In a little chapel overlooking the Del Mesa coastline, Cal watched his not-so-estranged father marry his second wife. And he couldn't be happier for him than in that moment. But maybe that had something to do with the gorgeous redhead on his arm.

As Cal walked them underneath the white roses twining around the aged wood archway, the springtime breeze carried salty sea air and the faint aroma of the native wildflowers through the propped-open double doors. All the other guests exited the chapel behind the blushing bride and the grinning groom. The newlyweds left for the reception in their vintage getaway car, and everyone else rushed to follow their lead. Cal and Madi were the stragglers, taking their time leaving the breathtaking chapel.

"—I did some digging on this place. Voyager's Peak Chapel is the oldest structure in Del Mesa. It's seen a century's worth of marriages while overlooking the ocean, the perfect view for sailors and their spouses to mark a sweet memory before they returned to the waters." Madi whispered despite no one else around them. She spoke softly as if not to offend the pristine sensibilities of the aged wooden walls blending into natural greenery and tinted glass.

At the right angle, the sunlight streaming through any of the windows might cast a faint glow on them, occasionally dipped in the colors of the rainbow. Flecks of pink or purple grazed across Madi's skin with the same reverence of Cal's hands, adorning her in unyielding favor.

Cal offered his arm to her as he escorted her out of the chapel. The late afternoon weather made perfect sense for the garden party dress code. "Sounds romantic."

"I'd think that's ideal for a wedding venue," Madi retorted, rolling her eyes at him. Her snort nearly pulled one from Cal. They walked up to the curb, waiting for Tommy to bring the car around. The reception would be held nearby at a gorgeous botanical and butterfly garden, full of cake and privacy to entertain the newlyweds. "The ceremony was beautiful."

"Yeah, it was," Cal agreed.

Madi's head leaned into his shoulder, careful not to smudge his dark blazer with any of her makeup. Cal brought her closer to burrow into his arms and keep him warm as the breeze swirled around them.

His eyes traced over her and the vibrant floral dress she had chosen. She looked like sunshine incarnate; her red hair spilled in fiery cascades down her bared shoulders, formed into Hollywood starlet curls, while her makeup glittered golden to match the dress. Who would look at him twice when a goddess clung to his arm?

Cal spent the whole ceremony sneaking glances at her, observing every little reaction on her face while her eyes remained glued on the ceremony. During that time, he let his thoughts wander but stumbled upon a conclusion as undeniable as "the sky is blue."

He wanted to spend the rest of his life with Madison Caldwell until they turned old, gray, and wrinkly. People always say that when someone knew, *they knew*. Cal knew this fact to be accurate, deep in his bones.

Not even a year ago, the old him would've balked and run far away from the idea of such a commitment. Maybe he left that commitment-phobe in the accident, lost in the wreckage. Or maybe, somewhere within his heart, a true romantic laid dormant until the sheer brilliance of Madi brought the light back in. Either way, the realization snowballed when Madi accompanied him to dinner with his dad and Jill the night before. Somewhere between the excellent wine and the hazy laughter of the two women, something shifted right into place, offering its name.

Hope. He called it hope. Hope that marriages *can* work when two people meet love and devotion to growth in the middle.

Hope that he might find the best way to have Madi in his life forever, never wanting to be without her light. Hope that, in the end, whether via marriage or civil partnership, Madi wanted him as much as he wanted her.

The two perked up as a familiar black car rolled up the steep, winding roadway to Voyager's Peak. Their ride was there, ready to whisk them away for a night of dancing, cake, and joy.

Madi tipped her face to catch Cal's gaze. "I'll probably need help later to get out of this dress. Would you mind giving me a hand with that?" she asked, her voice sweeter than honey, while she batted her lashes at him.

Cal chuckled. "Troublemaker." His mouth bridged the gap to snare her in a warm, comforting kiss. Yeah, he wanted to do life with her, and as they kissed, Cal mentally marked the thought for another day.

He had plenty of time before asking. However, he probably knew the answer from the look Madi gave him. Still, such a new revelation would be his secret to keep for a bit longer.

Epilogue

SIX MONTHS LATER—OCTOBER

"How's dinner looking?" Cal poked his head into the kitchen, hands tucked into the popped collar of his button-down. The muted green brought out undertones in his eyes, making them pop more than they already did.

Madi's head snapped up. She squatted in front of the stove with her favorite pink oven mitts, grasping the sizzling glass dish from the oven. "It's ready," she joked, plastering on a smile. She nudged the oven closed and slid the hot dish onto the counter before the heat blistered through the mitts.

"Smells amazing." Cal sidled over to her side, quickly wrapping her in his arms. Kisses peppered against her face and cheek, causing Madi to squirm. "Six months with you has been the highlight of my life."

Within the blink of an eye, the six-month anniversary of their relationship came and went in a blur of good memories. They committed to taking things at their own pace, slow in some parts and breakneck in others, chasing the good feeling. Although the two considered January their official start date, the world learned about them in April, so for the public, October marked six months. And oh, Cal decided to celebrate it in style.

Using a single photo—artistically shot but still showcasing Madi in her entirety—and a sappy, loving caption, Cal made their relationship public. He even tagged Madi in the photo, shouting from the rooftops that he chose her. They'd discussed going public and enduring the ups and downs of fame, which Madi accepted.

Fame and Cal were a package deal, so Madi took them both in.

Neither paid much attention to their phones after the relationship launch; they were too busy enjoying the second reason for celebrating: Madi had moved in.

Madi snuggled deeper into his arms, working on the pasta bake she had hauled out of the oven. Her spatula carved through the layers of broiled cheese, and the aroma of savory spices filled the whole kitchen. Much like the perfect pasta bake, her life had thrived since April.

She had the best job in the world, great friends, and a boyfriend who made her world more fun. What more could a girl ask for?

Knocking at the front door snapped Cal and Madi out of the moment, especially when the excited barking and whimpering echoed from the living room. Two dark blurs raced past the kitchen to pounce and jump at the door, setting off a flurry of barking.

"Arizona! Rhode! Don't scratch up the doors!" Cal exhaled. He relinquished Madi from his arms while going to handle their pups. Around three months, the two expanded their family with two loving shelter rescues—Arizona, a German Shepherd, and Rhode, a chocolate Labrador. Those were their babies.

Madi laughed at the overlapping sounds of playful barking and Cal shushing Alaska and Rhodes while he answered the door. "And the Ramseys are the first to arrive. Why am I not surprised?"

"Punctuality is a dying art, and I refuse to let it go," Daisy cackled from the other room. Madi could hear the muffled greetings and the eager barking from her dogs, who adored Jensen after the time he and Daisy helped pet-sit them. The click of heels approached the kitchen, and Daisy entered into view. "Need any help with setting up?"

"You aren't getting anywhere near messy food with that designer dress." Madi crinkled her nose, prompting laughter from the two. Cal had been right; Madi and Daisy got along like a house on fire and had met before in passing, unaware that they'd meet again.

"Oh, fine. Where would you like me to set down the antipasto?" Daisy shook the boxes she had brought for the potluck.

"On the counter is fine!"

As Daisy stepped past her, more greetings echoed from the doorway. Madi heard Sonia and Alaina—tasked with bringing a salad—enter next. Finally, Claire and Alex, who brought the dessert, closed out the guests' arrival. Each greeted Madi after having their fill of Cal and the dogs.

Claire lingered the longest, sliding the box of cannoli from *Buttery Bites* across the counter. "I picked these up, special order."

"You spoil me!" Madi gasped. She flipped open the box to admire the gorgeous cannoli packed in the box. "I thought Evan shut off his custom orders for the next few months. Something about a heavier influx of brides this season?"

"Including his baby sister, Gabriela. However, I mentioned they were for you, and he made an exception. I'd argue my negotiating skills helped, but this might've been all you," Claire teased. The two fell into a comfortable silence while working to plate food.

"Thank you. It adds a special touch to an already special night," Madi mused, and her eyes flitted past Claire when Cal leaned in the archway to the kitchen. Claire glanced over her shoulder and smirked.

"I'll leave you two for a moment. We'll be at the table," Claire told them, swapping places with her best friend before vanishing from the kitchen. The guests' conversations continued without the hosts, but neither would be gone too long.

Cal swept Madi into his arms, bringing his mouth shy of hers to breathe out, "I love you."

"Love you more," Madi promised, sinking her kiss into Cal's warm embrace. Fireworks erupted in her chest when he kissed back, coloring her world in a new light like the night they met.

Afterword

Grief is a funny thing.

As people, we grieve for things, people we've lost, and the life we imagine for ourselves. While this book does not fully explore grief, it does fulfill the last subcategory.

Cal grieves. Cal walks through each and every day while still learning how to digest his traumatic experience. As someone with my own traumatic experiences, some days can be an uphill battle to feel like yourself. You look at yourself and wonder where the version of yourself that you recognize went. You look for who you used to be because part of you hasn't accepted your new iteration. You mourn who you could've been, who you **wanted** to be. Those feelings of grief are valid, yet those often feel hard to talk about. It makes sense to miss others; it never compares to missing yourself or who you might've been in another lifetime.

Conversely, Madi walks into the future, chin held high and hopeful. She is the cliche light at the end of the tunnel. Even though her past experiences do undermine her at times, e.g., dating as a fat woman and struggling to feel desirable, she chooses to believe in the good. She becomes who I wish I could be, a little softer and a whole lot more eager to give the benefit of the doubt. She deserves a love as energetic, electric, and passionate as her heart. She was written for the women I've come to know who love with their whole hearts and yearn for the happily ever after society sometimes withholds from them.

This book became an exercise in catharsis. That's probably why it took me an extra month to write the damn thing, spending more time dragging my feet and learning lessons through my characters. Trying to write this book through 1) a mental health decline, 2) the worst physical pain of my life, and 3) when feeling burned out from academia culminated into the most frustrating creative experience. No matter how healed I thought I was, the reality was that my trauma still had its claws in me.

I let it hold onto me and keep me stuck while peddling the illusion of acceptance. So, as I close the doors to the Ridge, a place that reminds me of home and unrelenting comfort, I leave the reminders of the past in the past.

Like Madi and Cal, now more hopeful than they started, I am entering a new era of my life. This place has good things for me, and I have to believe that.

Acknowledgements

As any author knows, I couldn't produce any books without an amazing community behind my vision. As the Ridge closes its doors, completing its final story, I'm thankful for every person who made this journey as smooth as possible.

First, thank you to Melody, my cover designer for the Royal Ridge romances, who made magic from my Google Drive folders of references and half-baked ramblings about my vision for the covers. The sheer amount of love these covers receive from readers is because of you. Every time I see the books on my shelf, I can't help but smile.

Thank you to my alpha/beta readers Olive, Estelle, and Evelyn. Since meeting them, these three have supported me in every project I've published. Their support means the world to me, and I'm so lucky to be their friend. Also, follow Estelle and Evelyn on their social media pages (@estellegrantauthor and @evelynleighauthor) to keep up with their upcoming projects.

Thanks to my editing team, Cassidy and Sophie, for their work on this final project. I know I'm in safe hands with them both, and they honor my voice while refining the story's details. Every author knows how much work goes into editing, and having those people whom they can trust is integral.

Thank you to all the early access readers—ARCs—who gave this story a chance and visibility in the market. Having people eager to read my stories helps me stay focused on what I have. They leave their mark on me, and I hope my books stay with them in the future.

Thank you to my family and friends. We may have lost one of our own before publishing this book (my sweet Shanti), but no one let me collapse in on myself or implode. While taking a break for a few months and shelving projects, you never let me give up on being Cassandra.

Finally, I give a shoutout to 9-1-1 on ABC for altering my brain chemistry and keeping me sane while writing this book. I've fallen head-over-heels for this show and won't ever shut up about it. Also, #Buddiecanon2025.

About the Author

Cassandra Diviak is a 10x-published indie author in fantasy and contemporary romance. As a lifelong bookworm, books are her best friend and her greatest joy. In her final year of law school, Diviak knows the importance of words and how people use the written word as self-expression. While not at classes, filled with legal theory and the insatiable urge to cry about why she signed up for academic torture, Diviak is a cat mom, loves cooking, hosting book club with her internet friends, falling down internet rabbit holes out of sheer boredom, coaching other writers in how to find their unique story.

Diviak writes manuscripts at inhuman speeds, earning her the moniker of *Muse Cass*. She's thankful to spend so much time doing what she loves and building a community. She also welcomes you to follow the start of her brand new YA pen name (Cass Rougeau) beginning in Fall of 2025. The same storyteller but a whole new genre!

<u>CONNECT WITH CASSANDRA:</u>
Insta: @author.cassandradiviak
Threads: @author.cassandradiviak
YA Instagram: @cass.rougeau.books
Tiktok: @author.cassandradiviak
Website: https://cassandradiviakauthor.weebly.com/

Also By Cassandra Diviak

The Shadow and Soul Series

Shadow of the Beast (Book 1)
Soul of the Sorceress (Book 2)
Of Wild and Witchcraft (Book 3)
Of Death and Divination (Book 4)

The Laws of Love Duology

Love on the Docket (Book 1)
Love Thicker Than Blood (Book 2)

A Love at Royal Ridge

The Lies We Tell (Book 1)
The Games We Play (Book 2)

Standalone Romances

The Signature Move

<u>Anthologies</u>

Unapologetic Love: A Charity Anthology of Radical Resistance (Vol. 1)